Advance praise for

The View on the Way Down

'So compassionate, so heartbreaking. I found myself
revisiting moments in this novel long after I'd finished
reading it; the story wouldn't let me go.'
Shelley Harris, author of *Jubilee*

'*The View on the Way Down* is deeply moving – yet
unsentimental – and profound, and has a family secret
at the heart of it that will remain with you for a long time
after you finish reading. It is a novel that needed to
be written and which will touch many people . . .
A fine achievement.'
Mark Gartside, author of *What Will Survive*

'A wonderfully moving portrayal of love and pain
with a mystery right at its heart. I defy anybody to
read this book and not be touched in some way.'
Sally Brampton, author of *Shoot the Damn Dog*

'*The View on the Way Down* is a novel that deserves to
win awards as well as a huge readership. It's a wise, honest,
wonderful read that marks Rebecca Wait not just as a
writer to watch out for, but one to appreciate now.'
Daniel Clay, author of *Broken*

'Understated and compelling. I had tears in
my eyes at the end.'
Morgan McCarthy, author of *The Other Half of Me*

'*The View on the Way Down* is written with great
sympathy and an aching tenderness. Rebecca Wait's
evocative storytelling is alive to the tragedies and miracles
of everyday life, illuminating the grey area between
protecting and deceiving the ones we love.'
Laura Harrington, author of *Alice Bliss*

'Wonderfully written . . . highly sensitive . . .
thought-provoking . . . ultimately uplifting.'
Bookseller

The View on the Way Down

REBECCA WAIT

The View on the Way Down

PICADOR

First published 2013 by Picador
an imprint of Pan Macmillan, a division of Macmillan Publishers Limited
Pan Macmillan, 20 New Wharf Road, London N1 9RR
Basingstoke and Oxford
Associated companies throughout the world
www.panmacmillan.com

ISBN 978-1-4472-2469-3

Printed and bound by CPI Group (UK) Ltd, Croydon, CR0 4YY

...oks
...ews and
...sletters
...ses.

For my parents

And there they were again.

Later, they would recall this scene. Alone, they would study it for its secrets, trying to fit what they knew now with what they knew then. It was coming. Even then it was coming, even on that beach, years ago – only they didn't realize it.

But if they returned to that day, what clues would they find? They might remember that grey clouds were starting to gather in the distance, over at the far end of the beach. That the weather felt like it was about to break; the heat had grown cloying, muggy. Or they might look back at it all and see nothing but the washed-out yellow of the sand and the rhythmic sweep of waves.

The couple were sheltering from the heat in the bay of rocks, with a flask of tea and some sandwiches. Joe had a book open, and Rose held the baby on her lap, occasionally bouncing her up and down.

The boys were further off, down towards the sea, dishevelled and happy in their ragged T-shirts and swimming trunks. They'd decided to dig a hole, and it was proving slow work.

'You need to reinforce the sides,' Kit was saying. 'The walls keep collapsing in on themselves.'

I

'Why am I doing all the digging?' Jamie said.

'I'm overseeing.'

The hole had been Jamie's idea in the first place, but now it felt like Kit's. He had taken over, as he always did.

'We've hit water at the bottom now, which is a good sign,' Kit said, peering down into the hole.

'I'm glad you're such an expert.' Jamie stuck his plastic spade into the sludge at the bottom, and heaved it to one side. More slid straight in to fill its place. He dragged one foot out of the slushy sand with difficulty.

'It's like quicksand down here,' he said.

'Don't be stupid. It's not quicksand.'

'I said *like* quicksand.'

'Keep going,' Kit said. 'We need to get a lot deeper than this, or there's no point.'

'Are we heading for Australia?'

'Yup.'

They smiled at the old joke.

'Hand it over, then,' Kit said. 'I'll have a turn.'

He took the spade from Jamie, and grabbed his arm to haul him out of the hole. Scrambling towards him, Jamie stood on the fragile overhang and part of the wall collapsed.

'Jamie!'

'You pulled me up too quickly.'

Kit jumped in and set about repairing the damage.

'Did you know that sand deaths outnumber shark deaths in America?' Jamie said whilst Kit worked. 'I mean, people getting buried in the sand. You're more likely to get buried in sand and suffocate than to get eaten by a shark.'

'That's fascinating, Jamie.'

'I'm just saying. You'd think sharks would be more of a danger. You wouldn't think getting buried in sand would kill more people.'

'Probably all idiots like you, who don't know how to dig a hole properly.'

'I've done more of it than you!'

'Quality not quantity,' said Kit.

'We should probably make a move soon,' Joe was saying, further up the beach.

'I don't like to drag them away,' Rose said. She was kneeling now, playing with the baby, who was absorbed in scooping up handfuls of the loose, soft sand and letting it run between her fingers. 'Look – her first time on the beach, and she loves it. Don't you, Emma?'

The baby gave her mother a ponderous look, and then returned her attention to the sand.

'A bit longer?' Rose said.

'Alright.' Joe tried to return to his novel.

'Aren't the boys funny?' Rose said. 'They're just like little kids again.'

'They've regressed. Childhood associations of the beach, and all that.'

'It's nice to see them playing together.'

'I'm not sure they'd call it "playing".'

'Kit's being lovely with Jamie, isn't he? Helping him with his digging. Very patient.'

3

Joe mulled this over. He didn't think 'patient' was the first word he'd use to describe Kit.

'I've been a bit worried about Jamie,' Rose said. 'The age gap suddenly seems more noticeable, doesn't it? Now they're both teenagers.'

'Jamie will catch up,' Joe said. 'Give him a year or so.'

'Yes, I'm sure you're right.' There was a pause, then she added, 'Lovely to have a holiday all together. Before we know it, it'll just be you, me and Em.'

'Mmm.' He was absorbed again in his book.

Rose turned back to Emma. She helped her fill a little bucket with sand, and then empty it, over and over again.

She said, 'Shall we have fish and chips for supper? As a special treat?'

'Whatever you want,' he said, making it sound almost as though it were a treat for Rose, when in fact she was thinking of the boys.

It was so peaceful, watching Emma play with the sand, and her sons in the distance, serious with their spades. Rose wished they could stay there forever.

So the afternoon went on and they remained on the beach, as the breeze grew cooler and the sun went in, and the clouds in the distance thickened. The soft sand in the bay began to lose its heat, and the sea slunk its way further up the beach, slyly encroaching on them. There was a scattering of other holidaymakers further along the sand, but they were gradually thinning in number, until at last there was nobody left but the five of them.

Finally, Joe said to Rose, 'Tide's coming in.'

Rose got to her feet, scooping Emma up with her. 'I'll call the boys.'

Jamie was saying to Kit, who was still standing in the hole, 'When the sea comes in, we'll have a swimming pool.'

'No,' Kit said. 'It'll be ruined.'

And then the first drops of rain began to fall.

Part One

1

The rain should have disturbed him like it disturbed everyone else. It was wild, it was insistent. It hammered against the windows for attention. The customers had taken on a conspiratorial air, exchanging glances and huddling inside their coats, but he ignored them. He went round closing any open windows so the books didn't get wet, then returned to the Jewish History section where he was putting the new stock on the shelves.

Inside his head, he insisted on silence. It had been difficult, teaching himself to think of nothing. But he was patient and through hard practice it had become habit. Occasionally, when he was struggling – like now – he'd manage to withdraw. Sometimes he'd picture himself on an island, or alone in the desert. Now, though, he chose the woods. They were still and quiet, waiting to absorb him into their great silence. He stood still among the history books, staring up at the sunlight coming through the leaves.

He was wrenched away by someone touching his arm. Reluctantly, he left the shelter of the trees and turned to find an elderly man behind him.

Jamie was blank for a moment, then put on his work voice. 'Can I help you, sir?'

'I have a complaint about your Jewish History section,' the man said in precise, careful diction, as though he had rehearsed the sentence. 'I can't find any of the books I'm looking for. All your books are on the Holocaust.'

'Yes,' Jamie said hesitantly. 'I suppose most of them are.'

'It's absurd,' the man said. He seemed to gather courage as he spoke. 'Where are your books on Jewish culture, and music, and literature? You make it look as though the Holocaust is the only significant event that's happened to the Jewish people in their entire history. As if they don't have a rich and varied past regardless of that particular atrocity.'

Jamie said carefully, 'We tend to stock what sells, otherwise we lose money. Books on the Holocaust are always in demand.'

'Because people are fascinated by horror.'

Jamie didn't know what to say to this, so he kept quiet.

'I don't like it,' the man said. 'I don't like the way your shop defines the Jewish people by one awful thing that was done to them, and not by anything they've ever done for themselves. Do you see what I'm saying?'

Jamie nodded.

'To define us by what they did to us is to let them win. History should give equal weight to everything.'

'How can it?' said Jamie before he could help himself. 'Some things loom up and dominate.'

'Why should we only study what's considered interesting by people who don't care about the – the *big picture*, and only want the gruesome details?'

Was this really his main complaint, Jamie thought, that their History department lacked coherence? He was quickly losing interest in the discussion, but could see the man was still fired up.

Jamie put up a wall between them. 'We always appreciate customer feedback, sir. Do you have any suggestions of books we could order in to broaden the range of the section?'

He thought the man would be irritated, but he eagerly made Jamie an extensive list. Then he struggled back into his coat, his swollen fingers fumbling with the buttons, and went out into the rain. Jamie stuck the list up behind his desk with his other reminders. He knew he would never order any of the books. There wasn't enough room on the shelves. Besides, people wanted the horror.

The rain was still driving down in his lunch hour and he couldn't face going out for a sandwich. He got some crisps and a Mars bar from the vending machine and sat in the staff room reading an Alistair MacLean novel. He always kept an eye out for Alistair MacLeans, and he had a large collection now.

He'd chosen his usual chair in the far corner of the room, a position that usually didn't invite interruption. But just as he was biting into his Mars bar, a shadow loomed over him.

'What are we on now?'

Jamie groaned inwardly. Brian from General Fiction thought he'd found a kindred spirit in Jamie, whose passion for old thrillers he had noted early on. Brian himself was a Science Fiction and Fantasy man, but he'd observed the zeal of the aficionado in Jamie and seemed to think he'd soon enough be able to divert his energies towards a more deserving genre.

'*South by Java Head*,' Jamie said, without looking up from the page. He was aiming for damage control. Occasionally you could head Brian off by refusing to engage with him, like playing dead when faced with a grizzly bear.

'Any good?'

'Don't know yet. Chapter One.'

Brian sat down beside him, as ever a little too close. Resigned, Jamie closed his book.

'I think you should reconsider Ursula Le Guin,' Brian said.

'I'm just not sure she's for me, Brian.'

'A majestic writer,' Brian said. 'If you're ready for something a class or two above MacLean, that is.'

'I don't think I can handle anything much above MacLean.'

'What, too exhausted from slogging it out in History?' Brian chuckled. 'All those crowds of customers using up your brain power? They never make it up to the second floor, Jamie. You should try working in General.'

'The truth is, Brian,' Jamie tried as a last resort, 'I can't read very well.'

He shoved his book into his pocket and exited the staff room whilst Brian was still stammering an apology. Being robbed of those precious minutes of his lunch break made him feel childishly furious. He sneaked past the History Enquiries desk and seated himself in the little alcove between Jewish History and Military History to carry on reading, hoping Brian wouldn't track him down.

He became so engrossed in Chapter Two of *South by Java Head* that at first he didn't notice the young man and woman standing near him. Then the woman made some kind of movement – perhaps pushing her hair back from her face, or shaking the raindrops from her coat, he couldn't afterwards say what – and something familiar about the motion drew his attention. Jamie didn't look up from the page, but now he was acutely aware of the couple standing close by.

After a moment, the woman spoke, murmured something to the man which made him laugh under his breath, and immediately Jamie was frozen, unable to make out the words but recognizing something in the tone, something in the rhythm of that voice which erased the intervening years.

Alice Brown.

He saw her turn out of the corner of his eye, and could see her stop and stare. She was looking right at him as he sat in the alcove, with *South by Java Head* open in his lap.

When she started walking over, he stood up.

'Jamie?'

Her hair was cut into a short, neat bob and was its natural dark brown rather than the bright red it had been back then. But her face still had that fragile, questioning quality; almost childlike, especially now with its tentative expression. She was still beautiful. Of course she was still beautiful.

'It is you, isn't it?' she was saying. 'I thought it was.' She seemed nervous. Jamie wondered if he was too, but couldn't tell.

'Alice.'

'I can't believe it.'

Now he saw again her slow, wide smile. Jamie used to love the confiding quality in that smile, which made him and Alice co-conspirators whenever she caught his eye. Eventually he had realized she smiled like that at everyone.

'This is so strange,' Alice was saying. 'We've just been up to visit Mark's parents in Leeds and stopped here on the way back. And then it was raining, so you see—' She gestured as if to say, here we are.

There was a pause. Alice only seemed to be talking to fill the dead space between them. Jamie had realized after the initial shock that they didn't have much to say to one another, and he supposed that Alice knew it too.

She gestured to the man with her, and he came forward. Jamie looked him over. He seemed OK. Kind-ish. Not very good-looking.

'Jamie, this is my husband, Mark. Mark, this is my old friend Jamie.'

Her husband. Jamie took in the news quietly, then shook the man's hand. 'Nice to meet you.' He could tell from Mark's appraising look that he knew what Alice meant by 'old friend'. He wondered how much Mark knew. Probably a fair bit, from the careful way he seemed to be looking at him.

'We've been married four months,' Alice said, as though Jamie had asked.

'Congratulations,' Jamie said. 'That's brilliant.' He thought perhaps he was supposed to hug Alice at this point so he reached for her, but she stiffened and he let his arm drop. To cover the moment of awkwardness, he said, 'Alice, it's been forever.' This, he thought, would pass muster. It was the kind of thing someone else might say in a situation like this.

Alice corrected him. 'Five years. It's been five years.'

'How are you?'

'I didn't know where you were, Jamie,' she said, ignoring his question. 'Where have you been all this time?'

Jamie tried to meet her gaze. 'Here and there. You know. I've been working here a few years.'

'In a bookshop?'

'I'm in charge of the Jewish History section,' he found himself saying defensively.

'That sounds interesting,' Mark intervened. 'Do you know, I might excuse myself for a moment and go and have a look.'

Jamie pointed it out to him, silently hoping he was interested in the Holocaust. He noticed the protective way Mark touched Alice's shoulder before he walked away, and the look that passed between them. He thought, she'll be alright with him.

When they were alone, Alice said, 'It's so weird, seeing you again like this.'

'I know.'

'I waited for you to get in touch. I waited for ages.'

Jamie knew he should say something, but couldn't think what.

'Anyway,' Alice said into the silence. 'You can't do anything about it now.'

He thought this was probably true. There was another pause, more uncomfortable this time. Jamie decided to say after a moment, 'I really am sorry, Alice. There's no excuse.' He noticed the formality in his own voice, and thought how odd it was that he was talking to her like a stranger.

'But how are you, Jamie?' Alice said. 'Really?'

'I'm fine.'

'And your family?'

'I don't know.'

'Oh, Jamie.'

He said nothing.

Alice said, 'You know it doesn't make it go away, just pretending people don't exist.'

She would never forgive him, he thought. He didn't blame her, and it didn't matter; but he felt sorry for her.

Mark was coming back over. He said, 'You've got a good selection of books on Auschwitz.'

'Thanks.'

Mark turned to Alice. 'Darling, we should be getting off.'

Alice was rummaging around in her handbag, and eventually pulled out a business card. 'Keep in touch, Jamie,' she said as she handed it to him.

'You're an interior designer,' Jamie said, inspecting it.

'Not a very successful one,' Alice said.

'I thought you wanted to be an artist.'

She'd been looking at him narrowly, but suddenly she

smiled. 'People *are* allowed to change their plans.' Jamie felt her old charm working on him again.

'I mean it about keeping in touch,' she added. 'Don't disappear again.'

'It was nice seeing you, Alice,' he said. 'Good to meet you, Mark.'

'Take care of yourself.' Alice started to walk away, but at the last minute she seemed to change her mind. She murmured something to Mark, and left him waiting a little way away. Then she came quickly back towards Jamie and slipped her arms around him, putting her head against his chest. For a moment, the familiar gesture left him stricken. Alice had always had a special way of tangling herself in his arms. The next moment, she'd turned away and gone back to Mark without a word. Mark took her hand, gave Jamie a quick nod, and they disappeared down the stairs.

Jamie went and stuck Alice's business card behind his desk next to the old man's list of Jewish history books. He took a quick glance at the titles. *Resource and Ritual in the Ancient Near East*, he read. *The Wisdom of Solomon: Israeli Science and Discovery, 400–500 BC.* No use stocking that kind of thing, he thought. Nobody would ever buy it.

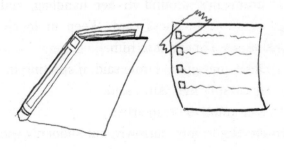

2

It was lunchtime, always an ordeal for Emma. She was hiding in the school chapel, or lying low, as she put it to herself. She sat in a pew at the back and stared up at the stained-glass cross in the window above the altar. It was made up of reds and oranges and yellows, with purple at the centre, so it looked like it was on fire. Rejoice in the glory of the Cross, she thought.

She didn't want to go to the canteen because she had no one to sit with, and besides, she shouldn't eat anything because she was fat. And she wasn't fat in the way other girls at her school were fat, which just meant that they were thin but worried about their appearance because it made them seem 'adult'. No – she was fat in the normal, rubbish way, where you have a double chin, and extra rolls of flesh on your tummy. She was genuinely fat, and surrounded by people pretending to be fat. It made her feel like she was losing her mind. Trust her to be fat in the wrong way.

The chaplain came in and smiled hello at her – he was used to her silent presence at the back of the chapel at lunchtimes. He disappeared into the vestry.

Sunlight was glinting through the coloured glass, setting it ablaze once more. Staring at the cross, Emma thought: Jesus went through life alone. He always had people around him, but really he was alone. Imagine how he must have felt as he was made to carry his cross to Golgotha. It struck her now what a disturbing part of the punishment that was – the condemned men made to carry their own cross-beams, sweating and exhausted, to their place of execution.

If Jesus had suffered all that, surely she could go through life by herself and not mind too much. She didn't need to be surrounded by people to do God's will.

Her stomach rumbled. She thought of fish and chips on the beach, the sand sticking to the grease on her fingers. She thought of the chocolate muffin and strawberry milkshake she had as a treat on Saturdays when she was little. She thought of creamy mounds of mashed potato with her mother's special onion gravy. How unfair that girls who were already thin could quite happily miss lunch and not even notice, whilst she was hungry all the time.

The chaplain reappeared. 'Ready for the Christian Union meeting tomorrow, Emma?'

'Yes.'

'What's your topic?'

'God's purpose for us.'

'Good.'

She sat there a few minutes longer, leafed through the hymn book and memorized the words to 'Be Still for the Presence of the Lord'. Then she thought she'd better go to lunch, even if it meant sitting by herself, because she was too hungry now to think about anything else, and at this rate she wouldn't be able to concentrate all afternoon. She had double Maths after lunch which was her worst subject; and Mr Lawson would be horrible and sarcastic when she got things wrong, and then everyone would look at her and she'd go bright red with the effort of trying not to cry.

It was quarter to one. Emma steeled herself. If she went to lunch now, she might bump into Kayleigh, who was also in the Christian Union and would probably sit with her.

She was in luck. She spotted Kayleigh by the entrance of the canteen, and ran to catch up, an undignified, huffing little run.

'Kayleigh! Are you going to lunch?'

She saw before Kayleigh could disguise it a slight look of irritation cross her face. Of course, Kayleigh didn't want her tagging along, but she put up with it because she recognized her Christian duty. Emma knew this, and to be honest she didn't particularly want to tag along with Kayleigh either, but she was short of options.

They queued together, and Emma said, 'I've picked some passages for tomorrow's meeting.'

'Cool,' Kayleigh said politely.

'I thought some St Paul.'

'Yeah, sounds good.'

Then Jasmine came up and Kayleigh started to talk to her, ignoring Emma. When they got to the front, Emma chose carefully. She wanted French fries, but it was too embarrassing for a fat person to ask for chips, so she got some roast potatoes instead and then took lots of pasta salad to fill up on, and some lettuce leaves and tomatoes so she looked healthy. She had to wait for ages at the salad bar because the cool group kept pushing in front of her, not even deliberately, probably, but just because she was so unimportant as to be almost invisible. She waited patiently for a lull, then loaded up her plate.

She went to find Kayleigh and Jasmine, but they'd already sat down with Harriet Jackson and Lucy Wright, and there was no space at their table. Emma hovered with her tray for a few moments hoping someone would ask her to pull up a chair, but nobody did, so in the end she had to go off and find a table in the corner by herself. She ate her lunch as fast as she could and left the canteen to go back to the chapel.

When Emma got home from school, her mother was on her knees in the kitchen scrubbing inside the oven. The surfaces were gleaming, and various cleaning products were arranged in neat rows on the kitchen table. A bad day, then. Emma put some bread in the toaster and poured herself a glass of milk.

'How was school, love?' her mum asked.

'Fine.'

'That's great, darling!'

It struck Emma that this was not exactly what she'd said, but she decided to let it go.

'How was Maths? Was it alright?'

'Fine.' She saw her mother looking at her, anxious for more information, and added, 'We did quadratic equations.'

'And did you have a CU meeting?'

'Nope. It's tomorrow.'

'And what have you got planned?'

'I think we'll do some St Paul.'

'And how are your friends?'

'They're fine.'

Emma took the toast and milk up to her room and sat down on her bed. She wondered when her dad would be home. Her mum was in fussing mode – it would be better if he wasn't around.

She tore the crust carefully off the toast and put it to one side whilst she ate the middle bit, licking the jam off her fingers. She was always, always aware of the danger. They probably thought she couldn't remember all the awfulness after Kit died. But it was part of her now – her dad's scary moods, her mum going for days without speaking. There could be no going back to that, so she tried to keep an eye on things.

She finished the crusts, and went to get her CU file from the desk. Looking at it made her feel better. It was a big pink ring-binder filled with plastic pockets where she kept all her notes and Bible passages and pictures. She liked how thick the file had got, and she found it satisfying to turn over the plastic pockets and look at all the successful meetings she'd organized in the past. The better prepared she was for tomorrow, the less likely Kayleigh would be to try and take over.

She got out her pad of paper and felt tips, and wrote the heading in bright blue: 'God's purpose for us'. She thought for a moment, then added below in pink, 'Paul's own life serves as example. Wicked Saul converts to

Christianity and accepts his mission to spread Christ's Word.' She hesitated, chewing the end of the felt tip. She wasn't happy with the phrase 'accepts his mission'. It made St Paul sound like he was in *Mission Impossible*. She crumpled up the page and started again. She had a rule of no crossings-out in her notes.

This time she wrote, 'undertakes the mission of spreading Christ's Word'. Then she paused again. She was finding it hard to concentrate today. Jamie was in her head. Sometimes she enjoyed imagining where he might be, and what he might be doing now, but today it was just making her sad.

She closed her eyes, and asked Jesus for guidance. He stayed silent. Sometimes it was like that. Emma wondered, suddenly, if Jamie believed in God. When he finally came back, she would ask him. She would remind him that God loved everyone, and He would forgive Jamie. And so would Emma, in the blink of an eye, if he just came home.

3

Emma was woken by her father hammering on the door.

'Time to get up,' he called.

Emma ignored him.

'It's *late*, Emma.'

'It's Saturday, Dad.'

'You've had enough of a lie-in.'

Emma picked up her watch from the bedside table and inspected it. 'It's 8.47.'

'Quite.'

Emma rolled out of bed and started hunting around the room for clothes. There was no point in arguing, and despite her grumbling she wasn't really annoyed. She adored Saturdays. No school and no prospect of school the next day either. Sundays weren't so good. A little bit of Monday always seemed to bleed in, however hard she tried to keep them separate.

The kitchen table was laid with three plates, and jam, Nutella and maple syrup. They always sat in the same places, round one end. It struck Emma that the table was too big for just the three of them. She took her seat along-side her dad as her mum brought over the pancakes; she'd piled them up on a plate with kitchen towel between the layers. There had been pancakes for breakfast every Saturday since Emma could remember. Her mum said a family breakfast, all together, made a good start to the weekend.

Emma helped herself to Nutella, and passed the maple syrup to her dad. They prepared their pancakes in silence.

Her mum sat down and began to pare an apple, which she cut into quarters and ate very slowly. She didn't like pancakes, and rarely ate breakfast herself. Emma noticed that she already had lipstick on, the orangey-red one that didn't look very nice. Her mother used to wear pink colours, soft shades, rose like her name, but recently she'd said she was trying a new look, a smarter one. Her make-up had got brighter and her clothes had got darker, and she didn't look much like herself any more.

'What have you got planned for today, Emma?' she asked.

'Nothing much.'

'You must have something in mind. A nice book to read?'

Emma shrugged and concentrated on her pancake. She could feel her dad tensing with irritation beside her.

'Any schoolwork to get on with?'

Emma's mood plummeted at the mention of school. She didn't reply.

'I thought we might go and look at the shops together this afternoon. Unless Dad wants to go on a family walk?'

'For God's sake,' Emma's dad said. 'Can't you leave her alone for a second? She's fourteen, she doesn't need you scheduling her day for her.'

Emma saw her mum freeze for a moment, a piece of apple halfway to her mouth. She shot a thought-wave at her father: I hate you. Her mum put the piece of apple into her mouth and looked down at her plate as she chewed. Emma watched her swallow and fix her face into a smile. 'I just thought it would be nice to do something as a family. We could go for a walk and then play Monopoly.'

Emma cringed in anticipation of her dad's response. But he only said, 'I'll be in the shed all day.'

'I'll come shopping with you, Mum,' Emma said.

She reached for another pancake, but as she picked it up her dad said, 'Don't you think two's enough?' Emma drew back her hand and stared uncertainly at her empty, chocolate-smeared plate. She felt humiliated, caught out in her greed.

Her mum said, 'She's hungry. Let her have another.'

Emma silently pleaded with her not to make it worse.

'Makes no difference to me.' Her dad got up from the table, muttered something about the shed and left the kitchen.

Her mum offered Emma the pancake plate. 'Go on, darling. If you want another, have one.'

Emma stared at the plate of pancakes. They'd gone a bit cold by now, and drops of grease stood out on their surface. She didn't want one any more, but she took one anyway and ate it miserably. She pictured herself as her father must see her, fat cheeks crammed with slimy chewed-up pancake. She kept the mess in her mouth too long, found it horrible to swallow.

As soon as she could, she said, 'I have to go and get started on my homework, Mum.' She was on her feet and heading out of the room before her mother could reply.

On the landing, she paused briefly outside Jamie's and Kit's old rooms. Sometimes, with the doors closed like this, she tried to pretend her brothers were still in there, playing on their computers or listening to music. It had worked in the past. It was usually easier with Kit, because his room had been kept exactly the same (though tidier now than when he'd been alive) – the same dark-blue duvet cover, the sports trophies on the shelf, the Spurs scarf pinned above the bed.

Jamie's room, though, had been cleared out and redecorated, with cream walls and a brand-new double bed. It had become the Guest Room, although no guest had ever slept there. It was more difficult to imagine Jamie being in there; hard to ignore the emptiness that seeped out from under the door.

Emma went into her own bedroom, deciding to distract herself by working on her board game. She got out the board she'd made from the base of a cardboard box, and her sheets of coloured card and felt-tip pens and glitter glue. This game, her project of several weeks, was based around the Harrowing of Hell. The players' aim was to help Jesus rescue as many lost souls as possible. She'd enjoyed working out all the aims and rules and designing the colourful base, but she was getting too tangled up in the theology now to feel confident about the final product. (Chiefly, if the souls were already in hell, could they really be rescued? Surely you couldn't be un-damned?)

Nevertheless, she set about outlining the squares on the board with different-coloured glitter, but after she'd done that she couldn't really think of anything else to add.

She'd already made her little Jesus figurine out of modelling clay, and dressed him in a loincloth made from a piece of bandage from the medicine cupboard and a red cloak she'd fashioned out of a scrap of velvet. She'd also made some poor men and women he could save, but she'd left them naked (part of their punishment). The game was almost complete now. This last stage of creation was never as exciting as the beginning. And it occurred to her that she wasn't sure what she was going to do with it when it was finished. Her mum would probably play it with her, but it wasn't really designed for just two people.

If Jamie was here, he'd play it with her as well. Jamie and Kit had always played with her when she was little. They'd been much older than her, which her mum used to say had made them protective of her. Emma enjoyed thinking about this.

She remembered Kit teasing her, when he met her around the house and pretended not to know who she was, pretended to think she was a burglar. Or he'd deliberately get her name wrong, making her giggle.

'Hello, Emmet,' he'd say.

'No, no,' Emma would reply in delight. 'That's not my name. You always say it wrong. It's Em*ma*.'

'*I'm* saying it right,' Kit would say. 'You're the one saying it wrong.'

And she remembered Jamie reading *The Hobbit* to her, doing all the different voices. He'd sung the dwarves' song about the Misty Mountains, making up his own tune and using a very deep voice which made her laugh.

She clung on to memories like this, but it had occurred

to her recently that perhaps they couldn't be trusted. If enough time went by, how could you be sure what was actually true and what you had imagined? Especially if nobody talked about any of it.

Emma tried to focus her mind on Jamie, to imagine what he might be doing. Maybe he was working as a journalist somewhere dangerous and exciting like Africa. Or perhaps he was living a glamorous life in Paris, drinking red wine on the banks of the Seine and painting. But it was Kit who'd been good at art. It upset her for a moment that she'd got confused, like she was forgetting them both or rolling them into one, so in the end she'd be left with a sort of composite brother who didn't resemble either.

She returned to Jamie. He hadn't liked Art, but he'd been interested in history. He'd studied it at university. Emma didn't like it much herself. They'd had a lesson at school on why History was an important subject, and Mrs Majithia had said it was because we need to learn from the mistakes of the past so we can stop awful things like the Holocaust ever happening again. Kayleigh had put up her hand and said sagely, 'Those who do not learn from the mistakes of the past are doomed to repeat them,' and Mrs Majithia had said, yes, that was a very *apposite* quotation and Kayleigh had looked pleased with herself. But as far as Emma could see, people could study the past until they were blue in the face and it still didn't stop them doing horrible things in the present.

Perhaps one day Jamie would turn up on television doing a series on the Tudors or the Nazis or something. And then she'd write to him and ask for his autograph.

She told herself again that he'd come home eventually. She was sure of it. Even if he didn't turn up on TV, one day he'd start to feel less upset about Kit, and then he'd come back for her.

The bit which she tried not to think about was that Jamie had left without even saying goodbye. How could he have done that, when her mum said he'd been so protective of her? It was when she remembered this that she came closest to understanding why her father was so angry.

4

Jamie woke early. The light where it came in between the curtains had a pale, washed-out quality, despite its aggressive brightness. It couldn't be long after seven.

He lay there for a few moments, accepting the presence of another day, letting its colour wash over him.

He needed to pee. His mind could freeze over, but his body was insistent in its demands. He headed to the bathroom, then made some tea and took it back to bed with him, where he read a few more chapters of *South by Java Head*. There didn't seem to be any reason to get out of bed, but he was bored with lying there.

The empty day ahead disconcerted him. He tried to make a timetable in his head. Shower. Put on clothes. Eat. Then . . . go out somewhere? He could go into town and buy some Lego. He tried not to do it too often, and to spread his custom thinly, frequenting several different stores. He didn't want them looking at him strangely, a grown man browsing amongst the toys. But he really wanted the Lego space station.

He was putting on his jacket when the doorbell rang. Jamie retreated into his bedroom and waited there silently until he thought whoever it was must have gone. But when he went back into the hall, the doorbell rang again. This time the person didn't take their finger off the bell and Jamie winced at the drawn-out, piercing shriek. A voice called through the door, 'Let me in, you bastard. I'm freezing.'

'For Christ's sake.' Jamie wrenched open the door and was forced back as a man pushed past him and stood in the hall, soaking wet and dripping onto the carpet.

Jamie looked at him with resignation. 'Hello, Sam.'

'You kept me waiting ages, and it's pouring with rain!'

'It's not raining again, is it?'

'It's always fucking raining in Sheffield.'

Sam hung his sodden coat on a hook and squelched through to the living room where he peeled off his soaking jeans and positioned himself on the sofa in his boxer shorts.

'No, please, make yourself at home,' Jamie said, following him through.

Sam was his closest friend from university – his only friend, these days. This was a tribute to Sam's tenacity. He had clung on where others had been cast off, exhibiting a determination and thick skin that defeated even Jamie.

'What are you doing here?' Jamie asked him.

'Checking you're still alive. Because you haven't been answering your phone. For *weeks*.'

Jamie glanced guiltily at the mobile on the coffee table. 'It ran out of battery,' he said. 'A while ago.'

'Well, it's funny you should say that, because lots of people were having the same problem, so the phone companies invented this magical thing called a *phone charger—*'

'Alright. Sorry.' Jamie paused. 'You can't stay.'

'Why not?'

Jamie said nothing.

Sam said, 'I'm not going to allow you to chuck me out when I've come all the way up from London. Even *you* wouldn't do that. Would you?'

Jamie sighed. 'Apparently I wouldn't.'

When Jamie had made them both tea, Sam produced, with great ceremony, a large, garishly wrapped parcel from his bag. He deposited it in Jamie's lap.

'Happy birthday.'

'It's not my birthday.'

'I know. But it *was* last month. Try to make these connections on your own, Jamie.'

Jamie picked up the parcel. It was a box, quite wide and flat. It felt heavy. 'What is it?'

'Open it and see. Jesus. It's like talking to an alien.'

Uncertainly, Jamie pulled off the wrapping paper. 'A PlayStation?'

'A PlayStation 3.'

Jamie inspected the box. 'You didn't have to get me a present.'

'I know,' Sam said. 'It was selfish, really. I didn't want to have to talk to you, so I thought we could play FIFA instead. I brought a second controller.' He produced a stack of games from his bag. 'These are for you, too.'

'FIFA?' Jamie brightened. 'I remember being a lot better than you at that.'

'Ah. But we're not in the heady days of FIFA 2000,

Jamie. Times have moved on. You'll be like Captain Hornblower trying to man a submarine.'

That evening, playing FIFA amongst the detritus of their Indian takeaway, Jamie said, 'I saw Alice a few days ago.'

'Alice who?' Sam's Agger tackled Jamie's Defoe just outside the box and angled the ball out to the wing. '*Strong challenge*,' the commentator observed, as the animated Defoe went down.

'Alice Brown.'

'Oh.' Sam went silent for a few moments, apparently concentrating on the game. 'Where did you see her?'

'She came into the bookshop. Just by chance.'

'Nothing's ever by chance with her.'

'She was with her husband.'

Sam raised his eyebrows. 'What was he like?'

'Seemed alright.'

'Alice Brown married.' Sam drew in his breath speculatively. 'Wonder if that'll last.'

Defoe was making for the goal again, but Sam blocked him easily.

'You've been practising.'

Sam acknowledged the compliment with an incline of his head. 'What did Alice say?'

'Nothing, really. It was – awkward.'

'I bet it was. Did she seem angry?'

'Yes.'

Sam took a swig of beer. 'I don't blame her, Jamie.'

Jamie didn't reply for a moment. On screen, Dawson scythed down Suarez. 'No point raking all that up now.'

'No, I agree. But will Alice?' When Jamie didn't reply, Sam added, 'She's not one to let things rest, is she?'

Jamie thought about it. 'You never liked her.'

Sam's eyes remained fixed on the screen. 'No, I never did.'

On Sunday morning they drove to the Peak District and walked for two hours in the wind and rain, both unsuitably attired in jeans and sweatshirts, much to the scorn of the serious, Goretex-ed walkers who crossed their path. They worked their way up Chrome Hill in puffing silence and triumphantly made their way along the ridge, breathless, chilled and damp.

Sam was in high spirits. 'Look at that view!' he shouted above the noise of the wind. His gesture took in the green, drenched valley and the neighbouring hills crouching under the onslaught of the weather.

Jamie nodded, pushing his wet hair off his forehead.

Sam shouted, 'You're lucky, living so close to all this. How often do you come out here?'

'Hardly ever,' Jamie shouted back. He became aware of Sam staring at him. 'What?'

Sam shouted something.

'What?'

'I said, that's a bit weird.'

'Why?'

'It's just – a shame, isn't it?'

'Typical Londoner,' Jamie said, turning to carry on along the ridge.

They stopped for lunch in a pub and ordered pints and a roast each, seating themselves by the fire to dry off. Sawing at a tough slice of beef, Sam said, 'I could do a better roast than this.' He speared a piece of Yorkshire pudding, contemplating it sadly. 'Look how dry this is. They need to watch their timings more carefully.'

'You're a bit insufferable sometimes,' Jamie said.

Sam didn't seem concerned by this. For a while, they ate in silence. The rain was growing heavier outside, beating against the windows with increasing urgency.

'How's life in the bookshop?' Sam said.

'Fine. Except for the customers.'

He hadn't intended this as a joke, but Sam laughed.

'I mean,' Jamie said, 'they're always asking you for things.'

'How unreasonable of them.'

'But it's stupid questions, like, where can I find books on Military History? – when they're standing right next to the Military History section.'

'You're so misanthropic. Maybe it's time to get a different job. Go somewhere new.'

'Can't be bothered.'

'Come on, Jamie.'

'It's a good job. They're going to put me in charge of Eastern European History. I'm going to order in loads of books on the Bosnian genocide. And maybe Vlad the Impaler.'

'Sounds like a right laugh,' Sam said. 'But how about moving down to London?'

'I want to stay where I am.'

Sam exhaled in exasperation. 'That's what you're going to end up doing. Forever.'

Jamie kept his eyes on his plate.

There was an uncomfortable pause, then Sam said, 'They haven't crisped up these potatoes very well.'

'I think they're OK.'

'I'm not sure they've even used the meat juices in the gravy. I have a horrible suspicion it's Bisto.'

Jamie shook his head, but smiled in spite of himself. 'You're very hard to please.'

'I'm not, though. That's the sad thing.'

Sam left in the late afternoon, promising – unprompted and uninvited, Jamie noted – to visit again soon.

Alone, Jamie wandered listlessly around the flat. He settled down for a while to play one of the PlayStation games Sam had left him, *Red Dead Redemption*, which intriguingly he found to be a Western. He was surprised at how violent it was. He thought of his and Kit's teenage years playing *Tomb Raider* – a much tamer proposition. But that, he thought, had been all about killing, too. It was just that they managed to make the deaths look real these days. You could blow a man's head off and see the fear in his eyes the moment before, the blood splatter on the ground behind.

He grew tired of the game and went through to his bedroom, wondering what to do next. The light outside was fading, spreading gloom through the flat. He supposed he should make some supper, but couldn't work up the energy. He pulled off his jeans and sweatshirt, and climbed into bed in the darkening room. The weekend was nearly over, at least. After a few moments of lying blankly, he roused himself, flicked on the bedside light and reached for *South by Java Head*.

5

Years ago, in the other life, Jamie had won four tickets to Blackpool Pleasure Beach in a charity tombola at his school fair. He and his friends had all bought tickets for 50p after being harassed at breaktimes and lunchtimes by the Year 6s, who were in charge of selling them.

Mr Winters was up on the wooden platform and asked for a volunteer from the crowd to choose the winning tickets. Jamie and his friends all put up their hands, but it was Jamie who was picked, perhaps because his mum had helped to organize the tombola.

His hands were so sticky from the gobstopper he'd been transferring between his mouth and his pocket that when he reached into the box to pick a ticket, a whole cluster of them stuck to his hand and he brought out about fifteen at once. Everyone laughed, and Jamie played to the crowd by waving his hand around as if trying to shake the tickets off. They stuck firm. Miss Wyatt came forward and picked one of them off and read out the number as the winning ticket. It took Jamie a moment to realize it, but then he said, 'That's me!' and drew out the ticket's twin from his pocket, where it had curled itself around the depleted gobstopper.

His mother said afterwards that he shouldn't have

accepted the prize because if you're picking out tickets and you choose your own, you're supposed to put it back and choose another one. And it was awkward, too, because she was the one who'd organized the prizes. But Jamie didn't care, because it was too late to give the prize back and he and his parents and Kit were going to Blackpool Pleasure Beach!

They went one Saturday in the summer holidays. Afterwards, their dad described the experience as 'like being mugged', but Kit and Jamie thought it was brilliant. They wandered round wide-eyed, dazed by all the bright colours, the swooping, hurtling rides, the crowds, the endless candyfloss and sweet stalls. Jamie rushed them from ride to ride and from stall to stall, bumping them through throngs of people. He was concerned, as always, with the passage of time, aware that they couldn't cram every activity into one day but seized by an almost hysterical determination to try. 'Come on, come *on*,' he'd say, as he chivvied them out of the exit of one ride and towards the queue for another. Kit told him to chill out, but kept up with him all the same.

Their parents dealt with it good-naturedly, used to their sons' sudden enthusiasms. They allowed themselves to be hurried along, insisting only that the boys sat down for a solid half-hour after lunch before being allowed to go on another ride.

But the excitement of the day began to fade for Jamie when they started trying to go on the bigger rides. Aged eight, he found himself just below the height-restriction for the rides that looked the most exciting. He went on the tiny Ferris wheel with his mother over and over again whilst Kit and his father went on huge, careering rides that promised the thrill of chaos. Kit went on the same roller coaster four times he enjoyed it so much.

'With the tickets *I* won!' Jamie complained to his mother as they went round on the Ferris wheel at a painfully slow pace for the sixth time.

'I know, love,' she said. 'But it wouldn't make it any better, would it, if Kit couldn't go on either?'

'It would,' Jamie said crossly.

Standing at the side and listening again to the urgent rumble of a roller coaster passing by without him on it, Jamie's fury at the injustice came to a head and he burst into tears. His mother comforted him with a big, colourful lollipop, and he was sucking tearfully on it when Kit returned, flushed and laughing, his hair standing up like the crest of an exotic bird.

'What's the matter?' Kit said.

Jamie was too sulky and humiliated to reply, or even to look at his brother, but their mother said, 'He's upset because he's too small for some of the rides.'

Kit looked at Jamie with concern.

'Don't worry, darling,' their mother said. 'Jamie and I will go on the dodgems again. You can look after me, can't you, Jamie? These big ones are a bit scary for me. Then we'll go and get some candyfloss, or maybe a toffee apple. How does that sound?'

Jamie licked his sticky fingers miserably and didn't say anything. He wanted a toffee apple, but not as much as he wanted to go on the big roller coasters.

'You really want to go on one of the big rides, Jamie?' Kit asked.

Jamie nodded.

'Come on, then.' Kit grabbed Jamie's arm and pulled him towards the space-themed roller coaster. Their parents followed reluctantly.

'No good, Kit,' their dad said. 'He's too small to be let on it.'

'Let's try,' Kit said.

Their mum looked unsure, but seeing Jamie's face, their dad said, 'Worth a try, I suppose.'

As they neared the front of the queue, Kit said quietly to Jamie, 'See the man in the booth? He's checking, but he can't see properly from where he's sitting.' When they had drawn almost level, Kit whispered, 'Stand on my foot.' Jamie did as he was told, clutching his brother's arm to take some of his weight and trying to look nonchalant. The extra few centimetres were all it took: the man in the booth nodded them on. Jamie and Kit kept very quiet, but exchanged delighted smiles as they passed through the turnstile.

The ride car was grey and shaped like a space shuttle. Jamie and Kit climbed into the front seats, their parents behind them, and brought down the T-bar restraints. After what seemed like ages, everyone else had got on, and there was a hushed, expectant pause as they all waited for the ride to start. Then the cars jerked and clunked into life, and Jamie felt a rush of pure joy as they moved off, quickly gathering speed. This was it: he was living on the very edge of life.

The roller coaster passed along winding tracks in the open air before rocketing into an enclosed tunnel and descending rapidly in darkness, with stars glowing on the tunnel walls. Being too small for the harness, Jamie slipped lower in his seat as soon as the car started to race down the sloping tracks, and was held by his harness half-sitting, half-lying in place, his arms jammed uncomfortably in the air. His legs were now wedged into the nose of the shuttle-car, and all he could see were the stars on the ceiling spinning round and round. But he shouted with excitement along with the others as the ride hurtled downhill.

As they emerged into the light and shot along the tracks towards the end of the ride, Kit glanced over and noticed the position his brother had ended up in. He laughed helplessly until they drew to a halt. The fact that Jamie then had to be prised out of his harness by the ride attendant became one of Kit's favourite stories.

Alone in his flat with the new PlayStation, Jamie saw it all again.

He'd been racing round different tracks ever since coming home from work, playing one of the games Sam had given him – a game which reminded him of *Mario Kart*, one of his and Kit's old favourites.

He allowed himself to think once more of the roller coaster, then tried to put it away. It was a happy memory, but it wasn't safe. This seemed the cruellest punishment of all – that he could rarely think of Kit without also thinking about what happened. Particularly when he was in a mood like this. He couldn't be certain, but he thought things had been getting worse since he'd seen Alice again. He could have done without that.

He tried to fill his head with silence, whitewashing the bright images of the theme park. Searching for safety, he managed to conjure up the woods. He stepped forwards; began to disappear among the trees.

6

Emma was furtively eating some cheese and onion crisps at the back of the chapel. She was the only person in there so there was no real need to be surreptitious, but it felt disrespectful to be munching on crisps in the House of God.

She had officially given up crisps, because her mum had put her on a healthy-eating drive. Rose said it would make Emma feel happier in the long run, and since Emma thought it would be good to feel a bit happier, she'd agreed.

They'd discussed it together and decided that Emma should start by cutting out crisps completely, and then gradually try to cut down on other unhealthy foods like cakes and chocolate; 'cut down on', her mother had said, not cut out completely – it was best to be realistic, otherwise there was no chance Emma would stick to it. Her mum had made her a healthy-eating chart which she was supposed to fill in every day, and when she'd got three gold stars, for three weeks of consistently healthy eating, her mum would buy her the kimono jacket she'd seen in Debenhams, which was made of the softest pale-pink silk, with a pattern of surging dragons embroidered in black.

Emma hadn't forgotten the healthy-eating chart when she'd stopped at the vending machine just now; she'd sinned with her eyes open. She was already regretting her decision. If she was honest and wrote it on the chart, that would be the end of the kimono jacket. But if she didn't, that would be a kind of lie – and pretending it wasn't, even to herself, would be another; God was probably counting them all up. The crisps had made her feel better for the first few mouthfuls, but they were making her feel much worse now. She licked her fingers and reached into the packet for the last few crumbled bits.

She'd needed something to cheer herself up. This lunchtime's CU meeting hadn't gone at all well, and Emma had ended up leaving early – something she'd never, ever done in all her time as a member. Then she'd passed the vending machine on the way to the chapel, and fallen into Temptation.

Everything had been different since Stephanie Morris started coming to meetings. Emma had feared the worst when she first turned up, because she was in Emma's class and was one of the cool group, who sat on the desks in the middle of the form room every breaktime and lunchtime so everybody else was squeezed out into the corners of the room, but nobody ever complained about it. Often they blocked the way to Emma's desk completely, and she'd have to say 'Excuse me', and then all of them would turn and look at her and usually not bother to move. Sometimes they'd talk really loudly about getting drunk, and the things they'd done with boys, and it made Emma feel embarrassed and a bit frightened.

All the same, Emma thought she'd better give Stephanie Morris the benefit of the doubt. After all, Zacchaeus was a hated tax-collector, but even he had wanted to see Jesus, and Jesus had looked up and seen him in the tree and said, 'Zacchaeus, make haste, and come down,' and told him he would stay at his house. So Zacchaeus was saved, and promised to give half his goods to the poor. And Jesus said, 'This day is salvation come to this house.' So perhaps it would be the same for Stephanie Morris. Emma had started to feel a bit hopeful, and had smiled kindly at Stephanie when she came to the first meeting. ('This day is salvation come to this room.')

But Stephanie hadn't been humble and promised to give half her goods to the poor. She'd just sat there playing with the ends of her hair and raising her eyebrows in a condescending way when Emma was trying to explain things. She'd brought Jenni Abbott with her to the next meeting, who was in the cool group too, and they'd started interrupting Emma to argue, or to bring up something completely different. Emma had looked over at Kayleigh, expecting her to be as annoyed as she was, but Kayleigh hadn't helped at all, just gone quiet, and nodded whenever Jenni or Stephanie spoke.

Emma had noticed that during discussions the others had started looking to Stephanie for a final verdict instead of herself. Even though Stephanie didn't know *anything* about the Bible. She hadn't even read it. She'd thought St Paul was one of Jesus' disciples, and when Emma had pointed out that of course he wasn't, Kayleigh had interrupted and said in an irritating, fake-apologetic voice, 'No, Emma, I think Steph's right – I think he was one of the disciples.' *Steph?* Emma thought. She had grabbed her

Bible and set about looking up the passages that would prove them wrong, but by the time she'd found them, the discussion had moved on and no one seemed interested.

It had all come to a head in today's meeting. Emma had been trying to talk about the Parable of the Prodigal Son, but Stephanie had interrupted to say she had something to share. She said she'd made a 'love list', because it made her feel closer to God. It was a list of the ten people she loved best and she read it out to them. She'd put God at number one, then Jesus at number two. Emma had had to speak up at this point.

'It doesn't really make sense to have Them separately,' she said.

'What?'

'Well, you shouldn't really say you like God more than Jesus. They're sort of the same. Jesus *is* God.'

'Jesus was a *guy*.'

'And he's God. You can't rank the Holy Trinity. Three in One.'

'This is *my* love list,' Stephanie said.

'But it's theologically misleading.'

'Ignore her, Steph,' Jenni said. 'Carry on.'

Stephanie went back to her list. At number three, she'd put her boyfriend Pete (she'd only *known* him a month, Emma thought, but she didn't dare interrupt again). Then came Jenni Abbott, and a few others from the cool group. Stephanie had even put Kayleigh at number ten. Emma looked at Kayleigh, who'd gone red and was clearly trying not to look too pleased. Everyone said it was a lovely thing to do, and Kayleigh suggested that they all make love lists.

Stephanie Morris said she'd make a new one, along with everyone else. 'Because it changes all the time,' she added meaningfully.

'But we haven't finished doing the Prodigal Son,' Emma said.

'This will make us feel closer to God,' Jenni said, without even bothering to look at her.

Emma had felt so furious she'd thought she was going to explode, so she'd pretended she had to go and see a teacher, grabbed her stuff and left.

Now she stared at the stained-glass cross and tried to concentrate on Jesus. It didn't matter how badly the CU was going as long as she didn't lose sight of the Lord. But she couldn't help thinking that Jesus wouldn't have rushed off and stuffed his face with crisps if there'd been a vending machine near Golgotha.

She tried to be sensible and think of a solution. She could ask Stephanie and Jenni to stop coming to CU meetings. They probably wouldn't listen, but if she *begged* them? No, that was ridiculous – that would make them laugh at her and then they'd go and tell everyone else about it. And worst of all, she'd look unchristian. She could start her own CU, a different one, and meet at the same time as the old one to make sure Stephanie and Jenni didn't come. But what if nobody came to her meetings?

There didn't seem to be an answer. She focused on the cross and silently prayed to Jesus. *O Lord God, Lamb of God, Son of the Father.* There was comfort in the old words. They insulated her from Stephanie Morris and Jenni Abbott and all the problems of the present. She could feel close to God without making a stupid love list.

The chaplain came in and seemed surprised to see her. 'Not at the meeting, Emma?'

She shook her head, glad the crisp packet was safely hidden in her lap.

'Why not?'

Emma shrugged.

The chaplain looked at her. 'Is everything alright?'

'Yes.'

Fortunately, he went on his way.

Emma bowed her head. She didn't feel at all well. A sharp ache had started up behind her eyes. She opened a hymn book at random, and found the words of 'Abide with Me' before her. She knew them by heart already, and closed the book, murmuring the first lines to herself. They were saddening and comforting at the same time.

> Abide with me; fast falls the eventide;
> The darkness deepens; Lord with me abide.

All at once, a memory was upon her which she couldn't place at first. She realized that she'd sung these words before, alongside Jamie, alongside her mother and father. It had been a heavy, grey day; everything drained of colour. Most of her memories from around the time of Kit's death were patchy, stitched back together scrap by scrap. But one thing Emma did remember clearly was singing this hymn, the melancholy of the music and the words.

Then there was another scene before her. Jamie and her father, making the air thick and black with their shouting.

Emma remembered the noise and her own fear but she couldn't recall the words. She'd run up to her room and eventually her mum had come to find her and said it was teatime, and when she went downstairs everything was quiet. Jamie was gone. It must have been the last time she ever saw him.

And something else was niggling at her now. The memory had thrown up a strange idea, a question that had never occurred to her before. If her father was angry because Jamie had run away after Kit died, why would he have been angry *before* Jamie left? Emma tried to think back to what she'd been told, but could remember nothing. And she knew she couldn't ask – it would lead to crying from her mum or shouting from her dad as it always did when Jamie was mentioned.

Sadly, Emma turned her attention back to the hymn, thinking again of Kit's funeral, and then of Kit himself. What she retained most vividly was her sense of shock at his disappearance, the startling discovery of how easy it was for someone to die. The flimsiness of the partition between life and death. You could slip through it, past it, under it, at any time.

She faltered at the final verse and opened the book again to remind herself. But the white of the page seemed to give out a painful glare and the words blurred into little black caterpillars that crawled away from her vision when she tried to read them. In the end, she had to give up.

7

When Emma got home from school, feeling sick and achey all over, her mother said straight away, 'You look white as a sheet.' Emma felt so sorry for herself that she burst into tears. She spent the next few days in bed with a crushing headache. Missing Thursday's CU meeting didn't bother her the way it would usually have done, and when her mum suggested she have a look through her special CU folder to cheer herself up, Emma said irritably that she didn't feel like it.

She had bad dreams at night which she could barely remember when she woke, sweating and disoriented. But they always involved people arguing, and were permeated by a frightening kind of rage.

It was a nasty virus, her mum said, and made her drink lots of hot squash. Even her dad was nice, and stopped on his way back from work to buy her some wine gums and a magazine. It was a teen magazine and he handed it over a bit awkwardly, saying, 'Thought you might be bored.' Emma didn't usually read magazines like that, because she didn't wear make-up or have boy troubles, but she was touched that he'd stopped to choose something specially for her.

Her return to school the following Monday was bad

enough, given that no one asked how she was or even seemed aware she'd been away. But it was when she arrived at the CU meeting that things really started to go wrong.

Emma thought it was weird that everyone else was already in the room, because she was early today, as always. But they were all sitting round the table with papers out. Confused, Emma checked her watch, but it definitely said 12.40, and the meeting didn't start until 12.45. She thought maybe her watch was wrong, but the clock on the wall said 12.40 too. She had a strange sense of the world tipping away from her.

'What's going on?' she asked Kayleigh. 'Has the meeting started?'

'Oh, yeah, it has,' Kayleigh said. 'We meet at 12.30 now,' she added.

'Why?'

'Well. You know. More time.'

'You didn't tell me.'

'You weren't here,' Kayleigh said. She didn't seem especially concerned. Emma felt everyone's eyes on her as she slipped into a chair.

Stephanie Morris said, 'So we're already making posters. What else?'

'We could do an assembly,' Kate Burgess said.

'And give out leaflets afterwards,' Nicki Butler added.

'What's this for?' Emma said, when there was a pause in the discussion.

Stephanie raised an eyebrow. 'The Message,' she said elliptically. Emma decided to keep quiet in the hope that what was meant by 'the Message' would become clear over the course of the meeting. She tried looking at Kayleigh for help, but Kayleigh was busy scribbling things down on the notepad in front of her.

'We have to bring the Word to as many people as possible,' Stephanie said, looking round at the others. 'That's what Jesus is asking us to do. Can't you feel Him in this room, asking us?'

Some people nodded.

'I can feel Him right now,' Jenni said. 'He's telling us we need more ideas for spreading the Word.'

'How about T-shirts?' Sarah Postill suggested, with a nervous glance around her as though she expected Jesus to emerge from the shadows any minute to pass judgement on her idea.

Stephanie thought about it. 'Yeah. They could say "What Would Jesus Do?"'

'Or "Thank God for Jesus",' Kayleigh said tentatively, adding, 'I saw that on a poster once.'

'That's good,' Stephanie said, and Kayleigh looked relieved and wrote it down on her pad.

'We could have a cake sale,' someone suggested. 'And call it "Bake for Jesus".'

Emma struggled with an increasing sense of confusion throughout the discussion. Finally, she forced herself to say, 'But – aren't we going to talk about the Bible?'

Stephanie turned and looked at her properly for the first time. 'We've talked about it and agreed that spreading the Word is more important,' she said.

Emma had a strange, fluttery feeling in her chest, but

she ploughed on. 'You have to understand what Jesus is saying before you can tell other people about it.'

'A true Christian already *feels* it.'

Emma felt her face getting hot. 'But this isn't what we usually do at meetings,' she said.

'Jesus hasn't put you in charge,' Stephanie said. 'If He had, we'd all feel it.'

There was a brief silence. Then Jenni said, 'Shall we read out our love lists?'

Something in the way she said it put Emma on her guard. Everyone started rummaging in their bags and producing their lists. Emma looked around at them, trying to work out what was going on.

'I'll go first,' Stephanie said, unfurling her piece of paper with ceremony. She began to read. Her list started with God at number one, then Jesus, as before. Emma waited for Pete's name but instead Stephanie began to name the other CU members, looking at each of them in turn and saying their name with a loving smile. She finished reading with the tenderly pronounced 'Nicki Butler' at number sixteen, having said everyone's name but Emma's.

Emma glanced around the table to see if anyone else had noticed she'd been missed out, but they were all staring at their pieces of paper and she couldn't catch anyone's eye. It was possible, she told herself, that it had been an accident.

'Your turn,' Stephanie said to Nicki, and Emma waited with growing unease. Nicki's list followed the same pattern, naming the other CU members one by one. Emma listened for her own name, then looked down at her lap in embarrassment as she was again missed out. As the others took it in turn to read out their lists, Emma realized that all this had been done on purpose, and must have been planned whilst she was away. *Why?* Because she'd argued with Stephanie at the last meeting? But why would everyone else go along with it?

It was Kayleigh's list that did it. Emma looked up expectantly as she began to read, sure that Kayleigh wouldn't betray her, but Kayleigh rushed through her list without looking up, and finished it without saying Emma's name. Emma looked at her beseechingly, but Kayleigh refused to meet her eye.

Emma didn't wait for the remaining members to take their turns. She was on her feet, shoving things back into her bag. Everyone watched her, but nobody said anything. For Emma, the world had become very quiet, as though she had water in her ears. She dropped her folder on the floor, sending loose pages everywhere, and had to scrabble around for them in the irrevocable silence of the room. Finally, she made it out of the door, head down, eyes blind.

In the weeks that followed, posters started going up around the school saying things like 'Jesus Rules' and 'Are You Saved?' and 'Spread the Gospell' (Emma noted the misspelling with contempt). Several others from the cool group had joined the CU by now, and they'd bought badges and bracelets from the Internet with slogans like 'GOD IS AWESOME' and 'WWJD' which they wore around school.

They held a big assembly, led by Stephanie Morris and Jenni Abbott, on how friendship was a gift from Jesus. And on Home Clothes Day they all came in wearing matching bright-pink T-shirts saying 'Someday My Prince Will Come', which, they explained to everyone, meant Jesus.

Emma had thought her involvement with the CU and its members would end after she left the group, but Stephanie and Jenni would often try to catch her eye and stare her down when they saw her, sometimes exchanging a whispered comment. It took Emma a while to work out what they were whispering. Then she heard Stephanie say the word quite clearly one day as she walked past her to get to her desk in the form room. It was 'infidel'.

Now, when any of the cool group passed her, they'd mutter 'infidel' to each other, and pretend to look at her suspiciously.

'I'm *not* an infidel! I'm a believer!' Emma burst out on one occasion, but Stephanie shrieked with laughter and after that the cool group would sing the Monkees' 'I'm a Believer' at her as well as calling her an infidel.

Emma told herself she could endure it. Jesus was on her side. *The darkness deepens; Lord with me abide.*

But she woke up each morning feeling sick. Sometimes she'd tell her mum she was too ill to go to school, and she might be allowed to stay off for a day or two. But she always had to go back in the end.

The cool group would be sorry one day, she thought. Emma wasn't sure how or when this would happen, but she did know that when the time came, she wouldn't forgive them. It would be too late for them, just like it was too late for Judas. He cast down the silver pieces in the temple and went away and hanged himself.

Jesus would forgive them, though. That was the problem. Emma was beginning to think He could be a bit of a pushover sometimes. At this rate, she'd end up in heaven with the entire cool group, forced to hang out with Jenni Abbott and Stephanie Morris for all of eternity.

It would be different if her brothers were still around. They could have come into school and sorted the cool group out. Kit and Jamie were cooler than anyone else. They would have made fun of Stephanie and Jenni and made them feel stupid. But it was no good thinking about that, Emma thought, with a prickle of anger that took her by surprise. Where was Jamie when she needed him? Hadn't she waited long enough? The truth was she'd been on her own for years, and memories and imaginings wouldn't help.

One day, she thought, maybe she'd get away too. She'd do what Jamie had done: walk out of her own life and never come back. But she felt a pang of guilt when she imagined abandoning her parents. However awful things were at home, she couldn't let them lose all their children.

8

It was raining again – Sam was right, it was always raining here – and Jamie wasn't feeling good at all.

There was something about Sheffield in the rain. It was greyer than anywhere he'd ever seen. Usually, he liked the way rain made everywhere look the same, the whole city uniformly sodden. But this time the rain wasn't helping. He wasn't sure if it was the sleeplessness or the drinking (he'd slipped into bad habits recently, needed to do something about it) – but either way he was starting to feel ragged. Looking for the trigger didn't help. What mattered was catching it before it got too far. Otherwise he'd be lost for days – weeks, even.

He braved the weather to go out to the toy shop, and began to feel calmer. He spent an enjoyable ten minutes browsing amongst the Lego models and then resolutely picked up the Lego space station and made his way to the desk to pay. He handed over his debit card and watched the woman slip the large box into a plastic bag. You could still see the colours through the plastic, bright blue and muted grey, and Jamie felt a surge of pleasure as he took the bag from her.

But once he was outside, he started to feel bad again. He had that tense, wound-up feeling – not a good sign.

The sky seemed to grow heavier, pressing down on him, and he stood still for a moment, aware of the nightmare rushing in his ears, of everything around him starting to slow down and himself starting to speed up—

Without warning, he recalled Kit's voice, handing out some brotherly advice.

'You need to relax, Jamie.'

Jamie remembered his own irritation at this comment. Leaning on the bar of their local, refusing to look at Kit, he had snapped, 'I am relaxed.'

'You get too intense about things.'

Now, Jamie tried to think what the conversation had been about. Alice, he thought. Kit hadn't been a big fan, had claimed that Alice was walking all over Jamie.

Jamie had said, with the self-righteous conviction of a nineteen-year-old, 'I love her.'

Kit said, 'Just be careful, OK?'

Jamie had been annoyed at the time, didn't see why Kit thought he had all the answers when he was only two years older. But he could see now that Kit had been on his side. One way or another, Kit had always been on his side.

This was getting dangerous. The sickness was rising in him and his hands had started to shake.

He put his head down and walked on through the rain, clutching the plastic bag with his new space station inside. He'd get the Lego home, then he'd build it.

But everything was breaking into pieces. His face was flushing hot and cold, his heart beating too fast. He recognized the symptoms of the panic attack moments before it hit him, and then the world lurched sideways, plunging him into the limitless terror, the pounding universe of panic. He leaned against the wall, trying to take deep breaths. He was drowning. He saw Kit again, but his face was turned away. He tried to go to the woods, but there was no escape.

He heard his father's voice: clear, vicious, and still unforgettable—

How could you?

Jamie crouched on the pavement in the rain, his head in his hands. He felt the cold water trickle into his collar and down his back, but it didn't revive him. His only thought was, let this be over. The nausea hit him suddenly and he turned just in time to vomit into the gutter. He knelt on the wet pavement, retching, trembling, tears streaming down his cheeks.

By the time the terror began to subside he was soaked to the skin. He stumbled the remaining distance home, stopping at an off-licence on the way. He could see how the man behind the counter was looking at him – ashen-faced and smelling of sick. Drunk, he was probably thinking. But he still sold Jamie the whisky.

At home, Jamie stripped off his clothes and got in the shower. He turned the water up so hot it almost scalded him and stood there under the onslaught, eyes closed, emptying his mind of everything but the sensation of the hot water pouring over him. He took the whisky to bed with him, began to feel it warm and unwind him. The anger was returning now, pulling the pieces of him back together. He thought of what he'd say to his father if he ever saw him again.

It was only as he was falling asleep that he realized he'd left the space station behind – left it lying on the pavement in the rain, next to a pool of his own vomit.

9

When Rose was a child, she'd heard her mother remark of her sister Millie, 'She'll make a lovely wife.' Rose had been thirteen years old, and was passing the sitting-room door with her friend Ginny when they heard Rose's mother make this observation to a visitor over tea.

Ginny had puffed out her cheeks and giggled. 'Thank God she wasn't talking about you! Can you imagine anything worse?' Ginny's mother was a feminist.

But Rose had been secretly mortified. She began to pick up on little comments her mother made, like 'Rose is rather clever', and 'She's doing so well at school'. The truth was that Rose was no cleverer than Millie. It seemed to her that nobody noticed whether or not Millie was clever because she was pretty, and everyone expected Rose to be clever because she was plain.

Rose didn't care that she was in fact quite good at Geography, nor that she was in the bottom set for Maths, whatever Ginny said about women needing to forge a career. Rose never wanted a career. All she wanted was to prove her mother wrong and not end up a spinster.

She was in her first year at nursing college when she met Joe at a friend's party, and she had instantly felt at ease with this quiet, serious law student. More than that – she'd felt as though she, for once, had the upper hand. Joe had seemed almost shy of her, and Rose decided that she must have reserves of charm she hadn't been aware of.

She'd been married before Millie, and was eager to show everyone what a lovely wife she'd make, what a perfect family she'd have. But in the end there had been no one to show, because Millie had emigrated to Canada a year later with what her mother described as 'an unsuitable man', and her mother had died of breast cancer the month before Kit was born. But perhaps it was for the best, Rose thought. Her mother had been spared the past few years, at least.

Sitting at the kitchen table with her cooling tea, Rose realized that she'd wasted most of the morning. She'd been trying to read her book since Emma and Joe had left, but for some reason she was finding it difficult to focus today.

She pushed back her chair and stood up. It was no use sitting here feeling sorry for herself when there was still plenty to be done around the house. For one thing, it was about time the oven had another clean. She put on her rubber gloves, armed herself with the oven cleaner and knelt down to make a start.

Really, she thought as she scrubbed, if her mother could see her now, perhaps she'd be proud. Rose had succeeded in making a lovely family home for Emma and Joe, even after everything. She was holding it together, keeping things ticking along. After all, a happy home wasn't about luck or circumstances. You had to create it for yourself.

She made herself scrub harder, because she was thinking about Kit again, and there were times when it was OK and times when it wasn't, and right now it wasn't. She saw his dark hair, his quick smile. She paused, her hand frozen on the oven door, almost winded from the pain of it. She was thinking of Jamie, too, because it was impossible to think of Kit without thinking of Jamie, because they'd always been together, and because what had happened was inseparable from Jamie, and Jamie was inseparable from what had happened. Where was he now? The ache in her chest was making it difficult to breathe.

She saw again the roller coaster car at Blackpool Pleasure Beach, saw the empty space beside Kit as it hurtled out of the tunnel. She would never forget the terror of that moment. How hard she'd prayed for it not to be true, for Jamie to be saved. The wild bargains she'd made, gripped by the conviction that Jamie had fallen out of the ride in the darkness. She could remember it vividly: entering the tunnel with her eyes fixed on the backs of her sons' heads, and then emerging into the daylight only able to see Kit's, and an empty space where Jamie had been.

For the rest of the ride, her fear was excruciating. Unable to move her arms because of the harness, and unable to be heard above the noise of the ride, she couldn't attract Joe's attention, and remained alone in her agony.

When the ride slowed to a stop, Rose had sat perfectly still – if she didn't move, didn't acknowledge it, time might stop. If she willed it hard enough, perhaps it might even go backwards. She could hear nothing but the pounding in her ears, and she watched the muted scene as though viewing it from a great distance. She saw Kit undoing his harness and stepping out of the car, and she watched as the ride attendant rushed over, presumably to verify that a child was missing.

Then the next moment the attendant had released the harness and she saw Jamie emerge, Lazarus-like, from the ride-car. Sound returned. The world sped up. She heard Jamie shout exuberantly, 'Oh *wow*, that was cool!' And Rose felt like she was shattering with relief, breaking into a million pieces with the shock of her reprieve.

She didn't tell any of them afterwards what she'd believed, stranded in the sky. She tried it out in her head, imagined putting it into words to tell Joe, but no way of phrasing it seemed adequate. No words could communicate what she had undergone alone, eighty feet in the air; panic that heralded a new scale of experience.

Now, Rose decided that the oven would do. She stood up abruptly, peeling off her gloves, and turned on the radio. There was some kind of gardening programme on, which sounded interesting. Gratefully, she focused her attention on the planting of tulip bulbs as she went to put the kettle on. Emma would be home in a few hours, and perhaps they would do some cooking together. And in a bit, Rose would pop in on Eileen Draper and see if she needed anything. The important thing, Rose thought, was to make herself useful.

10

Alice had arrived home from work earlier than usual, and was wondering what to do. Mark wouldn't be back for at least a couple of hours. She knew she should make the most of having the house to herself, but she'd never much liked her own company, had always felt she came to life around other people.

Perhaps this would be a good time to get out her water-colours, with the house quiet and empty. She hadn't finished anything for years, but at heart she still thought of herself as an artist. She liked the idea of Mark coming home to find her wearing one of his old shirts, with her hair loosely pulled back off her face, absorbed in sketching or painting.

But by the time she'd unearthed her sketchbook from the top of the wardrobe in the spare room, she'd gone off the idea, was unable to think of a single thing to paint. She went back downstairs to pour herself a drink.

There had been a time when she was bubbling with ideas, she thought as she sipped her wine, leaning against the kitchen worktop; when she could hardly look at anything without wanting to draw it. Alice had always regretted studying History of Art at university instead of trying to get into art school, but her parents had seen it as the safer option, and if she was honest, so had she. She'd tried to make up for it by sketching the whole time she was at university, ostentatiously taking her pad and pencils everywhere. She remembered lamenting to Jamie that she hadn't followed her dreams, but he'd said with a flicker of amusement, 'You can be an artist without having gone to art school, you goon.'

Thinking again of Jamie, she took a large swig of wine and sighed. It was probably like this for everyone, in one way or another – life didn't turn out the way you expected it to when you were young.

On impulse, she headed back upstairs and after scrabbling around in her desk drawer, found his letter. She'd thrown the others out in a fit of misery a few years back, but she'd been drunk and not very thorough, and this one had escaped the cull. She hadn't looked at it for a long time now.

Reverently, Alice unfolded the scrap of A4, and started to read. There was Jamie's voice as it had once been – lively, amused.

'Dear Alice,' it began. 'You think I'm making revision notes. You err. I'm writing to you instead. You should probably shoulder some of the blame if I fail my Medieval World module. I want you to be surprised when we get up to leave and I hand it to you.'

He'd written the letter in the library cafe not long before their first-year exams, with her sitting opposite him. She'd been stressed out of her mind – convinced she was going to fail. But Jamie was relaxed, as usual. And why not? Things came easily to him.

'*You* really are revising,' he went on. 'You have your Hogarth notes spread in front of you and your coffee cup's resting on a reproduction of "Gin Lane". The crone on the steps has a coffee-coloured halo now – I notice it every time you pick up your cup. You thought you'd like Hogarth, but you don't. You're frowning as you highlight sections. Grubby Hogarth isn't for the likes of you. Your heart's in Florence, in the Middle Ages, in the Renaissance; you're a Giotto fan.'

It continued, covering both sides of the paper in Jamie's exuberant, slanting hand. She kept reading, no longer noticing the scrappy edges of the paper.

'I think you might be starting to suspect me,' he wrote at the end. 'You just said, "You're not looking at your books much. What notes are you making?" and craned your neck to look. I put my elbow on the paper and said, "Practice essay." Very smooth. But you still look unconvinced. Not very trusting, are you? I think I'd better stop.

'I hope this letter's cheered you up, and taken your mind off Hogarth for a bit. I want you to be cheerful all the time – and always because of me. Love Jamie.'

Forget that imagined, quicksilver ecstasy. This was happiness; this was all it was. How could she have known, aged twenty and stressed about Hogarth in a cafe, that it would never get better than this – being surprised by a letter written right under her nose?

Alice folded the paper slowly and put it back in the drawer, but remained standing where she was. She looked up and caught sight of herself in the mirror, was disorientated by a sudden sense of detachment from her current life, her current self. How had she ended up here? She'd assumed back then that she'd marry Jamie. She could see now that she'd been young and impulsive (and, she had to admit, not always entirely faithful). But she would have given everything up for him. What would her younger self have made of that strange, awkward encounter in the bookshop?

Alice sat down slowly on the stool by the desk. She'd really believed for a long time that she was over it. But seeing him again after all these years had shifted something. Time was a coiled spring, forever contracting and expanding, and suddenly there seemed to be no way of getting him out of her head. But was that really surprising, she thought, when there was so much left unsaid? Perhaps once you'd loved someone like that, you never really stopped – even if it became a different kind of love.

She tried not to blame him. She knew it had been terrible for him when Kit died – no wonder he had to get away. But all the same, a part of her couldn't help feeling that most people wouldn't have treated her like that, however intense their grief – just disappeared, without even telling her. The abandonment had been so brutal, and so complete. No word of explanation. No contact ever again.

In the months afterwards, there had been moments when Alice felt like she was going mad, had wondered if she could have imagined their whole relationship. The way Jamie had behaved didn't make any sense. And at the back of her mind, too, was the knowledge that she wasn't the kind of girl men would usually forget.

She was shaken by the sound of the front door. An

hour ago she would have been relieved at Mark's return, but now it felt like an intrusion. She stood up and glanced once more at her reflection, steeling herself for a return to the world. She probably should have supper underway, since she'd been home first. Mark would end up doing the cooking again. He always said he didn't mind, but perhaps he did.

She went reluctantly downstairs.

'Hi, Mark.'

He turned, and she saw how tired he was. 'Hi, love.' He hugged her to him.

She hid her face against his chest. When she felt steady, she looked up at him. 'I haven't started supper,' she said. 'I was just about to.'

'What are we having?'

'I don't know yet.'

'You don't really want to cook, do you? Why don't we get a takeaway?'

He was being kind, of course, but she felt stupidly hurt. 'I can do it. I can cook something.'

'I know. I just thought you might not want to.'

'Well, I do.'

They had soggy cheese omelettes, with brown bread and butter. It wasn't very nice, although Mark pretended it was. She should have let him order the takeaway.

They had sex that night, which made Alice feel better. When they were making love she felt close to him again, and it was easier to forget Jamie.

71

Afterwards, lying awake beside her sleeping husband, Alice began to feel afraid of the darkness. It was that complete, essential blackness that allowed for no chink of light. She wasn't used to it – night-time in London was shot through with little threads of illumination. But Mark had put up new blinds recently, heavy and midnight blue, which warded off any infiltrating light. Alice imagined the darkness seeping into her, through her mouth, through her nostrils, as though it were trying to dissolve her.

She turned over and reached out to Mark, felt for the warmth of his back and pressed herself against it, trying to assimilate her own breathing into the steady rhythm of his. She hated being the one left awake. However irrational, it made her feel as though she had been deliberately deserted.

Against her will, her thoughts returned to Jamie. Five years of silence, and then he was hurled back at her without warning. Surely this had to mean something. It was as though she were being offered a second chance, an opportunity to understand everything – and it was simply a question of being brave enough to take it. She turned away from Mark and curled up on her side, staring out into the darkness.

11

Her forehead resting against the train window, Alice watched the pallid landscape gliding past. She was troubled again by a sense of dislocation, as though she'd stepped out of her own life. Perhaps she should feel guilty for the lie she'd told that morning, but she was lulled into a kind of numbness by the steady motion of the train, the drab day, the strangeness of her situation.

She'd told Mark she was going to stay with Lindsay, one of the few school friends she still kept in touch with. He'd been pleased for her, as she'd known he would be. Alice had asked if he minded being left on his own for an evening, but Mark had said of course not, she should go and enjoy herself. She remembered how his kindness used to move her when they'd first met, how often his generosity had taken her by surprise. She supposed she took it for granted now.

Alice wasn't quite sure why she hadn't told him the truth. She wasn't doing anything wrong, exactly. But somehow she hadn't been able to imagine explaining it. It seemed impossible, like having a half-formed thought forced out of you before you'd had a chance to understand it yourself. She could tell him about it afterwards.

The train started to slow, and Alice felt a lurch of anxiety as it drew into Sheffield station.

She found the city grey and bewildering and fleetingly longed for Mark's comforting presence. She sought refuge in the loos in Debenhams and spent a while tidying herself up and adding the final touches to her make-up, overtaken for a moment by the weird sensation that she was preparing for a job interview. She hadn't expected to feel this nervous. She and Jamie had been so close once. Now she couldn't imagine how he was going to react, what they might say to each other. But she was just here to ask for an explanation, she reminded herself. Nothing more complicated than that. Taking a last look at herself in the mirror, she left.

The bookshop seemed less romantic than she remembered it. The building had looked darker and more imposing in the rain, less insistently red-brick than it did now; and she hadn't noticed how garish the sign was last time. Alice had planned to take a few moments outside to gather her courage, but she found she was being jostled by a steady stream of passersby, and in the end had to scurry straight in and up the stairs.

She paused, though, before ascending to the second floor. Trying to calm down, she spent a couple of minutes dazedly browsing the French Literature section next to the stairs. She remembered the last time she'd been here, how she and Mark had stopped briefly on this floor so Mark could pick up a French grammar; he was going on a business trip to Geneva and was trying to brush up. Alice picked up *Madame Bovary* in translation and flicked through its pages. She'd never read the novel, but she recalled Jamie recommending it to her once. Now she wished she'd bothered to read it.

Alice replaced the book and went up the stairs.

Scanning the History department for Jamie, she experienced a moment of despair as she realized it might be his day off. The idea hadn't occurred to her until now. But then her gaze fell on the till and there he was. She watched as he neatly slipped a book into a bag and handed the customer his change with a small, mechanical smile.

He came out from behind the desk holding a stack of books and carried them over to a section labelled Eastern European History. Alice stood a little way off whilst he arranged the books on the shelves, unsure how to begin. She found herself scanning the spines of the books he was shelving, as if for clues. She could just about make out the words 'Vlad the Impaler' on one of them.

The longer she waited, the more difficult it became to speak. In the end, she forced herself to say his name.

Jamie turned, a slight frown on his face.

'Hi, Alice.'

His manner was reserved to the point of wariness. Alice fiddled with the clasp of her handbag, wondering what on earth she should say next.

'How are you?' she tried.

'OK, thanks.'

Alice was stuck again, and Jamie showed no sign of helping her. She gestured at the shelves: 'Those look interesting.'

'Yes,' Jamie said. 'They're selling well.' He turned back

to the shelves, and remained looking at them speculatively for a few moments.

As the silence between them lengthened, Alice started to panic. She said, 'I'm just in Sheffield for the day.'

'Is Mark here too?'

'No – he's in London.' She made herself add, 'I came to see you.'

He didn't say anything, but she thought she saw his shoulders tense.

'I just wanted to talk to you,' she said.

'About what?'

How could he stand there so calmly? 'About *us*,' Alice said.

Now Jamie seemed to be retreating inside himself. It was like watching someone turn to stone. 'I'm not really sure what you mean,' he said.

'I mean, everything that happened,' she said. 'The way you left.'

'It was such a long time ago.'

'It still *matters*.' Alice heard the break in her voice and was overcome by a sense of her own helplessness. She tried to get herself under control.

More calmly, she said, 'I know you were messed up, Jamie. I wish you'd let me help you. But surely you can see now that running away doesn't solve anything?' When he didn't reply, she swallowed and said, 'I just want to know how you could leave me like that.'

Jamie looked at her silently. Eventually, he said, 'I'm sorry, Alice. I suppose I was upset.'

'I *know*. I know how awful it was for you.'

'I don't think you do.' His expression was unreadable.

'I mean, I know how close you and Kit were.'

Jamie turned away from her. He stared hard at the shelves. Alice wanted to reach out and touch him, to comfort him as she hadn't been allowed to at the time. But there was something rigid in the way he was standing that made her afraid.

After a moment, Jamie said, 'I don't want to talk about this.'

Alice could hardly speak. At length, she said, 'Don't you think you owe me some kind of explanation at least? Do you realize how much you hurt me?'

'I'm sorry.'

'I tried asking your family, you know. When you stopped answering my calls. They said you'd gone away. How do you think it felt, having to hear that from them?'

He wouldn't look at her.

Alice paused, as something occurred to her for the first time. 'Do your family even know where you are?'

'No.'

'*God*, Jamie.' She stared at him in disbelief. 'What makes you think it's OK to treat people like that?'

'You don't know what you're talking about.'

His burst of anger surprised Alice. She took a step back, close to tears.

'Jamie,' she said. She put out her hand and took hold of his arm. 'You were everything to me.'

Momentarily detained, he gave her a quick look; for a few seconds, he was the old Jamie, sharp and challenging, and she felt a surge of hope.

'I'm not sure that's true,' he said.

'You know I loved you. I think I always will.'

Jamie looked at her wearily. 'Go back to your husband, Alice.'

She took a taxi to the station, clutching her handbag to her chest for comfort. She'd thought she was too tired and angry to cry, but she managed it a bit on the train back to London.

Old images bled together in her mind. She saw Jamie sitting across from her in the pub on one of their early dates; then again in the stark hospital corridor. She saw him in the cafe, writing her the letter, and then at Kit's funeral; silent, his eyes dead.

Jamie, she could see, had found his own release from reality, far away from his family, pretending none of it had ever happened. She was a remnant of his past, so he'd cast her off, without even considering how that would make her feel, or how it would affect the rest of her life.

Staring out at the fields flashing past, aware of each second taking her further away from him, Alice thought: this was never Jamie's decision to make. After Kit died, he was in no fit state to know what was best for him, or for anyone else. Imagine what his parents must be going through – not knowing where their son is, not having seen him for years. As the train drew into St Pancras, Alice made up her mind. She could at least give some answers to other people, even if there could be none for her.

It had only just gone seven and she couldn't bear the

idea of going straight home, so she wandered through the darkening streets for a while and finally ended up in a little pub. She sat down at a table in the corner and had two glasses of white wine whilst trying to read the paper. But her eyes kept blurring with tears, and after a while she stopped trying to brush them away.

She arrived home around nine, and opened the front door quietly. The lights were on in the sitting room and she found Mark sitting on the sofa in his dressing gown, reading a book of hers about Byzantine art. He stood up in surprise when she entered.

'I thought you were staying over!' he said. He looked delighted to see her, and the tight, painful feeling in her chest eased a little.

'I was,' she said. 'But I missed you.' And she walked into his arms.

12

Rose woke early as usual, even though it was a Sunday. But it would be no use trying to get back to sleep. She eased herself out of bed gently so as not to wake Joe and went downstairs in her dressing gown to make a cup of tea.

It was just starting to get light outside. She didn't mind this hazy in-between time, before the day had started but after the night had ended. And she didn't find weekends too bad as a general rule, with the family around and needing her attention.

Sunday was special, the most important part of the week. Rose sometimes liked to imagine how the day might unfold. They'd all get up early and have breakfast together, then get dressed in their best clothes and congregate in the kitchen. Joe would read the papers whilst Rose and Emma prepared the roast, and then they'd all sit down to eat the hearty meal together whilst chatting good-naturedly about nothing in particular. In the afternoon, they'd go for a long walk and when they got back they'd collapse on the sofas in the living room with mugs of tea or hot chocolate. They'd perhaps play a board game together in the evening, then have a light supper of bread and cheese, and watch a film.

She often played scenes like this in her mind. Unfortunately, it never seemed to work out the way she hoped. Joe would disappear off to his shed for most of the day, and Emma, too, was being rather difficult. She used to be happy to help her mother with the cooking or to sit in the kitchen chatting to her, but now she was often sullen and stayed in her bedroom for hours at a time. When Rose asked her what she'd been doing up there, or what her plans for the day were, Emma would just shrug, as if to say 'None of your business'. Rose was worried something was going on at school, but Emma was being very moody and wouldn't talk to her about it. She used to tell me everything, Rose thought. When did that stop?

When she'd finished her tea, she went back upstairs to have a shower, and then chose her colourful silk skirt and orange cashmere jumper to wear. It was always good to make an effort.

She'd been reading in the kitchen for over an hour before Joe appeared. Rose looked up hopefully, but he only said a brief, mumbled 'good morning', made himself a cup of coffee and took it out to the shed with him.

Rose waited until nine o'clock before knocking on Emma's door.

'Darling, are you awake?'

There was no answer.

'Emma?'

After a brief pause, she heard a sulky 'What?' from the other side of the door.

'Don't you think you should be getting up now?'

'Leave me alone.'

'But don't you want to be making the most of your Sunday? You've got school again tomorrow.'

'Go away!'

Rose went back to the kitchen. She put on the radio for company and set about the preparations for lunch.

The meal was to be a roast chicken with roasted vegetables and cauliflower cheese followed by apple-and-blackberry crumble and she wanted it to be really good. It was just what the family needed.

Once, Rose had enjoyed cooking for its own sake. It was the alchemy of the transformation that delighted her. Flour, sugar, butter and eggs became a sponge cake, soft and warm from the oven. A delicious steaming casserole was created from chunks of raw meat and vegetables with flour and stock. Egg whites and sugar – the most astonishing metamorphosis of all – became meringues: hard, sweet and crumbling. Rose knew it was an everyday kind of magic, but it was magic nonetheless.

These days she seemed to have lost the joy in cooking she used to feel. Perhaps it was just because she'd done so *much* of it, made so many meals for her family over the years. But she continued to work hard at it; now it felt more important than ever to get it right.

The phone began to ring just as Rose was flouring the potatoes. She allowed herself a huff of irritation as she wiped her hands and went through to the living room to answer it.

She picked up the phone, and a woman's voice said, 'Mrs Stewart?'

Rose assumed it was a salesperson, and waited for the

woman to make her pitch so she could tell her she wasn't interested and put the phone down.

Then the voice said, 'This is Alice Brown.'

Rose knew the name, but couldn't place it for a few moments.

Alice added hesitantly, 'I used to be Jamie's girlfriend.'

Her careful phrase struck Rose as pre-prepared. She felt horribly caught out, but she rallied.

'Alice! What a lovely surprise. How *are* you?'

'Well, fine,' Alice said, sounding a bit uncertain. 'I'm married, actually.' She paused again, apparently searching for something else to add. 'His name's Mark.'

'That's *wonderful*. Congratulations!' Rose sounded breathless, even to herself. 'And where did you two meet?'

'Oh. Through friends. Not very interesting, I'm afraid. How are you, Mrs Stewart?'

'We're fine, thank you, ticking along nicely. I'm just in the middle of making the Sunday roast, actually. Joe looks forward to it every week, and I wouldn't want to disappoint him. And Emma's at that age where she's always hungry. It leaves a lot of clearing up to do, of course, but it is nice to sit down and eat a special meal together. I expect you find that with Mark?'

'I don't cook much.'

There was a silence. After a moment, Alice said, 'I hope you don't mind my ringing—'

'But of course not!' Rose said. 'It's lovely to catch up with all your news.' She wanted to end the conversation, and wondered if she should mention the roast again.

Alice said hurriedly, 'Well, the reason I rang is that I know where Jamie is.'

If Rose hadn't pursed her lips, she thought she would have cried out. She gripped the phone, seeing his face again, as a child, grinning and mischievous, hair sticking up all over the place.

Alice was talking again. Rose made herself pay attention.

'He works in a bookshop in Sheffield,' Alice said. 'Mark and I were passing through a few weeks ago, and it was tipping down with rain, so we stepped inside, and there he was.'

Rose couldn't speak for a moment. She was moved by the idea of Jamie working in a bookshop. Was that what he'd been doing with himself all these years? He was safe and well, at least. That was something. That was everything, really.

'How is he?' she said after a moment.

'Fine. I think.'

'How did he look?'

This seemed to stump Alice. 'Like . . . he always looked. A bit older, I suppose.'

'He's twenty-six,' Rose said, almost to herself. 'He had his birthday in August.'

'I know. I remember.'

'Of course. Yes.' Rose tried to get a grip on her thoughts. 'Did you speak to him?' she asked.

'Yes.'

'What did he say?'

Alice went quiet for a long time. Rose was just beginning to wonder if she'd hung up when Alice spoke again. 'He said it was nice to see me.'

Now Rose stayed silent. There were plenty of things she could say, but she found it impossible to choose one. She felt peculiar, as though her heart had got too big for her chest.

'He doesn't know I'm calling you,' Alice said. 'But I had to tell you I'd seen him. He shouldn't be allowed to cut himself off from everyone. For his own sake, as well as yours. I think he'll be glad I've told you – in the end.'

She doesn't know, Rose realized. All along, she'd assumed that Jamie would have told Alice, but he clearly hadn't. Alice knew how Kit had died, of course – she'd come to the funeral, bless her. But beyond that, he'd told her nothing. Rose could hardly bear to think of Jamie's isolation.

'What's the name of the bookshop?' she remembered to ask after a minute.

'Sudbury's. It's in the centre.'

There was a pause, and then Rose said in a rush, 'Well, Alice, it was lovely chatting but I must get on now. I have to get the potatoes in the oven or they won't be ready in time for the chicken, and Joe'll never let me hear the end of it. Take care of yourself, and give my love to Mark. I'm sure he's very nice.'

'OK,' Alice said. 'I just thought you should know.'

'Thank you, it was a kind thought. Alright. Bye now.'

'Bye.' Alice sounded resigned.

Rose put the phone down.

She went very slowly into the kitchen, put the tray of

potatoes in the oven and checked on the chicken. Then she allowed herself to sit at the kitchen table for a few moments, doing absolutely nothing.

The chicken turned out succulent and tender, the vegetables were done to perfection and the gravy steamed, rich and thick, on their loaded plates. Joe and Emma both commented on how good it was, which was a triumph in itself; generally, they were silently appreciative. Both had seconds. *And* they still found room for large helpings of blackberry-and-apple crumble with custard.

Even Rose found that she had finished everything on her plate almost without noticing it. She used to enjoy food ever so much – a little *too much*, truth be told – but nowadays she was rarely hungry, and even when she was, she could resist the urge to eat. She found a curious strength in denying herself.

'Who were you on the phone to, Mum?' Emma asked over pudding, catching Rose off guard.

She calmed herself, and countered airily, 'When?'

'Before lunch.'

Rose thought more quickly than she knew she was capable of. 'It was Carol, from down the road, just ringing for a chat. She'd run into her ex-husband, you see, and was in a bit of a tizz about it. He's been rather ill, as it turns out.' She could have gone on talking, joining the dots of her story in ever more elaborate ways, but she forced herself to stop and take a mouthful of water.

She glanced cautiously at Emma over the top of her glass, but Emma seemed to have lost interest. Rose drew her secret around herself. It wouldn't change anything – not really. But her new knowledge eased the dull pain in her chest, that feeling of constriction she was so used to these days.

Soon she would have to tell Joe. Joe would be . . . well, she didn't know how Joe would be. There was a time when the mention of Jamie's name produced in Joe a rage so black and complete that he no longer seemed like himself. But that had been years ago. Neither of them had been keen to talk about it afterwards, and it had gone unmentioned for so long now.

The realization that she had no idea how Joe would react shocked Rose a little. Had it come to that? He must feel calmer about what had happened now, more resigned. But she didn't know for sure, and couldn't imagine asking him. Sometimes Rose wondered if he'd wiped Jamie out completely – made himself forget he'd ever had a second son. She could understand why he might have wanted to, but the idea distressed her. It wasn't so easy for a mother, she thought.

Watching Emma finishing the last of her crumble, Rose recalled one occasion just before Kit went to university. She'd been in the kitchen when she heard the sound of shattering glass, and had rushed out into the garden to see what had happened. She found Kit and Jamie standing guiltily by the greenhouse, Jamie holding a football. Her appalled gaze took in the smashed pane and the shards of glass around their feet. Emma was nearby, her thumb in her mouth and her eyes round at the destruction that had just taken place.

'Boys, did you just break that?' Rose said.

'Yeah,' Jamie said reluctantly.

'Which of you was it?'

'It was Emmet,' Kit said.

'Don't be silly, Kit. I'm not in the mood.'

Emma took her thumb out of her mouth. 'It's not Emmet,' she said. 'It's Em*ma*.'

'That's what I said. Emmet.'

Emma began to giggle. 'It's Em*ma*.'

'Shall we just compromise?' Kit said. 'I'll call you Peter.'

Emma threw back her head and laughed uproariously. Rose had to remind herself that she was meant to be cross.

'Kit,' she said. 'Stop changing the subject. Who smashed the glass?'

'Alright,' Kit said. 'It was me. I'm sorry, Mum.'

'His aim's not very good,' Jamie said, by way of explanation. 'You should see him take a penalty.'

'Well, at least I can put some force behind the ball,' Kit said. 'I really am sorry, Mum. It was an accident.'

Rose tried to carry on being annoyed. She looked at the boys, who were apologetic, but too cheerful to be properly contrite, and she looked at Emma, who was still chuckling – and instead she found herself thinking how absurdly wonderful her children were, even when they were being a complete nuisance.

Kit and Jamie had paid to replace the glass themselves afterwards, though she hadn't asked them to. She'd wondered if Joe would be annoyed, but he'd been relaxed about it. He said he was surprised the greenhouse had remained intact for so long given that the boys regularly seemed to use it for target practice; and besides, it was only a greenhouse, not a family heirloom.

Remembering this, Rose began to feel a little more confident about the conversation she needed to have with him after lunch.

At last, the table was cleared, the plates were in the dishwasher and the larger pans were piled up in the sink. Emma had disappeared off, saying something about having a project to finish, and Rose was preparing to tackle the washing up.

Joe lingered in the doorway, clearly feeling he couldn't leave straight away. Usually Rose told him brightly to go back to the shed and get on with his work, to leave all the clearing up to her. (She'd learnt to refer to it as 'his work', not his 'hobby'.) But today she needed him to stay.

'That was a really nice lunch,' he commented. 'The chicken was very good. Should set me up nicely for the afternoon.' He paused. 'Thank you.'

'I was pleased with the chicken,' Rose said, to keep him talking. 'It was tender, wasn't it?'

'It was,' Joe conceded.

'It's all in the timing, of course.'

'So you always say.'

Rose could see she was losing him. 'Did you enjoy the crumble?'

'Yes, very much.' Joe looked out of the window towards his shed. 'I should probably be getting on now—'

'Joe,' she said, which stopped him; they hardly ever seemed to use each other's names these days.

'Joe,' Rose repeated uncertainly. 'I had a phone call today. From Alice Brown.'

She knew he recognized the name because she saw his jaw clench. He stared at her, registering no emotion. 'What did she want?'

Rose felt her mouth going dry, but she had to go on.

'She saw Jamie recently,' she said. 'In Sheffield. He's working in a bookshop called Sudbury's. He's—'

'Why are you telling me?' Joe cut across her.

Rose flinched at his look. She'd allowed herself to think, in the moments before, that perhaps Joe might share her relief that Jamie was safe, even if he could never come back. Now she saw that she'd been mistaken. No one could ever know what anybody else was thinking. Nobody knew that better than her.

'He's fine,' she said. 'That's all.'

The silence was loud. It roared with shock. Rose didn't need to look at Joe's face to know that she'd burst through the wall of the dam.

'Rose,' he said at last, and she thought how once she'd loved it when he said her name, back when it had sounded like a secret between them. Now the single syllable chilled her. 'Never speak to me about this again,' Joe said. 'Do you understand?'

'Yes.' She wished she could look at him, wished that she could show him she was agreeing not because she was afraid of him but because she knew he was right, that it was better for each of them to live with this alone. But she found she couldn't lift her eyes from the buttons on his shirt.

Joe turned and went out of the back door, but he wasn't going to his shed. A moment later Rose heard the car start and drive away.

She leaned against the sink. Then she put her rubber gloves on and began to wash up.

13

Emma, listening at the kitchen door, had fled when she heard her father leave the room. She wasn't sure where Jesus stood on eavesdropping (she suspected He didn't encourage it) but she was finding herself less and less interested these days in Jesus' opinions.

She'd assumed from the way her mum had lied about the phone call that she must be having an affair. Her mother's flustered reaction when asked about it was enough to confirm Emma's suspicions, as well as the way she'd spoken really fast without looking anyone in the eye. Not a good liar, Emma concluded. Not the kind of person who should embark upon a torrid affair. Besides, she was much too old and should be ashamed of herself.

She was sure that her father must also have realized the phone call wasn't from Carol down the road and wondered what he would make of it all, so after lunch she'd waited anxiously by the kitchen door to see what would happen.

But she'd forgotten all about the affair when she heard Jamie's name. Emma had pushed her face closer to the door, hardly able to keep still in her shock.

Now, she slipped upstairs to her bedroom feeling dis-orientated, as though she'd suddenly woken up to find herself in the wrong family. It was clear from her dad's reaction that Jamie's reappearance was another thing that couldn't ever be discussed. A new topic to add to the list, which already included anything to do with Kit, and the fact that Jamie had left home in the first place.

But now he'd been *found*, Emma thought, sitting on her bed in wonder. They couldn't pretend he didn't exist. Not any more.

Her thoughts turned to Jamie himself. Why had he been hiding himself away for so long? She recalled the things she'd imagined about him in the past – they struck her as embarrassing and childish now. Of course he hadn't been somewhere exotic like Africa or Paris. He'd been in Sheffield all along, working in a bookshop called Sudbury's. Not so far away he couldn't have visited once in a while, or sent her a card on her birthday.

She was beginning to feel angry with Jamie for abandoning her, but fought against it. She thought of him reading *The Hobbit* to her, and picking her up and spinning her round when she was very little. Surely he wouldn't have left unless he had no choice.

Emma stood up, finding she couldn't bear to stay in her bedroom any longer. She went out onto the landing and hesitated for a few moments, unsure of where to go. Certainly not downstairs, which was saturated with the hostility of her father's departure. After a minute, she went into the Guest Room, hoping to be soothed by its blankness. But it was no good. The room's neutrality became oppressive rather than peaceful. It suddenly seemed to Emma that there was something brutal in the bare walls. She acknowledged now what she must have already known – that any trace of Jamie had been deliberately erased by her parents.

She fled from the room and stood rigidly on the landing. One of her brothers had died and the other had run away, and her parents would never talk about it, had never even tried to explain to her why Jamie had left, beyond saying he was upset about Kit. *Which we all were*, Emma thought. It wasn't a proper explanation – it never had been, only she'd always been too young or too afraid to question it. Well, she wasn't now. They had no right to leave her out of everything, as if she didn't matter at all; as if she hadn't suffered too.

She found her mother in the kitchen, sitting at the table. There was a cup of tea in front of her which she didn't seem to be drinking. Emma saw that all the washing up had been done, the surfaces wiped down, the dishes put away. The kitchen was spotless.

Emma came straight to the point. 'I know about Jamie. I heard you and Dad talking. I know he's in Sheffield.'

She'd expected a more dramatic reaction from her mother, some kind of shock or fear at Emma's revelation. But her mum only said in a strange, bright-weary voice, without looking at her, 'Do you, darling? It's good news, isn't it? He's fine and he has a lovely job and he's quite happy up there.'

'How do you know?'

'Alice said he was fine.'

'When are we going to visit him?'

After a long pause, her mum said, 'We're not, Emma.'

Emma leapt on this. '*Why not*? Why don't we ever see

him? Why can't he come home?' When her mother didn't reply, Emma pushed for a reaction. 'It's got something to do with Kit, hasn't it?'

'Emma, I don't want to discuss it. Leave it, please.' Her mum was trying to sound offhand and commanding. It was almost funny, as if she was doing an impression of Emma's dad. But Emma could see straight through it.

'It's cowardly not to talk about things,' she said. 'And it's not fair on Kit,' she added, in a flash of inspiration. 'If you don't talk about people, you forget them. I've almost forgotten Kit, and Jamie as well.'

She saw this hit home. Her mum said hesitantly, 'It's hard to talk about some things. Don't you see that, darling? Let's leave it now.'

'Why is it hard?' Emma said.

Her mum gave a shuddering sigh and looked down at her mug of tea. She didn't speak for a few moments. Emma was just about to say something else when her mum said, 'Do you know how Kit died?'

This unsettled Emma. 'Yes,' she said. 'He made a mistake with his medication. Some kind of medicine. He had an allergic reaction, or something. It was an accident.' She couldn't stop talking, filling up the threatening silence. As she spoke, she began to see how feeble these explanations were. Was this another thing she'd known all along? She looked at her mother in mute appeal.

'No,' her mother said. 'I'm so sorry, darling. It wasn't an accident. Kit took his own life.'

Emma was swallowing hard, feeling as though she had

something stuck in her throat. 'You told me it was an accident. *You told me that.*'

'You were nine when it happened. How could I have told you he'd done it on purpose?'

'You lied to me,' Emma said in disbelief.

'I just didn't tell you the whole truth. I was trying to protect you. I wanted you to have a happy childhood.' Her mum was wheedling now, pleading with her.

'He can't have done,' Emma said. 'He wouldn't.'

'He was very unhappy—'

'Why didn't you stop him?'

Her mother began to cry. '*I didn't know.* We didn't realize—'

Emma was backing out of the kitchen. She didn't want to know anything more. As long as she lived, she didn't want to hear anything else about Kit's death. She just wanted to be far away from it all. She could still hear her mother crying as she ran back up the stairs.

Emma spent the rest of the afternoon sitting in her bed reading the Bible as it grew dark outside. She concentrated mainly on the Psalms, picking out the most desperate and anguished passages she could find. Psalm 55 suited her needs best, and she recited it quietly to herself. *My heart is sore pained within me: and the terrors of death are fallen upon me.*

She tried not to think about what Kit had done, but she couldn't keep her mind away from it. It was impossible that funny, handsome Kit could have killed himself. Her mother had said he was very unhappy, but Emma was often unhappy herself. Kit's response to unhappiness didn't make sense. Emma found that she couldn't get any kind of handle on the idea: her imagination retreated before it, leaving her numb.

Perhaps it was more understandable now, she thought, that Jamie had gone away. She'd heard people say that suicide was selfish. Maybe Jamie thought so too, and was angry with Kit, and that was why he didn't want to be at home.

Emma was trying to leave God out of it, but couldn't help thinking about His wrath. Would someone who killed themselves go to hell? She wasn't sure she believed in hell any more, but the idea worried her all the same. St Paul said your body was a temple of the Holy Ghost, so he probably hated suicide. And it seemed to be mostly wicked people who killed themselves in the Bible, like Judas and Saul.

But Jesus is meant to forgive us, Emma thought. He came to save us, not to condemn us.

She realized it would be better to read something reassuring in the New Testament next, but instead she chose the story of Cain and Abel, then the tale of the great flood, and then the destruction of Sodom and Gomorrah. The stories frightened her more than they ever had before, but she wanted to be frightened. The world was a terrifying place, and there was no longer any point in pretending otherwise.

*

Much later that evening, when Emma went downstairs, she found her mother laying out a cheese board and some rolls. Emma thought her mum looked tearful, but she smiled at Emma when she saw her.

'Ready for some supper, darling? I was just going to come and get you.'

Emma nodded and slid into her seat. 'Where's Dad?' she said.

'He's gone out. I expect he'll be back any minute.'

Her mum had laid three places at the table, Emma saw. 'Should we wait for him?'

'If I were you, darling, I'd tuck in now.'

Emma helped herself to some Cheddar and a roll, and they ate in silence for a while. Her mum didn't seem inclined to make conversation like she usually did.

At last, unable to bear the silence any longer, Emma said, 'Do you think they had cheese in biblical times?'

Her mum didn't reply. She was staring at her plate, apparently lost in thought.

'Mum?' Emma repeated her question.

'Sorry, love.' Her mum shook herself and considered the matter. 'I think they probably did.'

They lapsed into silence again.

Emma had nearly finished her second roll when they heard the sound of a car outside. Her mum looked up, and put her roll back down on her plate. Emma watched her stare at the door.

A moment later, Emma's dad walked in. He stopped just inside the door. Nobody said anything at first.

Then her mum said, 'You're just in time for supper.'

He nodded. 'So I see.'

'There's a lovely Stilton.'

He came round to the table slowly and took his place. 'Thank you,' he said after a moment.

Emma realized that she'd been holding her breath, and made herself relax. She returned her attention to her roll.

Eventually, her dad said, 'Got much on at school tomorrow, Emma?'

Emma was immediately downcast, but she knew he was trying to make conversation, so she said, 'I've got double English, which is good, and Maths, which I hate.'

'I didn't like Maths when I was at school,' her mum said.

'But it's a useful subject to master,' her dad added.

Emma nodded.

'Sometimes it's good to persevere,' her dad said.

Emma swallowed her last mouthful of bread and escaped back to her room as soon as she could.

That night, she had a disturbing dream. She was walking through a field in summer and as she crossed it she noticed that the sky was beginning to darken. The next moment, the sun vanished completely and everything became murky and dim. Then she saw two figures coming out of the gloom towards her. As they drew closer, she realized they were Cain and Abel; Abel mournful and dripping with blood, Cain mutinous and desolate. Then she heard the Lord's voice, booming out through the darkness. *What hast thou done? The voice of thy brother's blood crieth unto me from the ground.*

Emma started to walk away from the terrible scene, but

the ghostly Cain and Abel followed her. And then the blood from Abel's wound gushed out in a sudden torrent and turned into a river like the first plague of Egypt, and swept the three of them up in it, and carried them away while the Lord looked on.

14

The cold was vicious. Jamie woke every morning to a transformed world, the ground glittering with frost and the tree-branches spray-painted white. Winter had taken everyone by surprise, creeping up soundlessly and then sweeping in with a merciless force. Being outside became an ordeal; the freezing air made Jamie's face smart and however many layers he wore under his coat, he'd arrive at the bookshop each morning bitten to the core by the cold.

All the same, he relished the drawing in of winter. Darkness fell early, and people kept to themselves. He looked forward to coming back to his flat in the evenings, putting the heating on, drawing the curtains, retreating into his cocoon of light and warmth.

Winter brought with it a strange nostalgia. He remembered his mother reading him Hans Christian Andersen's *Snow Queen* when he was a child, how frightened and obscurely excited he'd been by its warped vision of the world. He thought of the icy queen in a cloud of snowflakes like white bees, with her chilling kisses: numbing; obliterating memory; and finally, killing. He thought of the tiny splinters of glass in Kay's eyes and heart which made everything appear ugly and hopeless to him. A despair that couldn't be mitigated or reasoned with.

The slopes of Sheffield soon became perilous with ice. Making his way to work one morning, Jamie slipped, twisting his ankle. He limped through the day, wincing with pain whenever he put any weight on his foot. The worst thing was that it drew people's attention. Jenny from Second-Hand asked him with real concern if he was OK, and Sally, his colleague in History, suggested he draw up a chair and sit behind the desk. Jamie thanked her, but said he'd rather carry on with the stock reports. The bookshop was at its busiest at this time of year, with only a month to go until Christmas, and the throngs of people milling about the usually empty History department unsettled Jamie. He hated the idea of being stranded behind the desk.

As he was checking off the stock report in Eastern European History, he was accosted by a large, middle-aged woman dressed for the adverse weather conditions in an anorak and sturdy walking boots. Jamie had noticed her browsing in Medieval History a while back.

'I hope you don't mind my saying,' she said. 'But that looks painful. Your ankle. May I ask what happened?' She had a clipped, officious voice. It set Jamie's teeth on edge.

'I slipped.'

'Oh. I thought it might be from sport or something,' the woman said. 'Lots of ice around, though. You need to be careful.' When Jamie kept quiet, she said, 'You should go to the doctor's. Get it looked at. It might be a nasty sprain. Or you could strap it up. Quite tricky to do yourself, though.'

'Yes.' He paused, looking for a way to end the exchange. 'I might just wait for it to get better on its own.'

'But you'll make it worse,' the woman said. 'Walking on it like that.'

There was an uncomfortable silence, which Jamie decided not to fill. After a moment, the woman said abruptly, 'Well, I just thought someone should say something. Rather than let you do yourself a mischief.' She returned to Medieval History, and Jamie could see he'd offended her. She still bought a book on the plague years, although she pointedly gave it to Sally to put through the till.

Jamie had hoped for some peace at lunchtime, but unfortunately Brian had resumed jovial relations with him after a few weeks of awkwardness. He sidled up to Jamie in the staff room, as he sat in the corner reading *The Guns of Navarone*. Jamie tried pretending he was too absorbed in his reading to notice Brian standing over him. He turned the page determinedly, but there was no escape.

'You're making short work of that,' Brian said.

Jamie reflected that he could hardly object to Brian's patronizing tone; he had, after all, brought it upon himself.

'No long words,' he said.

'Is it a good one?'

'Yes,' Jamie said, his eyes on the page.

'They've made a film of it, haven't they? Starred, er . . .' Brian searched around in his memory, 'that fellow with the moustache. David Lean.'

'David Niven.'

'Ah, yes. He was in it, too.' Brian thought for a few moments. 'There was someone else famous in it, too. Cary Grant, maybe.'

'Gregory Peck.'

'Quite the stellar cast.' Brian sat down beside him. 'I'm completely disturbing your reading,' he said chummily, as if waiting for Jamie to demur and close his book. When Jamie ignored him and carried on reading, Brian said, 'I've had a bit of a think about some books that might suit you. Perhaps Ursula Le Guin isn't for everyone. But have you tried the Willard Price adventure books?'

Jamie shook his head.

'Now don't be put off by the fact that they're for young adults,' Brian said. 'They're what you might call *rollicking good yarns*.' He produced a book from his bag and handed it over.

Jamie inspected it. It was called *Volcano Adventure*, and the front cover depicted two wholesome-looking youths running away from an erupting volcano. Jamie had an unenthusiastic flick through under Brian's watchful gaze and murmured that it looked gripping.

'It *is*,' Brian said. 'And if you like this one, there are many more. I can lend you all of them. How about we set you a little target? You could try to get through one a week – or a fortnight if you think that's more manageable. I guarantee you, your reading speed will increase in no time.'

Jamie took in this suggestion in silence.

'See how you get on with this one first,' Brian said. 'And we'll have a chat about it next week.'

'Thanks,' Jamie said. 'That sounds very – motivating.'

That evening, as he was attempting to swathe his swollen ankle in several Tubigrips he'd bought in Boots, his mobile rang. Jamie considered ignoring the call, decided not to.

'Sam.'

'James. How are you keeping?' Sam asked.

'Fine.'

'Cold up there?'

'Yes.'

'Any snow yet?'

'No.'

'Make sure you wear plenty of layers.'

'Jesus, Sam.'

There was a silence, then Sam said, 'Just wanted to check you weren't snowed in and half-starved to death. I'd hate to be the one who found you.'

'You'd love it. You'd be in the papers.'

'Getting any better at FIFA?'

'Yes.'

'You could hardly get any worse.'

'I was out of practice.'

'You know if you just got an Internet connection we could play together online?'

'Yeah. Maybe.'

'Have you started playing *Grand Theft Auto* yet?'

'The bridge to the second island's just opened up.'

Then, feeling like he should ask Sam something, Jamie said, 'How's work?'

'Hellish. Plenty of money, but no time to spend it.'

'Sounds like a treadmill.'

'It is, Jamie.' Sam paused. 'How are you spending your time now the cold weather's closed in? You're not too bored?'

'Nope. I play on the PlayStation. And I read.'

He was also, although he didn't mention this to Sam, building up his Lego collection. He'd allowed himself more purchases as the temperature dropped, given how much time he was spending indoors. He always chose the ones he thought Kit would have liked best. His latest acquisition was the haunted house, which now sat alongside the cowboy ranch, the jungle temple, the Pharaoh's tomb and the Viking catapult on his bedroom floor. He still lamented the loss of the space station, but had decided to wait a while before buying the model again; at present, it was tainted by the terror of his panic attack.

Kit had rarely played with any of his Lego models after he'd finished them, although sometimes he'd let Jamie play with them. It was the construction stage that interested Kit – the challenge of precisely recreating the steps in the pictures, filling in the blanks brick by brick, noting the exact progression of each picture and mirroring it in his own model. The joy had been in the creation of splendour from disparate, unpromising plastic bricks; the magic which lay in the potential of things.

After he'd finished speaking to Sam, Jamie went through to his bedroom to have another look at his models. It gave him some satisfaction to contemplate which one he might buy next.

He thought of the Christmas when Kit had been given the remote-control plane. At the time, Jamie had felt upset on Kit's behalf because he himself had got *Donkey Kong Country* for the Super Nintendo, which was a much better present than a model plane. He'd felt so sorry for Kit that he even decided he'd offer him the first go on *Donkey Kong*.

But Kit hadn't been interested, and had spent all of Christmas afternoon assembling the plane with their dad, gluing little bits together, and studying the instructions. Neither of them had wanted to come and watch Jamie complete level one, and he'd had to settle for his mum. She was very impressed by how many bananas he picked up and said, 'Well *done*, darling,' when he cantered along on the rhino, but he couldn't help feeling that she didn't really get it.

On Boxing Day morning, Kit went out with their dad to fly the plane for the first time. Their dad said, 'Why don't you come along too, Jamie?' but Jamie still felt cross, so he said it looked boring, and stayed in miserably playing through levels five to ten of *Donkey Kong*. His dad and Kit came back at lunchtime, glowing and excited, saying the plane had flown perfectly.

That afternoon, once Kit had settled down to build his new Lego castle, and their mum and dad were reading the papers together, Jamie thought he'd sneak a look at the plane himself. He went into Kit's bedroom and picked it up, making it swoop around as though it were flying. And then, since no one had noticed him, he thought he might as well have a proper go at flying it, so he grabbed the remote control and went out into the garden.

Holding the plane in one hand and the remote control in the other, he launched the plane into the air. It glided along perfectly for a few moments, and Jamie started to enjoy himself. But when he tried to steer it, the remote control didn't seem to work. He jabbed desperately at the controls as the plane soared towards a silver birch tree, but with no effect. The plane smashed into the trunk, and Jamie watched in horror as it fell to the ground and lay there, a crumpled mess. A wing had come off, and the propeller had snapped.

Jamie was still staring at the crash-site with his mouth open when Kit came out and shouted, 'What have you *done*?'

'I'm sorry!' Jamie said.

Then he saw his dad coming out as well, and panicked. He dodged through the hedge at the bottom of the garden and sprinted across the fields and into the woods.

He carried on running without pausing or looking back until he was right in the heart of the woods in the Swing Den. He sat down on the ground and considered his position. It was freezing, and he was wearing a jumper but no coat. He knew he might have to stay here for a few days before it was safe to return. He'd have to eat berries to survive. Water wouldn't be a problem, because there was a stream running through the Long Den, which wasn't far away, but he didn't think it was going to be much fun. He thought of his family, who would probably soon forget all about him and sit down to turkey and mashed potato together – their usual Boxing Day supper. Jamie was shaken by his first experience of real, intense loneliness. He began to cry.

He was eventually distracted by the sound of twigs cracking nearby. Moments later, Kit appeared.

'Mum and Dad say you have to come home,' he said, looking at Jamie stonily.

Jamie stayed where he was, wiping his nose with the sleeve of his jumper. 'They don't want me.'

'Don't be stupid.' Kit stood with his hands in his pockets, half-scowling, half-relenting. 'Look, there's no need to cry about it. We can glue the wing back on, and Dad says he can get me a new propeller.'

Jamie said, very quietly, 'Sorry, Kit.'

And Kit said, 'Come and see my Lego castle. It's finished. I don't mind if you play with it – just don't break it.'

'Is Dad cross?'

'A bit. Not really. It was *my* plane, anyway. And Mum says supper's-nearly-ready-and-would-you-like-peas-instead-of-carrots?'

They set off back home, and Jamie offered as they walked, 'Do you want a go on *Donkey Kong*?'

'Alright,' Kit said.

'I'm on level eleven.'

'Nice.'

Remembering his brother now, Jamie found himself smiling.

Then, as if to punish his complacence, he recalled Kit's bedroom, the day the Lego was broken. He saw in his mind's eye the bombsite of destroyed buildings, his brother hurling handfuls of tiny bricks against the wall, the explosion of colour. Jamie himself, summoned by the noise, had stood silently in the doorway and watched.

After the crisis had passed, Jamie had tried to rebuild them for Kit, but he hadn't done a good job and the models looked lopsided and broken when he set them up again on Kit's shelf. And when Kit saw them he sneered, because he knew what Jamie hadn't yet learnt, that some things can't be rebuilt.

Jamie tried to push this final memory out of his head. He was grateful for winter. He absorbed its icy blasts and stored them up against the future. Days passed, but they took no time with them.

15

Emma should have grown suspicious that morning when she saw everyone huddled round the cool group's desks, looking at something. She noticed that Stephanie Morris was holding a bit of paper, which she slipped into her bag when she saw Emma coming. Pathetic, Emma thought. She saw some of them exchange knowing looks, but ignored them. Jesus had to put up with a lot more than knowing looks, didn't He? It was just a question of being brave and rising above it. It wasn't for her to judge people on earth – God would do that. And punish them, she hoped.

But God seemed reluctant to get involved. Where was He, for instance, at lunchtime? Emma was walking down the corridor to the canteen when she saw that people were congregating by the central notice board. At first she assumed the list of parts for *Cabaret* had finally been released. But then she saw the way they were looking at her as she approached.

In the centre of the board was pinned an A4 sheet of paper. At the top it said in large red letters, 'Attention!' and the title, 'Emma Stewart's Love List'. Below that was a list, with points numbered from one to ten.

Emma read it in silence.

1. Cake

2. Chocolate

3. Crisps

4. Pizza

5. Doughnuts . . .

Emma was aware of everyone's eyes on her. Nobody said anything except Olivia Thomas, who was in Emma's Maths set and said quietly to her, 'I don't think it's funny at all.'

The worst thing, Emma thought afterwards, was that she'd been too frozen with embarrassment to reach out and rip the list down. That's what she should have done, saying something light-hearted and mocking like, 'What a good use of time', and then walked away as though she couldn't have cared less. But instead she'd just stood there like a slow-witted cow in a field, staring blurrily at the poster as her eyes filled with tears. What kind of person sees something like that pinned up for everyone to see, and then walks away with their head down?

God was supposed to protect His own; but if He was trying to protect her, He wasn't being very effective. Emma thought of the 'Footprints in the Sand' poem that Kayleigh had made them read in CU once. Stephanie and Jenni and the others had used it again in one of their assemblies, and some people had actually *cried*. It was the one about the man walking along a beach, whilst scenes from his life flash across the sky. There are two sets of footprints in the sand for most of the journey, one belonging to the man and the other to God. But during the worst scenes of his life, the man notices that there's only one set of footprints, and complains to God that He abandoned him in his hour of need. But God tells the man that actually that was when He was carrying him.

Nauseating, Emma thought. And it didn't even make any sense. God must have done a crap job of carrying the man if the man didn't even notice, and those times were still the worst of his life, and he still felt abandoned by God. What was the point of God carrying you if you still had a rubbish time?

Emma stopped short, unnerved by her own subversion. But she was angry with God. He gave her no help, even though she'd been His faithful servant for years.

All the same, she kept going back to the chapel. It was the only refuge she had. The chaplain, probably noticing she no longer attended CU meetings, seemed intent on having a talk with her, but she dodged all his attempts until he appeared to give up.

That Sunday, her mum made a big fuss as usual about lunch, overruling Emma's dad, who had said he'd rather give it a miss today because he was working on something very important in the shed.

They all sat down at 1.30, and Emma's mum beamed around the table and said how nice it was to have a 'proper family meal, all together'. But they weren't really all together, were they? Emma thought.

Today her mum had cooked chicken breasts stuffed with cream cheese and pesto, wrapped in Parma ham, accompanied by garlic mashed potato and green vegetables. She said that it was good to have a change from a roast occasionally, and to try new things. She was trying out lots of new things these days. There hardly seemed to be a moment when she wasn't mixing and stirring and tasting, and asking Emma what she thought, before moving on to the next recipe. (What Emma thought was that she might not be so fat if she wasn't surrounded by food every second of every day.)

Emma remembered the horrible poster at school and was determined not to eat much. But the smell of it cooking was so delicious, and she was so hungry, that once the plate was put in front of her she started eating without even thinking about it. She realized halfway through her garlic mash, and tried to stop eating. She even put down her fork and made herself stare out of the window and recite a psalm. But her mum said, 'Are you alright, love? Your mash is going cold.'

Emma was still hungry and the delicious mashed potato was right in front of her. So the girls at school were right. When she was this greedy and fat it wasn't surprising none of them liked her. Tears ran down her face as she sawed at her chicken and crammed a large piece into her mouth along with a scoop of mash.

'Emma, what's *wrong*?' her mum said, sounding tearful herself.

Emma picked up the serving spoon and, still crying, reached towards the bowl of mash. Her dad took the spoon out of her hand. Emma hurled her empty plate across the room.

'Jesus, Emma,' her dad said.

Emma put her head in her hands and sobbed.

She was dimly aware of her father starting to clear away the plates before her mother put her arms around her.

By the time she'd calmed down, her dad had tidied away all the lunch things, including the pieces of Emma's broken plate, and had gone out to the shed. Her mum said, 'Can you tell me what's wrong now, Emma?'

Emma shook her head.

'Come on, darling.' Her mum paused, and then said, 'Is it something to do with what we talked about? About Kit?'

'*No*. I don't want to talk about that.'

'Then what is it, love? Is it something at school?'

'Leave me alone,' Emma said, pushing her off. 'Why would I talk to *you* when you never tell me anything?' She saw the hurt on her mother's face, but she didn't care. She ran up to her room, slamming the door behind her.

Later that afternoon, as she sat on her bed listlessly flicking through the Old Testament, there was a knock on her door.

'Go away.'

'It's me.' It was her dad's voice.

Surprised, Emma kept quiet. Her dad stuck his head round the door. 'Thought you might like a cup of tea.' Emma didn't really like tea, but she took the mug from him anyway. His gaze took in the open Bible next to her. 'Aren't you getting a bit old for that stuff now?'

Emma shrugged, refusing to meet his eye. Her dad hovered awkwardly in the doorway. 'Up to much this afternoon?' he asked.

'No.'

'I was wondering if you might want to come and help me out in the shed.'

Emma considered the matter in silence, and he went on, 'I thought you might be at a loose end, and – well, I could use someone to hold things steady.'

Emma had never been invited into the shed. It seemed to her more like a father–son thing, not a father–daughter thing, and she'd always assumed her father thought so too. But she was touched to be asked after all this time, so she put on her coat and followed him outside.

She'd been wondering how he was keeping warm in there now the winter had set in, but when he pushed open the door she saw that it was actually quite cosy, with an electric heater and a rug on the floor. Emma breathed in the sharp, smoky smell of sawdust and listened as her dad explained the array of tools and equipment set up along the two workbenches.

His latest project, he told her, was a magazine rack, and he outlined its intricacies in some detail. Emma didn't say much in return, but she nodded along with a thoughtful expression to show that she was concentrating.

The little twist he'd added, her dad explained, was that one of the wooden sides would be further forward than the other, for a slanted effect. He would fit pieces of sturdy plastic tubing between them to make slots for the magazines. Now, having sanded the wooden sides, he was trying to decide where the holes for the tubes should be drilled, and at what angle. He had to get it perfect, he said, as even a couple of millimetres off would be disastrous. ('Disastrous' seemed to Emma a slight exaggeration.)

They didn't talk much after that, beyond her dad giving her the occasional instruction, but Emma enjoyed herself. She supported each wooden side in turn whilst her dad made measurements, held up the tubing for him to check distances and watched him drill the holes in the wood.

By now it was growing dark outside and Emma realized she'd passed an hour or more without even thinking about school, or feeling miserable. But of course realizing that got her thinking about school all over again, and she started to feel sick and anxious. And now she felt bad about her mum, who was stuck in the house all by herself, and was probably upset because Emma had been horrible to her after lunch.

'I'd better go back inside, Dad,' she said. 'Got to finish my homework.'

'Alright, love.' He was so absorbed in the magazine rack he hardly noticed her leave.

Her mum was sitting at the kitchen table reading a book. It was a paperback and had a picture of two women drinking tea together on the front. Her mum read lots of books like that, about women drinking tea and going to the shops.

'Would you like me to make you a cup of tea?' Emma said.

Her mum was usually really pleased when Emma made

her tea. But now she was frowning, and seemed distracted by something.

'Mum?' Emma said. 'Tea?'

Her mum looked at her. 'Why were you in the shed?'

'I was helping Dad.'

'You know he doesn't like to be disturbed when he's in there.'

'He asked me to help him.'

'Maybe he said that out of politeness. You shouldn't go bothering him.'

'I told you, he invited me.'

Her mother paused for a moment, then said in a different voice, 'What's he making?'

Emma didn't want to tell her about the magazine rack. 'Just – woodwork stuff,' she said.

'Well, I'm not sure I'm happy for you to be in there. There's dangerous machinery.'

'So that's a no to the tea, then,' Emma muttered, and left the kitchen.

She went up to her bedroom, thinking of the smell of sawdust, thinking that she'd been happy in the shed. She began to see why her dad liked it so much. It was good to have somewhere to go that was almost a secret. It reminded her a bit of Kit's and Jamie's dens in the woods. They'd told Emma about them when she was very little – amazing dens where they could hide and which no outsider would ever be able to find.

One day, they'd agreed to show her. They'd taken her to the Long Den, a thin, rectangular clearing in the woods with a huge tree at one end which was brilliant for climbing; and the Water Den, an area where the stream that ran through the woods widened and tumbled over a miniature waterfall of rocks, the perfect place for making dams. The Swing Den was the boys' favourite, a beautiful green clearing right in the heart of the woods, with a sturdy oak at the centre. They'd hung their rope swing from one of its thick, solid branches. Jamie had lifted Emma onto the swing and given her a push and she'd loved the whoosh of the breeze as she swung back and forth. Kit had said it was more fun to swing higher and had given her a bigger push, but she'd panicked and let go of the rope, and tumbled off the swing. Jamie leapt forward and caught her in his arms so she wasn't hurt. Jamie had been annoyed with Kit, she remembered, but Kit had only shrugged and said what was the point in doing it if you didn't really go for it?

She'd visited the dens by herself a few times later on, but it wasn't as much fun on her own. She made some dams in the Water Den and climbed the tree in the Long Den, and then got terrified that she would get stuck up there and clumsily scrabbled back down as quickly as she could. She went to the Swing Den, too, but couldn't get on the rope swing without Jamie to lift her.

Emma thought, if only time could have stopped that first day they went to the dens. If only everything could have stood still. They'd all have been safe forever, and the awful coming things would never have come.

The last, ragged remnant of her faith vanished the following week. She was sitting in the chapel on Tuesday lunchtime trying to memorize the words to 'Lift High the Cross' when she heard the heavy oak door open and turned to see Stephanie Morris, Jenni Abbott and a couple of others file in, one after another. Emma closed her hymn book and watched as they went piously to a row on the other side of the chapel, pretending not to have seen her, and sat with their heads bowed in prayer.

Slowly, Emma got up. Let them not say anything, she prayed. Please, Lord. I'll be Your faithful servant again. Let them not say anything.

She started to move very quietly towards the door. She was almost there, and thought she might escape, when it came. The whispered hiss from all four of them, perfectly timed:

'Infidel.'

She had been half-expecting it, but she jumped all the same. They laughed loudly. Emma put out her hand to push open the door. One of them – she didn't know which – said, 'That's right. You shouldn't be here. The chapel's no place for infidels.'

Emma ran. She pushed through a crowd of girls in the corridor and blundered on, away from them all. She didn't stop until she'd made it to the loos and locked herself in a cubicle. Then the tears started, and once they'd started she couldn't get them to stop. She heard the bell go for afternoon lessons but she stayed where she was. She was missing French, but it didn't seem important any more.

She tried telling herself that she couldn't hate God because there was no God. But she still hated Him. She hated Him for letting things go so wrong, for not protecting her, for not protecting *any* of them. She hated Him for allowing Kit to die and Jamie to vanish, for making her mother so unhappy and her father so angry, and for always being silent, always unresponsive, even when Emma pleaded for help. Silently, she informed Him that since He never did anything useful, she'd manage without Him from now on.

That evening, she packed some clothes and food into a bag. The next day, she got on the bus to school, but instead of going in at the gates she turned and headed for the town centre, and then to the railway station. She had enough money in her savings account to get to France if she wanted to. But she wasn't going to France. She was going to disappear, just like everyone else.

16

When he came back from his lunch break and Sally said, 'There's someone here to see you,' Jamie thought, Oh Christ. Alice again.

'Where is she?' He was wondering if he could sneak off again before Alice saw him, and how he might explain this to Sally.

'Over there,' Sally said. 'In the Crusades section.'

Jamie looked, but couldn't see Alice. The only person browsing the Crusades stock was a chubby teenage girl.

'Where?' he said again.

'Right there. You're looking at her.'

Jamie was baffled. He stared at the girl, who was leafing through a large hardback entitled *God's Warriors*. 'What does she want?'

'*I* don't know, Jamie. She didn't come to see me.'

It occurred to him then that perhaps the girl wanted a recommendation on a book on Jewish History, or Vlad the Impaler, and had been pointed towards him by someone on the General desk downstairs. Reassured by this idea, he approached the girl.

'Can I help you?'

She dropped her eyes and looked down at the book she

was holding when he spoke to her. Then she held it against her chest and wrapped her arms around it.

Jamie stared at her. He'd been about to ask what kind of book she was looking for, but now the sentence dissolved in his mind. He glanced quickly around him, scanned the other sections, but could see no sign of his parents. His heart was beginning to beat too fast.

'I'm Emma,' the girl said.

Jamie nodded slowly. 'I know.'

'You didn't recognize me.' She said it flatly, without accusation.

'Not from across the room. I did when I came over,' Jamie said. 'As soon as I came over.' She bore very little resemblance to the skinny nine-year-old he'd left behind.

Emma put the book back on the shelf. She stared at the place where she'd put it.

Jamie searched for something to say, and for a way to conceal his shock. 'This is a nice surprise,' he said at last. Then, 'Are you here by yourself?'

She nodded minutely. She'd always been shy as a child, Jamie remembered – around strangers, at least. He thought he should say something to put her at her ease, but he didn't know what. 'You've grown up so much,' he came out with. 'You must be fourteen now?'

'Yes.'

'What are you doing here, Emma?'

She said something, but too quietly for him to catch.

'Sorry?'

'I've run away from home.'

Jamie tried to sound calm and matter-of-fact as he asked, 'When did you run away?'

'Today.'

He relaxed a bit. The police probably weren't involved yet, at least. He'd get her to ring up their parents, and then he could put her on the train home or something.

'I've come to live with you in Sheffield,' Emma said.

'I'm not sure that's a good idea,' Jamie said carefully.

'Why not?'

'Well, for one thing, Mum and Dad will wonder where you are and be worried.'

'We'll tell them I'm in Sheffield.'

'I don't think they'd like that very much.'

'You can't betray me,' Emma said. Her voice rose in desperation. 'I've come so far to see you, and I spent my savings on the ticket, and I travelled all the way up here by myself to look for you, and I got lost and had to ask loads of different people for directions.' She was growing tearful. Jamie began to panic. He glanced round, but no one seemed to be looking at them.

'It's OK. I don't want to betray you,' he said, echoing her odd phrase. 'Let's go and get a drink or something and talk about it.'

'I'm underage,' Emma said shakily.

Jamie almost laughed, but managed not to. 'I meant a non-alcoholic drink. Obviously. Like – a milkshake, or something.'

Emma considered this. 'I like milkshakes.'

'Yeah, I know.' On impulse, he added, 'Do you remember going for a milkshake on Saturdays when you were a little kid?'

She gave a small, tearful smile. 'I used to have a strawberry milkshake and a chocolate muffin. Mum took me.' She was looking at Jamie properly now instead of her shoes.

He said, 'Just give me a second to clear it with my colleague, then we'll go.'

He went over and said to Sally, 'Can you hold the fort for a bit?'

'Who's the girl?'

'My sister.'

'Come on, Jamie.'

'I'm serious. I haven't seen her for years, so I didn't recognize her straight away. I said I'd take her for a milkshake.'

Sally was looking at him with curiosity, and Jamie knew he was going to have to answer questions the next day. But he'd worry about that then. He grabbed his coat from behind the desk, and he and Emma set off.

They headed to the cafe side by side, Jamie slowing his pace so Emma could keep up. At one stage she slipped on a patch of ice and grabbed onto his arm for balance. 'You OK?' he said, righting her. She nodded, embarrassed, and took her hand quickly off his arm.

Out of curiosity, as well as for something to say, he asked her, 'How did you find me?'

'Alice rang up Mum and I overheard Mum telling Dad.'

Jamie tensed. After a moment, he said, 'What did Mum say?'

'That you were in Sheffield.'

'How did Dad – seem?'

'Angry.'

Jamie absorbed this silently.

'Why is he so angry?' Emma said.

Jamie shrugged. He felt himself growing cold, felt the first shivers of panic working their way down his spine. He had no idea how to have this conversation. He *couldn't* have this conversation.

'It's complicated,' he said at last. 'Lots of reasons.'

He quickened his pace, and she didn't ask anything more after that.

In the cafe, he ordered Emma a strawberry milkshake and was about to ask for a coffee, then changed his mind and asked for a milkshake as well. When he brought the drinks back to the table, Emma said conversationally, 'I see you've chosen chocolate. Most people prefer that, but I think strawberry has the better flavour.'

'You're quite the connoisseur, aren't you?'

She took this seriously. 'I like ice-cream-based milk-shakes best.' She took a small sip and smiled at him. She seemed to have got over her initial shyness. 'I think this is just Nesquik. But it's still nice because they've frothed the milk properly. Did you know that McDonald's use seaweed extract in their milkshakes? It's to thicken it.'

'I didn't know that.' Jamie felt he might be losing his grip on the conversation. 'You mean seaweed from the beach?'

'I don't know.' Emma took another sip.

Jamie said, 'Will Mum and Dad have realized you've gone yet?'

'They'll still think I'm at school.'

'Won't the school ring them?'

'Dunno.'

'Right.' Jamie was formulating a plan of action. He'd chat to Emma for a bit here, and then when the time seemed right he'd raise the possibility of her ringing home again. If she still refused to do it, he'd have to. But that wouldn't be ideal.

Emma interrupted his thoughts. 'Do you have any hobbies?' She said it so abruptly that Jamie wasn't sure he'd heard her correctly.

'Any what?'

'Hobbies. Things you do in your spare time. Do you read lots of history books?'

'Occasionally.' He wondered what else he could add. 'I have a PlayStation,' he offered.

'You and Kit used to have a PlayStation at home, didn't you?' She seemed pleased to have recalled it.

'It was Kit's actually,' Jamie said. 'I had the Super Nintendo before that. The SNES. We pretty much shared them both.'

'Do you still like football?'

'I don't watch it much any more,' Jamie said.

'Who do you support?'

'Spurs.'

'Like Dad.'

'Yes. And Kit.' Then, because it seemed to be expected

of him, he said, 'What are your hobbies? Apart from milk-shake?'

'I like to read. And I watch television. Sometimes I make things, like board games. And I used to like the Bible a lot. But I'm over that now,' she ended grandly. She'd finished her drink, and was fiddling with the sugar bowl. 'That's the trouble,' she said, when she saw Jamie looking at her empty glass. 'They go very quickly, don't they? Or they do with me, anyway.'

Jamie was starting to find her rather charming, in a strange way. He said, 'Do you want to tell me why you ran away?'

It was a bit hard to follow Emma's explanation because it all came out in a jumble, but he picked up something about horrible girls, and some meetings, and something called a love list, and Jesus.

'So are you being bullied?' he said awkwardly.

'Yes. And I've been abandoned by God.'

Jamie didn't know what to say to this. 'What about those girls?'

'They're bitches.'

'And they took over your club?'

She sighed. 'It wasn't a club. It was the Christian Union.'

'Right. Sorry. And they took over and stopped you coming?'

'Yes. They made that poster and they got everything about the Bible wrong.' Her voice wavered.

Jamie said, 'Have you told your form teacher?'

She shook her head, and a few tears slipped down her cheek.

'Have you talked to Mum about it?'

'She wouldn't listen,' Emma said, and Jamie was surprised by her anger. 'She never wants to hear about anything bad. Everything always has to be perfect and happy.'

Jamie was starting to wonder what he'd got himself into. 'I'll be back in a sec,' he said. He went up to the counter, but they didn't have any chocolate muffins, so he got her a chocolate brownie instead, and another strawberry milkshake, and hoped that would do.

He put them down in front of her and handed her a napkin.

She gave a small smile at the sight of the brownie. 'Thanks.'

'It'll get better,' Jamie said.

'It will, if I can live here instead.' But she said it with less conviction than in the bookshop, and Jamie started to see that perhaps she'd never really believed it would happen.

He capitalized on his advantage. 'It's very nice to see you. You know you can visit whenever you want.'

Emma ate her chocolate brownie in silence. Eventually she said, 'Do you remember taking me to see your dens when I was little?'

'Yes,' Jamie said. 'They were probably a let-down when you finally saw them, after the way we'd talked them up.'

'I liked them. They weren't a let-down.'

'I liked them too.'

'I went on my own a few times afterwards, but it wasn't as good.' She added, 'Nothing's as much fun on your own.'

Jamie didn't know what to say to this.

Emma said, almost inaudibly, 'I liked it when you were around. I wish you hadn't gone away.' She wasn't looking at him now, her shyness returning. 'Why did you leave?'

Jamie weighed up possible responses, then said briefly, 'Things were difficult at home.'

'Why?' she said.

Jamie tried to stay calm, weighing up his words carefully. 'We were all upset after Kit died. Things can get tangled when everyone's upset. It was a long time ago. Ancient history, Emma.'

'Is it?'

Jamie didn't answer her. They finished their milkshakes in silence.

He took her back to his flat in the end, on the strict understanding that she would ring their parents from there and tell them she was getting the next train home.

Whilst Emma made the call, Jamie went through to the kitchen and tried not to listen to the conversation.

Eventually, she called out, 'They're coming to collect me.'

Jamie was filled with dread. 'Where are they getting you from?

'Here.'

'Here?'

'Yeah. I told them what your street was called.'

Jamie dug his hands into his pockets and forced himself to relax his shoulders. Come on, he told himself. Pull yourself together. But the phrase carried an echo of his father, and he was shaken again by fear.

'Were they angry?' he said.

'Mum just sounded upset.'

He made himself speak calmly. 'I'm happy to take you somewhere more central to meet them.'

'I wouldn't want to inconvenience you,' Emma said.

Jamie was overcome by a strange feeling of unreality. So it was really going to happen, he thought. There seemed to be no way of preventing it. Perhaps it had been coming at him all this time, moving slowly towards him over the past five years.

He tried to imagine what it would be like, seeing his father again, having to meet his eye. Would there be some kind of scene? Jamie felt his stomach shrink at the idea. But it occurred to him that they probably wouldn't say much in front of Emma.

In any case, it wouldn't make a lot of difference what they said.

He put the TV on and went around the flat making nervous attempts to clear up. Then the absurdity of it struck him; as if having a tidy flat would be enough to placate them. He gave up and went to sit next to Emma on the sofa, tried to make himself keep still. For a while they watched *Friends* in silence.

Jamie glanced sideways at his sister. She seemed more cheerful now, but he felt saddened by her situation. She must have been desperate if she'd come all the way up here by herself to look for him. And he was sending her straight back to whatever misery she'd run away from. Still, what could he do?

'Do you want a biscuit?' he said.

'What kind do you have?'

'Ginger nuts.'

'I brought some chocolate digestives with me,' Emma said. 'And some Bourbons. They're in my bag.'

Weird, he thought.

After they'd eaten the biscuits, Emma asked to have a go on the PlayStation. They tried FIFA but Emma couldn't master the controls and said it was boring, so Jamie dug through the games Sam had given him and picked the racing game, which featured endearingly odd-looking cartoon protagonists. Emma got on with this much better.

'Was Kit good at games like this?' she asked. 'Or were you better?'

'I was way better,' Jamie said.

'I don't believe you.'

Their little cars raced round the tracks and Jamie noted with amusement that Emma unconsciously moved her whole body in line with the controls, leaning dramatically right when she steered right, and thrusting her shoulders forward when she accelerated. He subtly engineered it so that she beat him once or twice.

At the end of their fifth race, Emma put down her controller and said, 'What was Kit like? I remember some things, but I don't remember everything.'

Jamie thought for a moment. 'He was very funny.' He paused, realizing that this wasn't enough. 'He was a nightmare, sometimes.'

'Why?'

'He was – a bit of a troublemaker, I suppose. Sometimes he'd take things too far.'

'Like when?'

'Well.' Jamie searched for an example, unused to turning his memory loose. 'We were on holiday in Scotland one time – it was before you were born – and Kit talked me into borrowing this rowing boat. Only we were borrowing it without asking, so it was stealing, really. But we rowed out on the loch anyway, and it sank. Bit of a disaster.'

Emma was smiling. 'That was stupid.'

They were both silent for a few moments, thinking of Kit, and Jamie started to feel the old despair seeping back in. He was shutting himself down, about to suggest another race, when the doorbell rang.

'They're here,' Emma said, without enthusiasm.

17

Nobody spoke. But the air throbbed.

Jamie's living room felt much too small, with the four of them crammed into it; their parents on the sofa, Emma in the armchair, and Jamie on a chair from the kitchen.

Emma stared down at her glass of squash and tried to think of something to say. She was finding the situation unfathomable. The moment her parents had entered the flat, the atmosphere had shifted.

When the doorbell went, Jamie had got quickly to his feet. Emma followed him towards the hall, but hung back as he opened the door to reveal their parents standing on the doorstep.

Their mother's eyes widened when she saw Jamie, and she pressed her lips together as though she was trying to keep her face under control. Emma's father was behind her, his hands in his pockets, his face half-turned away.

There was a frozen silence. Emma stayed where she was in the living room doorway, glad not to be a part of this awkwardness. She saw that her mum's eyes were fixed on Jamie's face. Then her mum took a small step towards him and touched his arm.

'Hello, Jamie.'

Jamie seemed to draw away from her touch. He stepped back.

'Hello,' he said.

Emma watched her mum hesitate for a moment, then step over the threshold. Emma's dad didn't follow her.

'She's here,' Jamie said, gesturing towards Emma, and Emma had to step forward.

Her mum seemed to come back to life, and squeezed Emma into an uncomfortable hug. 'Darling, we've been so worried.'

Her dad said from the doorway, 'You've been extremely silly.'

Emma struggled out of the embrace. 'Sorry.'

There was another pause. Then Jamie said, in a voice which didn't sound like his normal one, 'Would you like a cup of tea? Since you've come such a long way.'

Their mum said, 'Yes, please,' at the same time as their dad said, 'We'd better be off.'

Seeing the desperate look her mum gave her dad, Emma said, 'You could just have a quick one?'

Her dad was looking at her mum. 'Alright,' he said. 'Just a quick one.'

Now, seated with their drinks in the living room, the whole thing was starting to remind Emma of one of those terrible visits they'd had to pay to Granny at the old people's home before she died – sitting stiff-backed in Granny's small, funny-smelling bedroom, those long, awkward pauses when Emma's parents had finished one boring topic of conversation (the weather / the traffic on the way) and had yet to find another (the neighbours / how

Emma was doing at school); and the whole while Granny never even seemed to be listening. She'd interrupt occasionally to ask Emma's dad something like, 'Are you Madeline's boy?' and her dad would have to say, 'I'm your son, Mother,' and Emma would squirm with embarrassment.

To break the silence, she said, 'Jamie and I went for a milkshake.' When nobody responded, she elaborated. 'And I had a chocolate brownie. I'd already had my lunch on the train, so it was a sort of pudding. Not a snack.'

Her mum said, 'That's lovely, darling.'

There was another silence. Emma looked at Jamie, and saw he was looking at their dad, who was staring steadfastly out of the window.

Emma said, to no one in particular, 'Jamie's in charge of the History department at work.'

'Only Jewish History and Eastern European History,' Jamie said.

Their mum said, with a big false smile that infuriated Emma, 'That's very impressive, Jamie.'

'It's not really,' Jamie said. 'They're not very big sections.'

'You must be doing very well for them to give you so much responsibility.'

Jamie said nothing to this.

Their mother said, 'This is a very nice, cosy little flat.' She looked around her and gave a little nod of satisfaction. 'It could perhaps use a splash of colour, couldn't it? What if you put up a few pictures? And perhaps you could get a cheerful rug to brighten up the sitting room?'

She broke off then, because Emma's dad had made an impatient noise that was a cross between a sigh and a snort. Emma tried to catch his eye to give him a stern look, but now he was staring down at his mug of tea. Her mum looked at him uncertainly, and then turned back to Jamie.

She said, 'It's nice to see you looking so *well*.'

Emma noticed with embarrassment that her mother's eyes were glistening, as though they were about to spill over. That would be the only thing that could make things more awkward, she thought. If her mother went and cried.

To distract everyone, Emma said, 'Jamie's got a Play-Station, and we played *ModNation Racers*. I won a few times,' she added.

'You were very good,' Jamie said.

'As good as Kit?' Emma asked, and they all seemed to go very still. She saw her mother look quickly at her father, and then at Jamie, and Emma knew she'd said the wrong thing.

Jamie said after a pause, 'Kit and I never played that game – it came a bit late for us. But you were pretty impressive, Emma. Way better than I was the first time I played.'

He was being nice at least, Emma thought. She'd rather stay with him than go back with her parents and have to see Stephanie Morris and Jenni Abbott again.

Her mum was still looking at Jamie. She couldn't seem to take her eyes off him. She said, 'It's very cold up north, isn't it, Jamie? Do you feel the cold much?'

Jamie said, 'I don't think it's any different here to back

home.' Emma saw her mother's face change when Jamie said the word 'home'. Jamie didn't seem to notice.

Their mother talked on about how the garden was doing, and how she was having to get used to driving the new car. Then her dad drained his mug and said, 'We should make a move.'

There was a short silence. Emma's dad got up and started putting on his coat.

'Come on, Emma,' he said. 'Get your stuff.'

Emma got up slowly and reached for her bag.

'Is that it then?' Jamie said. He was looking at their father.

Their dad ignored him and said to Emma and her mum, 'It's time we went.'

'Is that it?' Jamie said again.

Emma thought that Jamie's voice sounded different now. It had an edge to it that hadn't been there for the rest of the day. And his face looked different too. She didn't like his expression.

Emma's mum said she'd just pop through to the kitchen and wash up the cups for Jamie, but Jamie told her to leave them. He turned back to his father. 'Is that all I get?' he said. 'Five years, and that's all I get?'

Their father said, 'I don't know what you expected.' He turned to Emma and her mum. 'Come on.'

'Dad—' Emma said imploringly, not wanting the day to end like this, but he only said, 'Let's go.'

Emma looked at her mum, but she'd already put on her coat and picked up her handbag.

Emma said, 'When can I come and see you again, Jamie?'

He didn't seem to hear her.

Her mum went up and touched Jamie's arm. 'Take care, darling.'

Jamie looked at his mother, and his face lost some of its hardness. 'You too.'

Emma's dad had got the front door open now, letting in a blast of icy air, but Emma saw that her mum was still gazing fixedly at Jamie. Emma thought she was about to say something serious and important; but all she said in the end was, 'Make sure you wrap up against the cold, won't you?'

Jamie said he would.

Emma said again, 'When can I come and see you, Jamie?'

He answered this time. 'Any time you want.' He smiled at her, but he looked sad.

She said as she moved towards the door, 'You could write to me if you want. I like getting letters.' She didn't know why she'd said that; she never got any.

Jamie said, 'Maybe.' Then he added, 'I hope the school stuff sorts itself out.'

Her parents were outside now. Her mum was waiting for her on the doorstep, but her dad was already striding towards the car.

'Thank you for the milkshake,' Emma remembered to say at the last minute.

'Thank you for the interesting fact about seaweed,' Jamie said. He raised his hand briefly. 'Look after yourself.'

'Bye, then,' Emma said, as she followed her mum down the steps. The last sight she had of Jamie was of him standing alone in the middle of his sitting room, a dirty cup in each hand, watching them go.

Part Two

I know you won't read this. You'll have worked out who it's from by looking at the postmark, and you'll already be angry. Perhaps you've opened it anyway, out of curiosity. But I bet by the time you get to this point you'll have had enough. Am I right? Yes, you're crumpling up the paper – and now you're hurling it towards the bin. Look – there it goes. Then you're off, storming out of the room. And I'm alone again.

So now I suppose I'm free to say whatever I want.

Perhaps it was stupid, but I thought that if enough time went by you might begin to understand why I did it. But you haven't forgiven me. And what I want to say is, I haven't forgiven you either – I haven't forgiven you for not forgiving me.

*

When you came to my flat, you wouldn't speak to me. Five years, and you were still as angry as the day you told me to leave. That threw me off balance. I keep turning over and over in my head what you must think of me – but I can't imagine.

Why do you blame me? Do you think that without me Kit would still be alive?

I could tell you, if you want: how it all seemed to me. What the view was like from where I was standing. But I'm not sure there's any point now.

*

Sometimes, in my head, I'm able to reason with you. But when I try to write it down, all I get is this blinding rage and I can't remember what I wanted to say.

When I'm alone with my thoughts, I try to tell you that I acted for the best. But in the face of your silence, I find it hard to remember whether that's true.

*

No reply from you. Am I disappointed? I don't know what I expected.

*

I got a Christmas card in the post the other day. I tore it open, thinking it might be from you. But it wasn't. It was from Emma, with a sweet message. Mum had signed it at the bottom, too, which made me feel strange. It seemed both loving and cowardly of her.

Do you want to know what my plans for Christmas are? Somehow I seem to have become one of those people who gets asked that from time to time, always with a measure of pity. I'm not sure how it happened; I don't think I ever gave the impression I wanted company.

A girl at work invited me to a boozy Christmas dinner with her and her friends. They probably need another man to make up numbers, or else I'm a concession to one of her more desperate single friends. The other invitation was from Sam, whom you might remember. That was more difficult to get out of.

Tomorrow, I'll do a roast chicken if I feel like it, or have one of the pizzas in the freezer. I've got two bottles of wine to get through, and plenty of whisky. I have a couple of DVDs, my PlayStation, and a new book on the Crusades to keep me occupied. My day will be fine.

Another Christmas without Kit. If you're reading this, that's what you're thinking. Well, so am I. You think you're the only one entitled to grief. But I miss him too.

Merry Christmas, Dad. I expect all your replies are lost in the post.

*

I worked on New Year's Day, with a crashing hangover.

'Wild party?' Sally, my colleague, asked, as I sat blearily behind the desk.

'You could say that,' I said, not wanting to tell her that I'd actually spent the evening drinking myself into a stupor whilst playing *God of War III* on the PlayStation.

Do you remember that time we celebrated New Year in the pub? Kit and I were both underage, but Kit got hold of a bottle of White Lightning from somewhere and got smashed outside with a couple of school friends. But it was me who ended up throwing up before midnight.

You were furious, because I was only thirteen. You blamed Kit, who was too drunk to exonerate himself, but actually, Dad, it was my fault. I was sloping round the pub on my own whilst everyone got drunk around me, feeling sullen and left out, when I bumped into a middle-aged woman who had bags and bags of Cadbury Mini Rolls with her. I still haven't managed to come up with a plausible explanation for that. She had at least ten plastic bags full of them, and she was handing them out all over the place in a state of giddy, drunken benevolence. I think I must have eaten about twenty of them, which, alongside all the Coke I'd drunk, made me feel really ill. And that's how you came to find me being sick in the Gents, and marched both me and Kit home in disgrace.

I was too embarrassed to tell you the real reason for my illness. And I certainly wasn't going to tell Kit, who asked me the next day how on earth I'd managed to get drunk. I shrugged mysteriously and said that I had my ways. He treated me with a new-found respect after that. For a bit, anyway.

Interesting how quick you were to assume Kit had been a bad influence on me. He was innocent this time, but he did have a talent for getting me into trouble, didn't he?

*

There are so many things I'd like to explain to you, Dad.

Something I've been thinking about recently is how often Kit came through for me. You might not have

146

realized it back then – you thought he gave me a hard time, and you were right, mostly. But he looked out for me, too, and I think if you appreciated that, you might begin to understand what I owed him.

One time, for instance, when I was at primary school, I confided in Kit that I was having some trouble with a kid called Jordan Farrell. Jordan was stealing the crisps out of my lunchbox every day and eating them himself. Kit had just gone to secondary school and seemed streetwise, so I thought he'd know how to sort Jordan out.

Kit thought so too. 'We're going to get him,' he told me, and approached the task with the single-mindedness and self-importance of the professional. I was impressed.

Together, we took a packet of Monster Munch, opened it at the bottom, and tipped in huge quantities of cayenne pepper and chilli powder, taken from Mum's spice rack. Then we carefully resealed the packet using Superglue from your odd-job drawer and shook it to distribute the powder evenly.

'This plan is dynamite,' Kit said. (He used to come out with lots of old-fashioned phrases like that, didn't he? They were lifted from the TV programmes we used to watch.)

The next morning, I left my bag hanging up in the cloakroom as usual, with my lunchbox containing the poisoned Monster Munch inside. At lunchtime, the crisps were gone.

When I got to the canteen, everyone was talking about how Jordan Farrell had just puked and been taken out. The kids who'd seen said it was brilliant, and described the projectile sick in graphic detail. After lunch I heard that Jordan had been sent home.

I began to worry that he might die. Would I get sent to prison? I wondered if I'd get a lighter punishment if I confessed now. Should I drop Kit in it too? I thought I probably would if it meant I'd get off more lightly.

When I got home, I told Kit what had happened. He was delighted. 'Told you it would work,' he said.

'Work? He could die!'

'He won't. It's only chilli powder. It's not anthrax.'

'What's anthrax?'

'What we'll use next time.' Kit winked at me.

I began to wonder why I'd asked for his help in the first place. He always took things too far.

I went to school fearfully the next day, but Jordan was there in assembly as usual, apparently not dead after all. And when I went to get my lunchbox I found my Quavers still there, untouched.

Jordan Farrell never stole my crisps again. But I haven't forgotten the terror I felt when I thought I was going to be arrested. I'm not sure crisps were worth that kind of fear. But I can't really blame Kit. As I said, he was just trying to help me out.

*

Thank you for your note. Sorry to ignore your request, but I had to write again. I seem to have so much more to say. I would never have suspected it, until I saw you.

It's strange, because I seem to have got out of the habit of conversation. But look at me now.

Has it ever occurred to you that what you're doing is far worse than anything I did? I didn't act out of hate, but that's the only thing driving you. You haven't even tried to understand, have you? It's like you want to hate me.

*

Sometimes when I was little and had that horrible Sunday-evening feeling, you'd remind me that one day I wouldn't have to go to school any more, and I'd be able to choose my own job – something I'd enjoy and be good at, and then I'd never dread Monday mornings ever again.

I don't dread them now. Usually, I welcome them, though I suppose I wasn't always aiming to work in a bookshop. There was a time when I wanted to be a journalist.

But don't worry – I'm not unhappy. My job suits me fine, although it has its irritations.

Today was tedious, for example. An endless succession of people wanting recommendations – many of them not even sure what period of history they were interested in.

It culminated with a woman asking me to help her choose a book for her daughter. Something to 'get her started'.

'Get her started on what?' I said.

'On history,' the woman said. 'Something to spark her interest.'

'What sort of areas might she like?'

'Oh, I don't know,' she said. 'Not all those wars, anyway. Something with more human interest.'

'Something on Georgiana, Duchess of Devonshire?' I suggested. 'She might like the film.'

'Maybe,' the woman said. 'But I was thinking of something with a bit more substance.'

I wasn't really sure what she meant by this. I said, 'How about the Holocaust?'

She lit up. 'Yes. Good idea. Something to show her how important it is to study history.'

Wearily, I took her to the Jewish History section and suggested a couple of titles. Another satisfied customer.

I went back to the till faintly irritated by the whole exchange. I'm losing my patience with history. People expect studying it to impose order and meaning, to give past events a pattern – to reveal something to us. But it's impossible to explain the scuppered stretch of time behind us, or to predict what's going to happen next. The truth is, the world's about to run off its rails at any minute, and nobody will admit it.

*

Sam came to visit on Saturday. We went to the pub for lunch, but it wasn't a great success. I wasn't in the mood for company. Sam tried asking me more about Emma's visit, and you and Mum coming to collect her, but I made it clear I didn't want to talk about it. There's a lot he doesn't know about our family, and I haven't felt like enlightening him.

I'd assumed he'd stay over as usual, but in the afternoon he said he had to be getting back.

As he was going out the door, he said, 'You should spare a thought for Emma.'

I said nothing.

'You've had a shit time – but remember, so has she.'

'I'm not responsible for her.'

'Of course not. You're not responsible for anyone, Jamie.' He left without another word.

*

Do you remember that time we were staying in a cottage in the Highlands, and Kit and I came in soaking wet one afternoon? Kit lied to you that day, Dad.

The truth is, Kit and I hadn't really been for a swim in the loch. We'd stumbled across a rowing boat on one of our exploring trips, hidden away in a rickety old shed which stood on the banks of the loch. Kit decided we should borrow the boat for the afternoon. In my defence, Dad, I did protest at the time that going about borrowing other people's boats was probably frowned upon. But I was quickly overruled. Kit called me boring and old before my time.

He said, 'Jamie, you have to take some risks in life occasionally, or you'll never have any fun.'

'What if the owner thinks we're stealing it?'

Kit snorted. 'We're not going to make much of a getaway, are we, rowing very slowly across the loch?'

'Dad will be furious,' I pointed out.

'How's he going to know?' Kit said. 'As long as you don't lose your cool and blurt the whole thing out – which would be just like you, actually – we'll be OK.'

Resigned, I grabbed one side of the boat and helped him lug it down to the water.

Kit's rowing technique was splashy and inefficient, but he got us out to the middle of the loch before too long. It was pretty exciting, being afloat on the cold Scottish water, with the green hills at our backs and the woodland in front of us.

'This is the life, isn't it?' Kit said, rowing us in a circle using only one oar, and I laughed out loud as we spun round.

Then I realized my feet were getting wet.

'Kit, the boat's leaking!'

Kit looked down. 'That's just water from the oars.'

'No, look!'

Slowly, Kit considered the situation. 'I'd better row us back.'

He spun the boat again and started rowing us back towards the edge of the loch, but already the water was up to our ankles and the boat felt low in the water.

'We're going to sink,' I said.

'Stop being such a doom-monger, Jamie.'

But before Kit could get us back to dry land, water had started coming over the edges of the boat, and then it disappeared very quickly from under us, leaving us shocked and gasping, treading water in the freezing loch.

Kit grabbed hold of me and started to swim back to the shore, dragging me along with him.

Soaking wet on the bank, we surveyed the area of water where the boat had disappeared. Not so much as a ripple remained.

'How are we going to explain this?' I asked Kit.

'We won't,' he said simply. 'We were never here.'

I was uncomfortable, but didn't fancy explaining to you and Mum what had happened, and having to pay for the boat. So I agreed to keep quiet.

Kit made us run round the loch twice to warm up and try to dry off a bit, and then we went shivering back to the cottage. I was nervous about what you and Mum might say when you saw our wet clothes, but Kit told me to leave it all to him.

I'd half-convinced myself that perhaps you wouldn't even notice we were wet when we got back, but the first thing Mum said when she saw us was, 'Boys! What have you been doing?'

Kit said smoothly, 'Jamie tried to have a swim in the loch, and got into difficulties. So I had to go in and save him.'

I was too surprised and outraged to contradict him.

You said, 'What on earth were you thinking, Jamie?'

I shrugged sulkily.

'Well, go and have showers and get into dry clothes,' Mum said. 'You're probably covered in leeches.'

We went off, and I hissed to Kit as we went upstairs,

'Why couldn't it have been you who went for a swim, and me who rescued you?'

'That wouldn't have been very believable, would it?'

'Well, thanks a bunch,' I said furiously. 'Thanks a bunch, Kit.'

See what I mean about Kit getting me into trouble? It used to drive me mad when we were growing up. But I suppose he was also good at getting me out of it – and that's the main thing.

*

Sometimes it feels too hard, puzzling over causes and outcomes and intentions on my own.

If I had somebody else to talk to about Kit, Dad, I could leave you in peace. But who else is there? And if I get no peace, why should you? You took my peace. You and Kit, between you.

*

Sorry about my last letter. I wasn't myself. I'm a mess when I haven't slept. Have you ever gone for a week with no sleep? Everything goes very quiet. Time moves so slowly that you think it might actually have stopped. Then it leaps forward in one sudden, dizzying bound, and you realize you have no idea what happened during the last few hours, where you were, how you got home.

One thing keeps me going: I've seen this incredible Lego castle in the window of the department store near

Sudbury's. I stop and look at it every day on my way home from work, dazzled by its size and magnificence. It has sturdy-looking turrets and battlements, crenellations, a solid outer wall, a workable drawbridge and a portcullis. The detail is astonishing. It's peopled by a motley crew of archers and swordsmen, complete with a princess to guard. It costs over a hundred pounds, an unbelievable amount of money for what's really a toy.

Do you remember the day Kit smashed up all his Lego models? I don't know why that still bothers me so much, after everything else that happened. But it felt like the end of everything. Did you know I tried to rebuild the models for him afterwards? I did my best, but they didn't turn out very well. And it was stupid to try, really, because I couldn't even find all the pieces.

*

I see him everywhere these days. Walking through town on my way to work, I see him. He's a way ahead of me in the crowd, but I recognize his hair, his clothes, the way he walks, and I follow him. I find myself ten minutes later standing outside a cafe, staring through the glass at the stranger I've followed. I keep on watching him, as if he might change before my eyes, until he catches me looking, and I have to leave.

Standing behind the History desk, I see him again, browsing amongst the bookshelves – the dark hair, that red checked shirt he used to wear. And then again, stopping at the off-licence on the way home – there he is, queuing in front of me. And I have to hold myself together – I tell myself it isn't him. I force myself to keep quiet, because there have been too many disappointments already today and I can't face this one head-on. So I queue quietly behind him, and I wait for him to turn. I wait and wait, and by the time I see his face I've half-convinced myself it is him, and I catch a glimpse of that sharp nose and those dark eyes, and I think, yes. Then I see him properly – and of course, it isn't him. It never is.

I bought the Lego castle today, Dad. That was all I meant to tell you when I started this letter. I got lost, for a moment, when I picked up the pen.

*

Construction has begun. The castle is beginning to take shape.

At present I'm working on one of the towers and the section of the main wall to which it's attached.

It delights me, how it all starts off so simply; a myriad little pieces, each so unimposing on its own. Even the base doesn't come in one piece. But the builder – the craftsman – gradually unites them, until they make a magnificent whole; brick by brick; layer by layer.

I have a vision of the castle in my head. It hardly seems that I'm following instructions now – more like I've composed them myself, and the conception on the front of the box is my own. I build grey brick upon grey brick, I fuse sections with overlapping bricks.

At times I'm so focused on each small stage that I

hardly notice the building coming alive, growing upwards and outwards – until suddenly I take a step back and it takes my breath away.

*

With each brick added, something else snakes out of its hiding place and lays itself, scaly and fat, across the front of my mind.

Do you remember a particular time when Kit started to seem different? Often these days I find myself searching for it, for the distinct moment when everything began to slide out of our control. I know it's pointless; I know the change was gradual, and perhaps it came and went. You wouldn't have noticed it unless you knew what to look for.

Now, of course, we know the signs. And they didn't all come at once, I'm sure of that. They crept up on us stealthily, one by one, and by the time they'd become impossible to ignore, it was too late to head off the danger.

Dad, I think you must look for it, too. The moment we should have stepped in.

If we had realized at the time, though, would anything have been different? I don't believe it would. I wish you could see that; though I suppose it's not much of a comfort.

*

Perhaps you remember some things differently to me. In some ways I like that idea, because doesn't that mean we have more of Kit left? But it worries me too. How can I trust my own version of Kit if it's different from yours? Of course, our memories shift and alter. They're rewritten and overwritten. Think of the sadness of that, Dad. All that lost truth.

If I could keep him still in my mind, like an insect preserved in amber, then I could rest. But of course he won't keep still for me. He moves about. He slips away.

*

All kinds of things we should have noticed earlier.

Do you remember how much Kit used to sleep when he was in his teens? It came and went in phases, I think. But sometimes on school mornings I'd be ready to leave before he even emerged from his room, groggy and silent, and then we'd have a massive dash to catch the bus in time. Fairly often we missed it, but Kit was indifferent. We'd go home and get Mum to drive us. Occasionally Kit would slope off into town instead, and I'd have to get the public bus to school alone. At weekends, he often wouldn't appear until long after lunch.

Kit's behaviour didn't seem odd at the time, did it? Teenagers are supposed to sleep a lot. I was always more of an anomaly, wide awake as the sun came up each morning. Kit was the normal one.

But I can tell you the exact moment it started to seem odd to me. One night Kit had disappeared off to his room after supper, and I wanted to go and borrow a CD off him. When I went and knocked on his door there was no answer. I assumed he must be downstairs watching TV, so I pushed open the door and put on the light. There was Kit, in bed asleep. He stirred as I entered, roused by the light, and squinted up at me.

'Kit,' I said, surprised. 'Are you OK? Are you ill?' I couldn't think why else he would have put himself to bed before 8.30.

'No. Go away,' he said, with drowsy irritation. 'Why did you wake me?'

'Why are you in bed?'

'I'm tired. Fuck off.'

I went away, puzzled and annoyed. 'Kit's in bed,' I informed Mum in the kitchen.

'Well, it's a nice place to be, isn't it? A nice place to read.'

'He's not reading. He's asleep.'

'Is he ill?' Mum said, putting down the plate she was washing up.

'That's what I said. But he says he's tired.'

This seemed to reassure her. 'He's working on his A levels, it's very tough. It's not surprising he's a bit worn down.'

'I think it's weird.'

'Well, I'm sure you'll understand when you come to do your A levels.'

'Kit hardly does any work! I'm working way harder on my GCSEs than he is on his A levels.' I stomped off, angry with Mum and even angrier with Kit for being rude and antisocial, and still managing to be the favourite.

He was down for breakfast at the same time as me the

159

next morning; it was a school day, and Mum had managed to drag him out of bed. I waited until Kit yawned and then asked him sarcastically, 'Didn't you get enough sleep last night?'

He ignored me and went on eating his cereal. But I was watching now, and I noticed that these early nights continued. In fact, they got earlier and earlier. Kit would sometimes be in bed by 7.30, even at weekends. He didn't seem to want to see any of his friends in the evenings, and certainly not his family.

Over the last few years, I've thought of the sleep thing as purely physiological, a side effect of the illness that was creeping up on him. But more recently something even more obvious has occurred to me: that Kit simply couldn't bear to be awake. Every moment of consciousness was painful. How stupid, that I couldn't understand that until now.

There were other things as well. Or perhaps that's hindsight talking. I'm not sure how far to trust my memory. Looking back, I find plenty of signs, but how can I be sure they were there in the first place? I load memories with significance these days; heap up meaning upon meaning until the memory buckles under the weight.

For instance, when he started in the sixth form, Kit stopped hanging out with me the way he used to, which I now take as a sign that he was already becoming withdrawn. But maybe that signified nothing more than the fact that we were growing apart. Perhaps I was going through an annoying phase, and he didn't want my company. Can I really assume that just because someone didn't want to spend time with me, they must have been ill? Kit would have something to say about that, I feel.

Dad, I turn all this over in my mind, but I can't get a clear answer. I look for the first cracks appearing, and I can see where they widen into rifts, but I can't see where they begin.

*

I keep expecting to get another note from you, coldly telling me not to contact you again. I know I've been getting carried away recently. I'll try to write less often – perhaps just once a week. It's hard, though, because I think about it all the time now. What happened to him. What we could have done. It still defeats me.

Perhaps you just throw my letters into the bin unopened – that would be easier than telling me to stop. But that's not what I'd do. I'd read them – perverse curiosity. That's what makes me think you're reading this now, Dad. Despite everything, I think I know you fairly well.

*

There was no one moment when the universe shifted. It wasn't a sudden, brutal quake in the night. It was a slow drifting of the landscape so that for ages things hardly appeared any different, and then one day you look around and realize that the world has altered cataclysmically whilst your attention was elsewhere.

I don't know when this happened for you, Dad. For me, I think it was the day I walked into the sitting room and found Mum there with Kit, apparently having a row. Kit looked furious, but Mum just seemed bewildered.

She said, 'Mrs Simpson told me you missed your coursework deadline, too.'

'She's a bitch,' Kit said.

I hovered awkwardly by the door, half intending to retreat, but part of me wanted to see Kit not getting away with something for once.

Mum said, 'I don't understand why you haven't done the essay. You've had weeks.'

Kit wouldn't answer.

'Well,' Mum said, 'you're going to sit down at the kitchen table right now and start it.'

Kit looked almost tearful. I was astonished.

'What's wrong, Kit?' Mum said. 'You're so good at English. You got an A-star at GCSE.'

'I hate it.'

'You have to do the coursework or you'll fail your A level.'

Kit burst out crying.

I left, horrified and embarrassed, but I heard Kit's jumble of words as I went up the stairs. 'I can't do it,' he said. 'It's too hard. I can't do it.'

Nothing was the same after that. The world had been changing for months, but I hadn't noticed till then. The crying got worse over the next few weeks. I stayed away from Kit as much as possible, and let you and Mum handle it. Sometimes you couldn't get him to go to school.

I remember one day when he kept saying he couldn't do it, over and over again. You shouted at him to pull himself together. Not very helpful. But I don't blame you.

It's always frightened me, how quickly things seemed to go wrong. But there was nothing quick about it, really – that's all in my head.

I've got used to thinking of it in terms of Before and After. There was a period when we had Kit. Then we lost him – long before he died. It used to help me to keep them separate in my head, because then I could let myself think of Kit as he was, without it being contaminated by everything that happened.

That doesn't work now. The more I think about it, the more I start to see the After bleeding into the Before. I see signs in every memory. I can't stop myself seeing them, however much I try to block them out. They're all I ever see.

*

There were times when Kit seemed OK – normal. There were occasions at dinner when he'd be funny and relaxed, teasing Emma, or chatting to you about the football. The odd day where he'd go out to see his friends, or challenge me to a game of FIFA, or a kick-about in the garden. It was all too easy, back then, to focus on the good moments when they occurred.

We should have paid more attention to the times when he shut himself in his room all day, or when he sat hunched over the supper table, silent and barely eating.

Mum would chide him sometimes for bad manners, and mostly he wouldn't even look up. It was like someone drab and pale had sneaked in and replaced the Kit we knew.

Days like that should have screamed at us.

But in the end it was as though we couldn't spot it for ourselves. There was one particular evening when we were all in the kitchen. You and Mum were standing by the counter, you with a beer and Mum stirring something at the hob. I was down at the other end of the room, sitting with Emma whilst she showed me some pictures she'd done that day (she would be starting school the following year, and liked to say she was 'getting ready'). Kit was the only one missing, up in his room as usual.

I was only half paying attention to Emma. At the same time, I was listening to the conversation you and Mum were having.

Mum said, 'Mrs Macdonald rang. She's noticed Kit hasn't been himself recently. Apparently he's been very unhappy at school.'

You said, with a mixture of concern and irritation, 'Does she think it's something we're doing wrong? Does she think we're mistreating him in some way?'

'No, no,' Mum said. 'Nothing like that. She didn't say it was our fault.'

'I don't know what's got into him. What did you say to her?'

'I said that, more or less. The thing is . . .' Mum paused, staring down into the pan, and it was then that I realized she was nervous. I started paying proper attention. 'Mrs Macdonald was rather worried about him.'

'We all are,' you said.

'But she seemed to be taking it quite seriously. She thinks he might be ill.'

'Ill?'

'She thinks we should take him to the doctor.'

You snorted. 'What could the doctor do?'

Mum was stirring faster now. She said, 'Mrs Macdonald thinks Kit might have depression. She said we should take him to our GP.'

You went silent for a few seconds. Then you shook your head. 'Sounds like an overreaction.'

Mum stopped stirring and looked at you. 'But he's not himself, Joe, is he? He's so down all the time.'

'I know. But he's seventeen, and he's got important exams coming up. It's not surprising if he's a bit low.'

'Well.' Mum looked away from you and went back to her stirring. 'I've made him an appointment. I'm taking him on Friday.'

You took this in slowly, then shrugged. 'Alright. At least it'll keep Mrs Macdonald happy.'

I listened quietly from across the room. Privately, I agreed with you – dragging Kit off to the doctor's did seem like an overreaction. I thought the doctor would tell Kit to get out more, see people, that kind of thing. Then we'd all be reassured.

I regret our innocence back then – but I also envy it.

I couldn't stop thinking about Kit's trip to the doctor after that. The idea of depression was alien to me. It seemed shadowy and threatening, and I didn't see what it had to do with Kit. Depression was associated in my mind with the dull or the weak, a vision entirely at odds with Kit's energy and humour.

When I got home from school that Friday, I went to find Mum in the kitchen.

'How did it go at the doctor's?' I said, without preamble.

'Oh – it was alright,' Mum said. She seemed flustered; perhaps she hadn't realized I'd overheard your conversation. 'Dr Newman was very kind.'

'What did she say?' I was expecting to hear that Kit was fine. As you'd thought, a load of fuss over nothing.

Mum hesitated. 'Well, she thinks Kit might be depressed, actually. But it's nothing to panic about. It's more common than most people realize, apparently.'

Emma caused a momentary distraction then by bounding up to me and grabbing me round the legs.

'Hello, sausage,' I said, lifting her up.

'Hello, egg,' Emma said.

I wondered if I should take her out of the room, given what we were discussing. But I decided she was too young to understand any of it anyway, so I put her down next to me and said to Mum, 'What did Dr Newman suggest?'

'She gave him some pills. Antidepressants. And she referred him for counselling – psychotherapy, she called it. Only the waiting list is eighteen months, so I don't think he'll get any.'

'Does he really need drugs?' I said.

Mum was looking uncertain. 'The doctor said they'd help.'

I trailed off to my room. It seemed a weird idea to me, treating sadness with medicine. But there was something else bothering me now. It was the beginning of a realization: that this was about more than sadness. I thought back to how Kit had been over the past few months. He was fine some of the time, yes. But his mood could plummet at any moment. I wondered what that must be like for him. Slowly, these pieces were beginning to fit themselves together in my head, along with the doctor's comments. Of course something was wrong with Kit.

I wasn't there when Mum told you about the medication, so I don't know how you reacted. I can imagine, I think. But Mum must have overruled you somehow, because Kit began taking antidepressants every day after that.

I didn't notice much difference at first. Not for a long time, actually. The following months were bleak for him, and for all of us. The drugs seemed to help a bit, keeping Kit's mood stable for longer periods than before, but he still had some very bad days.

Even you, Dad, had accepted that Kit was ill at this point. I don't think it was the doctor's diagnosis that did it, or the follow-up appointments, or the increase of Kit's dosage. I think the only thing that could have changed your mind was seeing his suffering for yourself, having to stand by and watch him struggle through it.

*

167

My castle has conical roofs on some of its towers which look more Transylvanian than English to me, although I'm no expert. It's the kind of castle I could envisage belonging to Vlad the Impaler. I can see him now, sweeping imperiously along the battlements, ordering another volley of arrows, issuing terrible threats to his archers whilst his victims languish in horrible dungeons hundreds of feet below.

I visited Bran Castle when I was in Romania with Sam during our first university holidays – Dracula's Castle. Do you remember the postcard I sent you? Not that Bran has anything more than tenuous links to Vlad III, who, in turn, doesn't have anything more than tenuous links to the popular conception of Dracula. Still, it stuck in my mind as Dracula's Castle, as the Romanian tourist board intended it to.

My castle looks more impressive than Castelul Bran, even though it's not finished. It's darker, sturdier, more symmetrical – everything about it is stronger. It squats closer to the ground.

I've ordered lots of books about castles for the History department, under the guise of expanding the Medieval Europe section. I'm working my way through them slowly. They're not selling well, unlike my Vlad books.

Another thing. My castle has flags flying proudly from each of the main towers, some blue and some yellow. What's the significance of that, do you think? Someone like Alice, with her History of Art background, would tell you that bright blue was an expensive colour – a beautiful, rich, noble colour. Woad, lapis lazuli, indigo. In Christian art, the Virgin Mary is dressed in blue – a holy colour.

But yellow? I'm more uncomfortable with that. It could show light, hope, associations with Easter, maybe. But Giotto painted Judas Iscariot swathed in yellow. Alice had the poster on her wall at university.

What does it all mean, Dad?

*

He came back to life before our eyes. It wasn't exactly the reawakening of Lazarus – it was slower, far less dramatic. But all the same, he was returned to us.

You probably think no one noticed how much you tried to help. But I did, Dad.

Kit hadn't picked up a book for months because he couldn't concentrate. He used to race through novels, but now they were too difficult for him. So you came home one day with a stack of second-hand Alistair MacLean books: simple enough to read, even for someone whose mind was in pieces.

Kit looked dubious, but he picked one up and started to read – and that was it. He was off.

Another thing you did, Dad. You got Kit that portable radio so he could listen to the cricket wherever he was in the house, whether he was in the kitchen with Mum, in the TV room with me, or just in bed in his room. It always seemed weird to me that Kit was into cricket, since none of the rest of us ever showed any interest. But I noticed,

Dad, how you forced yourself to follow the Test series that summer, so you could discuss it with Kit.

He wasn't the same, of course. Even by the time he went back to school to do his A levels – a year late, now – he wasn't the same. He was anxious and self-conscious a lot of the time, when he'd always been so irritatingly assured in the past. And often he was quiet, as though all his energy was being channelled inwards, all of it going into keeping his head blank and silent.

*

Remember the day Kit was offered his place at UCL? We spent the evening celebrating. You'd bought champagne, and fizzy apple juice for Emma, and we all toasted the future. Mum got a bit tearful and Kit put his arm round her.

He said to me, 'Don't expect all this when you get a university place, Jamie. I've always been the favourite.'

You frowned at him and said of course we'd have champagne again when I got my offer.

Kit grinned at me, and mouthed, 'It'll be cava.'

That was a great evening, wasn't it? Nobody said it, but there was a sense of relief that the bad times were behind us, and Kit was back on track.

He thrived at university. That was how Mum put it, and I agreed. He enjoyed his course, he loved London, and every holiday the house would fill up with his friends, and the occasional girlfriend. When I went off to Warwick the following year, Kit told me it would be the best time

of my life, and based on what I'd seen of his first year,
I believed him.

By then, I hardly ever thought about those strange
months during his A levels. I'd confidently consigned it
to the past; a subject I wasn't particularly interested in
at the time, despite the History degree I was doing. I still
wondered, occasionally, where it had come from: that
sudden, frightening dip. It seemed too strange to
understand.

I don't think we were wrong in thinking Kit was happy
for most of his time at university. But would we have
realized if he wasn't? I think there were times when his
illness was very well disguised. That was partly him and
partly us. If we didn't see any more signs back then, it was
probably because we weren't looking the right way.

*

Sam called my mobile at lunchtime today. He'd already
rung the History department asking for me, and wanted
to know why I hadn't been going into work.

I told him I had flu. He suggested coming up to visit
next weekend, but I said I was busy.

'Sure you are,' he said. 'I'm getting a bit sick of this.'

When I didn't say anything, he put the phone down.

I turned the mobile off and crawled back under the
covers. No one can reach me now.

The truth is, I don't want to talk to anyone but you.

*

I was with Alice the night I got the phone call from you. We were in the second term of our second year. It had only just gone eleven, but we'd been up late the night before and were already in bed, just falling asleep, when my mobile rang. I remember the irritation as I fumbled to turn it off.

Then I saw it was you calling, and for some reason – because how could I have known what was coming? – I was filled with dread.

'It's my dad,' I told Alice, who'd raised herself sleepily on one elbow. I answered the phone.

You said, very carefully and precisely, 'Jamie. Don't worry because he's going to be fine, but Kit's hurt himself.'

For a brief millisecond after you said it, I had a vivid picture in my head of Kit stubbing his toe. But of course it wasn't a figure of speech to express a random accident, like 'Kit's hurt himself falling off his bike'. The reflexive carried a sinister weight of intention.

Alice was watching me as I spoke on the phone. When I hung up, she said quickly, 'What is it? What's happened?' Alice was always a sponge for other people's emotions. She couldn't help herself. If someone else cried, she would cry. If someone around her suffered a tragedy, it became Alice's tragedy as well. I used to like that about her. I saw it as a sign of supreme empathy.

We caught the train to London together. Alice held my hand for the whole of the journey, and didn't try to make me talk.

When we arrived in the A & E department a couple of hours later, a nurse told us to follow her. The place was brightly lit and hurt my eyes. It was full of drunks, and one man was staggering around, shouting slurred abuse at the receptionist. I kept a careful hold of Alice.

The nurse took us to a cubicle and we slipped through the curtain, and there was Kit, white-faced and semi-conscious on the bed, a drip attached to his arm. He was wearing a hospital gown, and his wrists were bandaged almost up to the elbows. You and Mum were sitting on plastic chairs next to the bed and Mum had Emma on her lap, wrapped in a blanket, with her head sleepily resting against Mum's shoulder.

Alice murmured, 'I'll go and get everyone a coffee,' and disappeared, tactfully leaving us alone.

You both looked exhausted, and Mum had been crying. Kit moved his head slightly when I came in, and seemed to look at me for a few moments, but then closed his eyes again.

'Is he OK?' was the first thing I asked.

You nodded briefly. 'He'll live.'

I pulled up a chair beside you and we sat for a few moments in silence.

'Fucking hell,' I said, to no one in particular.

Mum said, 'His flatmates found him. They'd gone out for supper, but they came back early. One of the girls went to knock on his door, and . . .' Her voice trailed off, and she turned to look at Kit.

'They're waiting for his paracetamol level to come back,' you added, 'then they'll admit him to a ward.'

You both seemed to feel the need to explain things to me, but I was barely listening. Mainly, I was wondering what would have happened if Kit's flatmates hadn't come back early. After a moment, I said, 'So he took paracetamol?'

'Among other things. But he vomited a lot of it up.'

'And his wrists?'

'He missed the major arteries,' you said.

'Bit of a botch job, really,' I said. I felt a sudden, mad urge to laugh, thinking what Kit's scathing response would be if he were conscious.

Alice came back in, precariously holding four polystyrene cups. She handed them out, and I gestured for her to pull up a chair next to me. She leaned her head on my shoulder and I told her, 'He's going to be OK. Just a bit of a scare.'

We sat in blank silence for a while. I suppose we were all in shock, trying to work out how this could have happened to someone in our family. It seemed like a mistake, as though we'd accidentally gone off-script or something. And I was thinking, how could Kit have done it? What was going through his mind as he swallowed all those pills?

It was then that I remembered I'd texted him just a few days before about the Spurs match, and had a reply from him. He'd sounded cheerful, had fancied our chances in Saturday's game. This disturbed me more than anything else. What could have changed so dramatically between then and now? Or had he already been planning his own death when he texted me?

I studied his unconscious face, tried to get some sense of who my brother was. It was a weird sensation, looking at someone you've known all your life as though they were a stranger. But it was like Kit had shut himself off from me through this one, unbelievable act.

I said, 'I thought he was alright now.'

'So did we,' you said. 'He seemed fine – he seemed happy.'

There was another long silence, eventually broken by Mum. 'We should have realized,' she said. Her voice was dead.

I never told you much about my visit to Kit a few days afterwards, did I? I didn't really feel like discussing it at the time. Mum was keen for me to go, but I was apprehensive.

You'd both warned me that Kit would be uncommunicative, and not to take it personally. This didn't sound promising. To be honest, I didn't want to go at all. I had no idea what I'd say to Kit when I saw him, or what kind of state he'd be in. The whole situation embarrassed me. What do you talk about with someone who's tried to kill himself? Kit and I hardly ever discussed our feelings with each other – it wasn't how our relationship worked. But I couldn't exactly waltz in and start chatting about the football. Plus I had an essay due in which I'd barely started, and it was preying on my mind. I could have gone to see my tutor and explained, but I didn't want to talk to anyone about what Kit had done.

I was angry with him, of course. Furious with him for frightening me so much. I think that was my main problem, but I didn't realize it then.

Kit had been moved to a different ward by now, and I

had to ask a nurse to help me find it, which she seemed to find irritating. She strode briskly down the main corridor, pointed wordlessly at a door, and then huffed back the way she came. 'Thanks,' I said to her retreating form.

I hovered for a moment outside the door, trying to prepare myself; but this didn't seem to be helping, so in the end I just went in. I tried to ignore the other patients staring at me as I wandered down the ward in search of Kit's bed, feeling increasingly self-conscious and out of place. I started to panic when I couldn't find Kit immediately. But then, just as I'd decided I'd have to go back and find the scary nurse again, I saw him, right at the far end of the ward, by the window. He was looking the other way, out at the hospital grounds. All I could see was the back of his head.

I went and sat by his bed. 'Hi, Kit.'

He delayed a moment, then turned to me. 'Hi, Jamie.'

He looked wrong. His face was pale and his movements were slow, but there was something else that was wrong, too, only I couldn't say what. His wrists were still bandaged, and he was hooked up to an IV drip. I glanced at his hand where the cannula had been inserted and then looked away, almost phobically. I was annoyed with myself for being surprised that Kit looked ill; in all my concern about his state of mind, I'd forgotten the damage he must have done to his body.

'How are you feeling?'

'Bad,' he said.

'Like, sick?'

'A bit.'

'Headache?'

'Yes.'

Already, I seemed to be boring him. I tried asking about the hospital food, and told him a bit about what I'd been up to at Warwick, but he didn't seem interested. I was starting to feel like an idiot.

After a bit, I said, with forced cheerfulness, 'They think you'll be able to go home tomorrow. Just a few more hours on the drip. You must be sick of it.'

Kit said, after a pause, 'They said I have to have a psych assessment before I'm allowed home.'

'Like, with a psychiatrist?'

'Well, I doubt it'll be with a dermatologist, Jamie.'

I was pleased at this bit of sarcasm. Kit sounded more like himself.

'So what will that involve?'

'I imagine they'll just ask me, did I mean to kill myself, and I'll say no, and then they'll ask, will I try to do it again, and I'll say no. And then I'll be discharged.'

His indifference unsettled me. I hesitated, then made myself say, 'Did you mean to do it?'

Kit didn't reply.

I gestured at his wrists. 'Did that hurt?'

'Yes, Jamie, of course it bloody hurt.'

'I just – I don't—' I couldn't get my words out. I wasn't even sure what I wanted to say. I was trying to ask how he could have done it, I suppose. What was going through his mind.

'I just don't get it,' I came out with in the end.

He looked at me. 'I know you don't.'

I waited, but he didn't say anything more, just turned his head to look out of the window again. He seemed to have withdrawn from me completely. I remembered now the sudden crashes in Kit's mood during his A level year, and I was surprised at myself for having shut them out of my mind so completely. I watched my brother stare sightlessly out of the window.

'I was worried about you,' I said.

Nothing.

'Spurs lost to Bolton,' I said. 'Shit game.'

Nothing.

'We need to sort out our defence.'

When Kit still didn't reply, I sat in silence for a few minutes, thinking perhaps he needed some time to gather himself, and get whatever awful blackness had overtaken him under control.

After a pause, I said, 'Do you want to have a rematch on FIFA of our Spurs–Arsenal showdown when we're both home?'

'Alright,' Kit said eventually.

I was relieved to have got a response from him. 'I'll be Spurs,' I said.

'No, you can be Arsenal.'

'I was Arsenal last time.'

'Yeah, and it's better that way,' Kit said, 'so we can keep Spurs winning.'

I smiled, but Kit seemed to lose interest again after that. He didn't speak much for the rest of the visit beyond saying he was tired. My embarrassment began to return as I sat in excruciating silence, wondering how long I had to wait before I could leave. Kit didn't seem to care whether I was there or not. He was irritating me, and I felt guilty for being irritated.

But then, when I was finally – with huge relief – getting up to leave, he muttered something I didn't catch.

'What, Kit?'

He said it again. 'I've made a fool of myself.' In his voice, complete certainty.

'No, Kit. No one thinks that.'

'I think it.'

'You're not well.'

'I couldn't even manage to kill myself.'

I thought he was going to cry then; in fact, I think I was almost hoping he would. I wanted him to show some kind of emotion instead of this unending blankness. But he didn't. He just sat there, propped up on his pillows, looking away from me.

'You're going to be OK,' I told him.

No reply.

'You're going to get better.'

When he still didn't say anything, I tentatively put my hand on his shoulder. 'We'll all help you. I'll see you at home,' I added. He remained unresponsive.

I thought, my visit hasn't made the slightest bit of difference, and now he won't even say goodbye. I started to walk away, angry and hurt and embarrassed by the whole thing. I looked back at him, to see if he was looking after me, to see if he'd even noticed me leaving. But he was staring straight ahead. I thought I was still furious, but instead I was surprised by an urge to go back to him and put my arms around him – hug him before I left.

I didn't go back. I put my head down and carried on walking.

*

I had a good time yesterday evening clipping my Lego soldiers into their armour and finery, their cloaks and helmets and breastplates, fixing shields and swords, axes, pikes and crossbows into their expectant hands. I've fitted out the horses, too, with their saddles and battledress, put their riders in place. I have a fearsome army marshalled in my sitting room.

Today I've been working on the most exciting part of all: the drawbridge and portcullis. Let me tell you how the drawbridge works, Dad – it's quite clever, and I think you'd appreciate it. It has two little bars clipped into it on either side to work as a hinge, and tiny chains attached at the other end, connected to levers. You push down on the bar above the drawbridge which connects the levers, the chains are pulled taut, and the drawbridge moves on its axle and is pulled closed. Simple and neat.

The portcullis doesn't look particularly formidable – that's my only complaint. It's just a rectangular barred grid, with no sharp spikes at the bottom. And there's only one, whereas plenty of castles had two portcullises. You could trap invaders between them and bombard them through the murder-holes with burning wood, and boiling liquids. (Common misconception, Dad, the idea that boiling oil was used. Oil was much too precious in medieval times to be wasted.)

The castle isn't finished yet, but it won't be long now. It'll look magnificent anyway, but it'll seem all the more so to me for having seen it rise up from nothing. I'll derive the same kind of satisfaction from my castle as you must from all the things you've made in the past – the dining room table, for instance. Perhaps you can't fully appreciate any finished form without having seen its origins, especially if you're responsible for them.

*

I know I said I didn't mind, but sometimes I wish you'd write back. Just to remind me that you were there, too. You witnessed it all. It's lonely, looking at it on my own.

Do you ever feel that, Dad? I suppose you've got Mum to talk to, if you want to. I don't remember you being much of a talker, though.

*

Still nothing. Stupid to have asked.

*

When I moved back home after university, Kit said, 'Living with your parents again? Bit tragic.'

This was a complicated joke, and I didn't know how to respond to it. Kit had been living at home for over a year by then, and was seeing Dr Ransom once a fortnight. You and Mum must have struggled to afford the fees, but you weren't going to risk the NHS waiting list again.

I think the sessions with Dr Ransom and the medication were helping a bit, or perhaps it was just the passage of time, but either way it was a slow process. I know you and Mum were disappointed that Kit hadn't managed to complete his degree, although you hoped he'd go back one day.

I was apprehensive about moving back home after graduating, but I didn't have much choice since I had no job lined up. I'd been trying to get an internship at a London newspaper, but it was more competitive than I'd realized, and so far I'd had no luck. I could tell you weren't particularly impressed. One son treading water was enough for you; you didn't want two.

On top of that, I didn't know how I was going to deal with Kit's moods. When he was bad, he'd alternate between distraught and hostile. I suppose you remember.

'I'm sorry, Jamie,' he said once, after he'd goaded me into yelling at him, calling him a bastard. 'Everything's so awful I just want it to be worse.' This didn't make much sense to me at the time, but I'm starting to understand it now. In this kind of mood, Kit wanted to make us all hate him. It was around this time that he smashed up his Lego models.

I felt particularly sorry for Emma, living there all the time with no refuge. Perhaps it was just in my head, but when I'd gone home during the last holidays, I'd thought she seemed rather withdrawn, and had lost some of her usual spark.

But actually by the time I moved home, things were way better than I'd expected. There were still days when Kit was quiet and stayed in his room, but other times he'd be fairly cheerful, sometimes chatting to Mum in the kitchen, but more often helping you out in your shed. You always used to say how good Kit was with his hands, and how creative he was. It annoyed me at the time because I was useless at things like that, and hardly ever got invited into the shed. It even made me hate you a bit when I was younger, for always seeming to prefer him. But you probably just thought I wasn't interested. And I wasn't, really – Kit liked to make things, but I could never see the point back then. Kit could watch you for hours, silently absorbing the techniques you used, or work patiently away at his own bit of wood until he'd got it perfect. I always got fidgety after ten minutes, and gave up with the work half-done. But I still wanted to be asked.

I didn't mind now, though. I was just relieved that Kit was getting better. He beat me at FIFA again, dragged me off to the woods to get some exercise, and interrogated me about my relationship with Alice, which he didn't approve of.

He was becoming interested in art again as well, which used to absorb him when he was younger. When he was recovering, feeling just about alright but not up to leaving the house much, he started producing those amazing collages. Do you remember them? Kit would be really disparaging if anyone commented on them or praised them. He'd say he was just messing around, that he

needed something to fill the hours. ('Is it art therapy?'
I asked him once. 'Fuck off,' Kit said.)

But I knew he was taking it more seriously than that.
Kit didn't do things by halves. It was brilliant to see him
intent on a project again – it reminded me of the way he
was with his Lego models when we were kids.

I remember being struck by one collage in particular.
It was on a huge piece of black card, and showed nothing
but a man standing by himself on the dark background:
simple enough, really. But when you looked more closely,
you noticed that the man was made entirely out of odds
and ends, scraps and rubbish – things I was surprised Kit
had kept: countless tickets from trains, museums, cinemas,
theatres, and various holiday mementos, along with pieces
cut from postcards and leaflets. Every shred offered up a
memory: the collage was flooded with the past. There
were photos of us as children, too, sometimes with you
and Mum in the background. There we were on the
swings, on the beach, on holiday in the Lake District,
worked in among the odds and ends, our faces staring out
from amongst the clusters of train tickets to Marylebone
and Paddington, glossy images of the Eiffel Tower and the
Colosseum, a postcard of the Bayeux Tapestry.

Over the top of it all, Kit had stuck layers of what
looked like tracing paper, but which he explained to me
was Mum's sewing-pattern paper. ('Don't tell her,' he
added. 'I think she's looking for it.') It gave the collage a
faded, aged appearance, as though the whole thing were
being viewed at a slight remove.

All this hoarded experience. From it, Kit had created

a man of scraps, a man of bits and pieces, who looked stronger than the sum of his parts. I'm not sure how he captured the grace of the man's movement out of those fragments, but he seemed to be dancing. There he was, a jumbled, composite man, dancing away by himself, standing out against the black background.

I don't know what happened to that collage, Dad. Do you have it at home somewhere? I often think I'd like to see it again.

*

Do you remember the meal Kit and I cooked for Mum's birthday that year?

It was all Kit's idea. He marched into my bedroom on the morning of Mum's birthday and announced, 'James, dig out your chef's hat. We're cooking dinner tonight.'

I agreed, pleased to see Kit enthusiastic about something. I suggested we do a roast or something, but Kit said, 'I've already decided on the menu.'

'How come you get to decide?' I said, irritated by his officious manner.

'Because I'm the Head Chef.'

'I thought you told me to dig out my chef's hat.'

Kit paused. 'You can be the Sous-Chef.'

'Brilliant.'

'We're making spaghetti with a creamy chicken and mushroom sauce.' He held out the recipe book, open at the relevant page. I had a careful look, and decided I approved.

'First we need to go and get the ingredients,' Kit said.

'Right.'

'I've made you a list.'

It took a moment for this to sink in. 'Wait. You've made *me* a list?'

'Well, there's no point in us both going,' Kit said.

'Why can't you go?' I protested.

'I'm an erratic driver.'

I think I probably argued for a bit longer, but of course in the end it was me who went out to get the ingredients. Emma came with me, wanting to be in on the plan. She rushed round the supermarket grabbing bottles of Pepsi and party hats and bags of sweets and other things which she claimed were vital to the success of our 'party'.

That evening, we asked Mum to stay out of the kitchen, telling her we were making her a surprise supper. I started chopping up the mushrooms whilst Kit fried the chicken and Emma tried to blow up the balloons she'd forced me to buy.

'This is going to be a gourmet feast,' Kit said.

Emma laughed, and let go of the one balloon she'd so far managed to inflate. It whizzed round the kitchen doing a high-pitched whine and Kit caught it just before it landed in the frying pan.

He was undeterred even when our chicken and mushroom sauce refused to thicken.

'Perhaps we put in too much stock,' I said.

Kit tried adding more cream cheese, but this didn't seem to help, so he stirred in some flour.

'Looks a bit lumpy.' Emma had come over to inspect it.

I told her to pipe down, and Kit carried on stirring.

Now the sauce seemed to be runny and lumpy at the same time. Kit remained upbeat, claiming it would be fine like this – 'sort of like it has dumplings in it.'

'Looks gross,' Emma said.

'Be quiet, Emmet, or I'll liquidize you and stir you in,' Kit said.

After a bit more hopeless stirring, Emma was despatched to fetch you and Mum and lead you to your seats.

I went to drain the spaghetti, but in my haste tipped half of it out of the colander into the sink. I looked round furtively and realized no one had noticed except Kit, who shook his head in disgust.

'You're the worst sous-chef I've ever worked with.'

I picked the rogue spaghetti out and put it back in the colander and we served it up with the runny-lumpy sauce.

'What a treat to be cooked for by you boys,' Mum said.

'Perhaps you should try it first,' I said.

Mum beamed at us, and heroically began to eat.

I'm sure you'll agree, Dad, that it was a fairly disgusting meal, though both you and Mum denied this at the time. But I still remember it as one of the best evenings in ages. We all stayed sitting round the table long after we'd finished eating, and everyone was in a good mood. We sang 'Happy Birthday' to Mum and produced the cake I'd picked up in the supermarket (a wise decision). Kit was brilliant company and made us all laugh like he used to, and we were all thinking, yes, we're getting back to normal. Maybe the bad times are over.

That's what was so cruel – we thought he was getting better.

*

Kit and I didn't talk much about his illness, but I do remember one conversation we had in the pub at home, not long after Mum's birthday meal. Sam had come to stay for a few days, and I'd introduced him to Kit for the first time.

I was nervous about whether they'd get on, and felt oddly protective when I thought of either of them exposed to the judgement of the other. But to my relief they hit it off immediately, united mainly by a shared delight in taking the piss out of me.

The Spurs game was on in the pub (the incredible 5–4 defeat against Arsenal – you must remember that game) and I was trying to concentrate, but Sam and Kit were more intent on swapping embarrassing stories about me. They both became hysterical with laughter as Sam related the time in the third year when we got back late from a football dinner, only to discover that we'd both forgotten our keys and that our other two housemates were away staying with their girlfriends.

'So Jamie gets it into his head,' Sam said, 'that it's a good idea to try to climb in through our bathroom window – which, by the way, was really high up and about the size of a cat flap – and he ends up getting his head stuck and dangling there for half an hour shouting, "I don't want to die like this!"'

Sam and Kit both collapsed whilst I stared grimly at the television screen.

Kit said, 'I've never forgotten the time when we were teenagers and were sitting in the park at around lunchtime, and this girl came up who Jamie fancied. What was her name again, Jamie? That girl in your class in Year 10? Fit, with the dark hair.'

'Suzie Chamberlain,' I said, through gritted teeth.

'Yeah, that's it. Anyway, she comes up and starts chatting to me and Jamie, and Jamie's trying to be really cool about it. And he's actually doing alright, for once. Then Suzie says she has to go because she's meeting her friend in town for lunch. And as she walks away, Jamie decides to call something after her, only he can't decide between "Have a nice lunch" and "Have a nice day", gets himself confused and ends up yelling after her, really cheerily, "Haaave luu-unch!"' Kit said this last part so loudly, and with such extravagant jollity, that several people in the pub turned to look at us. I put my head in my hands.

'How did she react to that?' Sam said, wiping his eyes.

Kit said, 'She was pretty nonplussed. She was like, "Yeah. I will. I will have lunch." And I don't think she ever talked to you again, did she, Jamie?'

'No,' I said. 'Thanks for bringing it up.'

'It seems like your life's been pretty embarrassing, Jamie,' Sam said. 'One humiliation after another.'

'That's about the size of it.'

Kit said, 'Remember that New Year's party where you threw up at 11.30, in front of Dad?'

This seemed a bit unfair. 'I was only thirteen.'

'It's impressive really, that you managed to get hold of any alcohol at all, with Mum and Dad prowling around.'

'I didn't,' I admitted at last. 'I ate too many Cadbury Mini Rolls.'

This kept them going until half-time in the game, and at that point I decided I needed a break. I downed the rest of my drink and said, 'I'm going to the bar. Same again?'

They nodded. As I was walking away, Kit called after me, 'Haaaave lunch!' and this set them off again.

When I came back, Sam had gone out to have a cigarette, leaving me and Kit alone. I set the pints down.

'You seem to be getting on well with Sam.'

'Nice guy,' Kit said. 'Funny. Funnier than you, anyway.'

'Impossible.' I gestured at the TV. 'Don't think this one's over yet. Not that you were watching. I'm actually feeling pretty tense. We've started brightly but not sure how long we'll keep Henry and Bergkamp at bay.'

'Still, at least they're playing Cygan,' Kit said. 'We'll always have a chance with him on the pitch.'

We drank for a while in silence. We were both on our third or fourth pint by then, and I was starting to get to that relaxed, expansive stage before outright drunkenness. This enabled me to say to Kit after a moment, 'You're on good form at the moment.'

Kit accepted this phlegmatically. 'I'm feeling OK.'

Looking back at the next thing I said, I cringe at my own stupidity. 'So you think all that bad stuff's behind you?'

'No,' Kit said.

'You think it might come back?'

'I don't know, Jamie.'

I was starting to feel emotional – the drink, I suppose. 'Just promise me one thing, OK? Promise me you won't try to hurt yourself again.' I paused, embarrassed to find my voice unsteady. 'It was so terrible.'

Kit was drinking his beer thoughtfully. After a minute, he said, 'Sorry. It must have been.'

'It was,' I said. 'You can't put us through that again. Just promise, alright?'

Kit said, 'I can't promise.'

'You have to. How can the rest of us carry on, worrying about you all the time?'

'Look, Jamie,' Kit said. 'If it gets that bad again then I might want to get out. You can't imagine it. I need to have an escape option.'

I couldn't think of anything to say. Fortunately, Sam reappeared at that moment, saying, 'I've remembered another one!' He started telling Kit about the time after a football curry I'd run out in front of a learner driver. Kit and I were both grateful for the distraction.

'Jamie claimed he was helping them practise their emergency stop,' Sam said. 'We dragged him away, but he kept on shouting, "They have to learn! They have to learn!"'

Kit laughed, and I was relieved to see our conversation hadn't ruined his mood. After that we couldn't think of anything except the drama at White Hart Lane, witnessing one of the most spectacular matches I've ever seen as Spurs fought to withstand Arsenal. Kit and I were almost beside ourselves as our hopes were dashed by Pirès and then revived by Kanouté, then dashed for good by the final whistle. Even Sam, a staunch Liverpool fan, was agog at the rapidly changing scorelines. What a second half, Dad. You watched it at home on Sky, and Kit and I shared our disappointment and disbelief with you when we got back from the pub. Remember that?

(I don't really follow football any more, by the way, but I see Spurs are having a fairly good run. I wonder if you still watch the games, now Kit and I are no longer around.)

That night, I put the conversation with Kit out of my head. I told myself it didn't matter that he'd refused to promise, because it would never come to that.

*

Things are falling into place with my castle. I have yet to fly the blue and yellow flags, but the walls and towers and battlements are complete, along with the entrance, drawbridge and portcullis.

I wish you could see how strong I've made my castle. I think even you might be impressed. Perhaps if you saw it you'd think I was as good with my hands as Kit was.

Sometimes I think about crawling inside and sheltering within its solid grey walls. I've been experimenting with hiding recently. I crouched down behind the History desk yesterday and stayed there, pretending to be looking for something. And I can always hide in my flat. But it never seems like enough. If I was in the castle, no one could follow me.

There are places I can't follow Kit either. Dad, I think it's best these letters stop now. You probably never read them, anyway.

*

Sorry I stopped writing to you for a while. I got tired of never getting a reply. And I was tired of lots of other things, too.

But something strange happened today. I was mooching about in American History when Sally came over and said, 'Someone on the phone for you.' I assumed it was a customer, or perhaps Sam, though he hasn't been in touch for a while now. But then Sally said, 'It's your sister.'

Surprised, I went over to the desk to take the call.

'Emma?'

'Hi, Jamie,' she said.

I waited for a few moments, and when she didn't speak, ventured, 'How's school?'

'Terrible.'

'Those girls?'

'Bitches.'

We were both silent for a few moments, then Emma said quickly, 'You know how you said I could come and visit whenever I wanted? Well, can I come up this weekend?'

I felt sorry for her – it must be lonely for her at home by herself. But I knew I couldn't have anyone visiting me. I told her this weekend wasn't good because I had to work, and that Sam was visiting next weekend.

'Can I come after that?' she said.

'I'm not sure Mum and Dad will be happy for you to visit,' I tried. 'I don't want to get you into trouble.'

'But it was Dad who told me to ring you,' she said.

I was so surprised I didn't reply for a few moments. Then I said, 'Why?'

'He just asked if I was in touch with you,' Emma said. 'I said I was a bit, and he said perhaps I should give you a quick ring. To see how you were.'

'So he didn't want to talk to me himself?'

'No, don't think so.'

'But he suggested you should?'

'Yeah.'

I was mulling this over throughout the rest of our conversation. I agreed that Emma could come up in a few weeks, and that I'd let her know which weekend I was free. Might just have to go through with it this time. It's not that I don't want to see her, Dad. I miss her sometimes. But it's all too difficult, isn't it?

The strangeness of the incident galvanized me into action. I think I've been in a kind of stupor over the past couple of months. But when I got home from work today I immediately scrabbled around for some paper and a pen so I could write to you. I hope I can find a stamp. I've thrown a lot of things out recently, including all my writing paper (you'll notice this letter's on pages torn from a notebook. I hope you don't mind). I messed up my flat a bit. But I'm alright now. I feel better.

Why did you ask Emma to ring me? I know you won't write back and tell me – I'll be left to puzzle over this

on my own. I wish I knew what was going on in your
head.

*

I'm trying to pull myself together, Dad. Honestly, I am. The
castle helps a bit.

*

I didn't know what Kit meant at first when he said, 'It's
starting again.'

We were in the TV room, watching *The Simpsons*.
I looked round at Kit, but he was still staring at the
screen. I said, 'What's starting again?' Then I realized
what he meant. I turned off the TV.

'You mean you think you're getting ill again?'

'Yes.'

'But you've been fine for ages.'

'Yeah, I have,' Kit said. 'And now it's starting again.'

'You're having a bad few days,' I said. 'That's all. It's part
of the recovery.'

'No. I'm not on the way up, Jamie. I'm on the way
down. I can feel myself slipping.'

'You'll be alright.'

'I'll never be alright,' he said. 'It's there, waiting for me.
And soon it's going to close in again.'

The way he was talking frightened me. I said, 'OK.
What can we do? Let's get you an appointment with
Dr Ransom, he could increase your dosage—'

'It won't make any difference. We've tried it all. There's

nothing anyone can do.' Kit looked away from me then, looked out of the window and up at the sky. It was late-afternoon and the light was a magnificent soft gold. Spring was on its way – there was warmth in the air again and the sky was restored to a bright blue after the washed-out winter grey. Very quietly, Kit said, 'You should see the view on the way down, though. It's beautiful.'

He sounded distant, as though he was already lost.

Once, I didn't know what to say to Kit when he talked about the view on the way down. Now I think I'm looking at it too.

*

I kept asking Kit how he was feeling over the next few days, but he'd only say, 'The same'. He hadn't told you and Mum – that much was clear from Mum's continued good mood – and I didn't tell you either. I should have done, of course. But that would have meant accepting it was true.

Kit and I went to the woods one day, and tramped through to the Swing Den. I swished idly back and forth on the rope swing and Kit sat nearby on the ground.

It was a bright, warm day, and Kit was gazing around the clearing. I thought he looked peaceful – contented, even. I started to think that perhaps he was going to be alright after all.

Then he said, 'I don't think I can do this any longer.'

I dropped off the rope swing onto the ground. 'What do you mean?' I crouched down beside him. I already knew what he meant.

Kit looked scared now, and the strange calm of the past week was gone. I realized he was frightened of me – of my face, whatever my face was doing.

'What do you mean, Kit?'

'I won't survive this.'

'You will.'

'No one can survive this.'

'Stop it, Kit.'

I thought that if I refused to discuss it with him I could bleach the meaning out his words, freeze out their implications.

'I'm tired,' Kit said.

We didn't speak on the way back, although Kit tried once or twice. He said, 'Jamie, I just want it to be over,' but I didn't answer. Kit was close to tears. He said, 'I'm trying to explain it to you. I don't want it to be a shock—' but I cut him off, told him viciously to shut up, to shut his fucking mouth. I'd never spoken to him like that before, and it shook him into silence.

Back home, he asked me not to tell you and Mum what he'd said, or even that he was feeling bad. I said I wouldn't, but I did, straight away – as soon as he'd gone to his room. Mum was out shopping, but I went straight out to your shed and told you, 'Kit says he's ill again.' Not, Kit's ill again, but Kit says he's ill again. I was so angry I wouldn't even admit I believed him. You said, 'Are you sure?'

'He's talking about killing himself.'

Your face froze. 'Jamie, what did he say?'

'He said, he can't survive this.'

You were already pushing past me out of the shed and running towards the house.

'You're welcome,' I said, alone in the shed.

The next day, you took Kit to Dr Ransom, who doubled his sessions and talked about changing his medication. Kit had worked his way through several different drugs by now, but they weren't having much effect. That's how he ended up on one of the old-school tricyclic antidepressants (a 'last-resort drug', as Kit optimistically termed it). We were told to keep a careful eye on him.

If Kit was angry at my betrayal, he never showed it. I was avoiding him most of the time anyway. I'd got my job in the cafe in the week, and would usually go to stay with Alice or Sam in London at weekends. You thought I was being selfish, abandoning my brother when he needed my support the most. And I was – but I couldn't let myself think about what Kit had said.

I did end up spending one particular Saturday with him, though. I was staying at home that weekend, and you and Mum had gone out to do the weekly shop, taking Emma with you – you were going to take her for a milkshake afterwards. That's how it came about that I was the only one at home when Kit jumped off the roof.

I never gave you all the details, did I?

Once you, Mum and Emma had gone out, I sat

downstairs for a while watching TV by myself. I was bored and irritable, pissed off with my life. I was trapped at home with no decent job in sight, no prospect of moving to London to join my friends, and everything overshadowed by Kit's misery.

I wallowed in self-pity for a while, until it occurred to me that Kit probably wasn't too thrilled about the way life had turned out, either. Then I thought I'd go and see what kind of mood he was in, ask if he felt like a go on the PlayStation.

I knocked on the door of his room, but there was no answer, so I went in and found Kit in the act of hoisting himself out of his bedroom window onto the sloping roof below. I reeled in shock.

'Kit—'

'Go away, Jamie.'

'Why don't you come downstairs?' I said. 'Play FIFA with me?' A completely moronic thing to suggest to someone climbing out of an upstairs window, but I couldn't think what to do.

'I don't want to play FIFA. I want to be left in peace.'

He was out on the roof now, and I moved to stand by the window. I was really frightened. The fall was about twenty feet, and there was concrete below. But Kit didn't look as I imagined someone would look when they were planning to harm themselves; he didn't look desperate or mad. He just looked very determined.

'Kit, come back in. It's dangerous.'

'Go back downstairs.'

That's when I knew he was going to do it. I made to climb out after him but he was on the edge of the roof now, and said, 'Stay where you are.'

'Please. Don't do anything now. Wait a bit. Come back inside.'

'It has to be now. Or I'll lose my nerve.'

I was almost crying, but a part of me couldn't really believe it was happening. 'You'll hurt yourself,' I said, stupidly.

'I'm sorry. Really, really sorry. Tell Mum and Dad.'

'Don't do this to me.'

'Jamie, I'm trying not to.' I could see he was on the verge of tears, too. 'Go back downstairs. Tell yourself you never came up.' His face was set. 'Too much pain,' he said. And, 'Sorry,' again.

He waited a moment, and then, when I didn't move, he jumped.

In the ambulance, I tried to think what I'd say to you and Mum. Was it my fault? I wondered if I should start by apologizing. I couldn't think straight. Since you'd left the house, the world we knew had spun away from us. I didn't recognize this new ground.

I wished you or Mum were with me. I felt like I was dissolving, evaporating in the stale air of the ambulance. I needed someone else's presence to confirm my own.

I called your mobile from the hospital. You answered the phone very calmly and deliberately on the third ring, as if you knew something had happened.

I said, 'There's been an accident,' and the world changed again.

*

If Kit had died that night, things would be different between you and me. Sometimes, I try to work out if I wish he hadn't survived the fall.

Because whatever I'd thought, waiting in terror at the hospital, you didn't blame me then. When you came into the waiting room, the first thing you did was hug me. Then Mum did the same. She said, 'Are you OK, darling?' I shook my head and you said, 'You know this isn't your fault,' and I started to cry.

Kit had multiple fractures to his legs and a crushed vertebra, but he hadn't hit his head, and he didn't die. As history teaches us, outcomes defeat intentions.

Over the months Kit was in hospital, I often found myself thinking, What's the point? All those operations, all that energy and effort going into fixing his body, when all he wanted to do was destroy it.

I knew by then that Kit would succeed one day. Everything had shifted the moment I saw him disappear over the edge of the roof. I would never again tell him he was going to be alright.

I put off visiting the hospital for several weeks, and you and Mum didn't press me. You probably thought I was angry with Kit for what he'd made me witness, or too traumatized to see its results, but it was more complicated than that. Though the doctors said Kit would make a full recovery, I knew now that he was slipping away from us, and there was nothing anyone could do. We couldn't make him want to live, or be able to live.

*

The castle's complete.

I thought I'd have more time, Dad – but everything is at an end.

Part Three

1

If Emma looked back at the last six months, she had to admit that she'd expected more than this. It had been naive of her, obviously. ('Naive' was a word she'd encountered a lot in Literature Club, and was determined not to be any longer.) But she was younger then, and you *were* naive when you were young. Now she was fifteen and she could see that it was stupid to have expected things to change, when all her experience of the past few years had told her that things never changed, but went on in their grey old way until it made you want to scream, or run away and become a missionary.

That was another thing she'd been stupid about. There was a time when she'd dreamed of escaping to do the Lord's work far away. But you couldn't just run away to Africa and be a missionary. It wasn't practical. In a fit of irritation with herself, Emma had thrown out the last board game she'd made, even though it had been one of her best efforts: complex, satisfying and artistically accomplished. It had been missionary-themed, and she'd called it *The Lord's Song in a Strange Land*. The rats at the landfill site were probably playing with it now, fighting over who got to be St Paul.

It almost embarrassed her to remember how different

she'd thought things would be once she found Jamie. What had she expected him to do? Magically transform her life? Make her thin and stop the girls at school being horrible to her? Jamie hadn't made the slightest bit of difference, really. She never saw him, and he still hadn't got back to her about when she could visit, even though he'd said he would. If she was honest, he'd been a bit of a let-down.

Nevertheless, Emma had contemplated asking her parents if Jamie could come to her birthday dinner. It was a special occasion, because fifteen was an important age, and Jamie was family after all, and it was *her* birthday. But in the end she'd decided it wasn't worth asking. She knew what the answer would be, because her parents were still weird about Jamie, and there was no point in making things uncomfortable when you wouldn't gain anything from it.

All the same, her birthday had turned out really well. One of the best moments was when she opened up a soft parcel from her parents and saw a glimpse of shining pink silk, and then the kimono jacket she'd wanted ages ago slithered out onto her lap in all its gorgeous finery.

'I can't *believe* it!' Emma said, and saw her mother look radiantly happy for a moment.

Emma hesitated briefly, aware that she hadn't earned the jacket like she was supposed to through her healthy-eating chart. But it was so beautiful that she decided she didn't care. She held it up to admire it for a few moments, then slipped it on over her jumper.

Her dad handed her another parcel, and said they'd got

her this as well. Emma tried to gauge the present through the wrapping paper. It was round and solid; she could rap her knuckles against it. She pulled off the paper and found herself holding a shiny wooden apple, its sides polished and smooth, made from a light-coloured wood. It even had a little wooden stalk at the top, and the bottom was slightly flattened like a real apple's, so it could stand upright on its own.

Her dad explained that he'd made it out of wood from the apple tree, which he'd cut down last year. Emma remembered being annoyed at the time – she used to climb that tree when she was little. She didn't know he'd saved any of the wood.

'An apple from the apple tree,' she said, turning it over and over in her hands, loving the smooth feel of the wood and the swirling pattern of the grain on its sides.

'It's not much really,' her dad said. 'Just an ornament.'

'It's *lovely*,' Emma said, and meant it.

He handed her a final present, small and strangely shaped, saying, 'I thought it needed some company.' The parcel contained a wooden pear, made out of a darker wood and polished smooth like the apple.

'It's laburnum,' he said. 'Not wood from a pear tree, I'm afraid.'

Emma adored her wooden fruit. The apple and the pear now sat side by side on her chest of drawers, and the lovely silk jacket hung on the back of her door. Emma looked at them contentedly. The Bible said it was wrong to be materialistic, but why not, if things could make you happy? Didn't the Bible want you to be happy?

For her birthday dinner they had sausages and mash (Emma's request). Her parents had bought some champagne, too, to mark the occasion. Emma wasn't sure she liked the taste very much but it felt special to be having champagne. Her mum had put some more presents around her plate – little things to unwrap, like earrings and a couple of CDs, and bath salts and some lip gloss. Emma never wore make-up, but she liked the sparkly, peachy colour of the gloss and thought she might try it.

She hadn't been sure if Jamie would remember her birthday. He didn't seem very reliable, and men weren't supposed to be good at remembering things like dates anyway. Plus, there was nobody to remind him.

But a parcel had arrived a couple of days before her birthday. Inside was a small present wrapped in blue paper, and a card. Emma opened the card straight away to check it really was from Jamie and was relieved to discover it was. It had a short message inside:

Dear Emma,

Happy birthday.

Wasn't sure what to get you, sorry if it's not much good.

Take care.

    Jamie

Then Emma thought she might as well open the present straight away, too. It turned out to be a necklace made from brightly coloured beads that glinted and sparkled as Emma held it up. It wasn't the kind of thing she would usually wear – it was a bit garish, and seemed a little young for her, really. She felt momentarily disappointed, but then rallied. She had been younger when she went to find Jamie in Sheffield. He wasn't to know how much she'd grown up since then. What mattered was that he'd sent her something. He'd remembered her birthday, and he'd gone into a shop and chosen something, and then gone to all the trouble of wrapping it up and posting it.

Her dad walked in at this point and saw her with the necklace. 'That's nice.'

So Emma said, just to see what would happen, 'Jamie sent it to me. For my birthday.'

She'd thought her dad might react angrily, but he only said, 'Was there a card?'

'Yes. But he didn't say much. Just, Happy Birthday.'

Her dad said, 'May I see?'

Emma showed him. He cast his eyes over it and nodded, but more to himself than to her, Emma thought. She said, 'I might go and visit him soon. Just for the day.'

'Mmm.'

'He said he'd tell me when I could come,' Emma said. 'But he hasn't yet.'

'He's probably busy,' her dad said, and didn't seem to want to talk about it any more.

Emma wrote Jamie a thank you note a few days after her birthday:

Dear Jamie,
    Thanks for the necklace, it's brilliant! I had a nice birthday. Mum wanted to make something fancy for

dinner but I wanted bangers and mash so she made that instead, with some really nice, posh sausages – several different kinds. And we had chocolate cake for pudding which Mum had made, with really thick icing and milk and white chocolate decorations on top.

Emma paused – was she going on about food too much? She continued carefully:

I got some nice presents, too. Although yours was the best, of course. And it was Saturday so I didn't have to go to school! Which I still don't enjoy very much. The girls in the CU have a very naive idea of Christianity.

When can I come and see you? We could have milkshakes again, if you want. There's a new place that's opened up in town that does loads of different sorts like Bakewell Tart and Creme Egg and Strawberry Cheesecake. I went last week with Mum, and I had a Rolo one. Perhaps there's one in Sheffield, too. You could go on your lunch breaks.

Love,

Emma

She waited for ages, but Jamie never wrote back. She felt stupid, because she'd wasted all this time – *years*, really – wondering about him and hoping he'd come back, when all along her idea of him was wrong, and he wasn't what she'd imagined at all. Perhaps her memory was to blame, or perhaps it was Jamie himself who'd changed. Either way, she missed the Jamie she'd had in her head and sometimes wished he hadn't been replaced by the real one.

But in some ways it could be a relief to accept your life as it was, to give up on the idea of it ever being different. Because you did eventually get used to things being bad, and then you didn't notice as much. School, for instance. Emma still got that sick feeling when the bus pulled up each day, but she expected it now and didn't try to fight it. Some of the cool group still hissed 'infidel' at her, but she expected that, too; sometimes she barely even registered the insult.

Nevertheless, Emma had made a few changes herself. She'd started going along to Literature Club with Olivia Thomas, for one thing. Mr Lawson had moved Olivia a few weeks ago to sit next to Emma in Maths and after that Olivia and Emma had started chatting a bit more. And then Olivia had invited Emma along to Literature Club, on Monday and Thursday lunchtimes. It clashed with CU meetings, but that didn't matter since Emma wasn't in the CU any longer.

Miss Griffiths ran the Literature Club, which was another plus, because she wasn't boring like some of the other teachers. Over the past term they'd been doing Jane Austen, and *Northanger Abbey* in particular. Miss Griffiths had pointed out how Catherine Morland gets everything wrong because she's young and naive and has read too many novels, but that the reader's on her side all the same. They'd done some popular gothic novels from the time as well, and Miss Griffiths had read passages out to them in a breathless, dramatic voice which made everyone laugh at how silly the stories were. Miss Griffiths said that in a hundred years people would probably feel exactly the same about the *Twilight* saga.

Emma and Olivia spent a lot of their time discussing books. Emma had loved *Northanger Abbey*, but Olivia said *Mansfield Park* was more 'adult'. This made Emma feel like she should prefer *Mansfield Park* too, but she'd found it long and slow-going. They decided that they'd both read *Persuasion* at the same time so they could discuss it as they went along, and after only a week they were already on chapter nine.

The cool group were still acting all holy, but they were less pushy about it now, and hadn't done an assembly for ages. Emma didn't mind them having Jesus these days. She never went to the chapel any more, though occasionally she still thought about God. She couldn't tell whether or not she missed Him. It occurred to her that maybe she'd got so used to missing people that this was another thing she didn't notice any more. But perhaps missing people was one of those things you were never supposed to get used to.

2

Sometimes, he didn't think about it. Shut away in the warmth of the shed, intent on some project – a set of wooden bowls, the chess set he'd been working on for over a year – he could go for maybe an hour or more without thinking about it. Miraculous, it seemed to him.

But it was never enough. It always came over him again. Better out here than in the house though, where Rose's nervous, hovering presence seemed to permeate every corner, her obsession with cleanliness, her attempts to play happy families. Talk about shutting the stable door after the horse has bolted. It drove Joe mad, made him hate her, and himself too. Best that he kept to the quiet of his shed where possible.

He'd gone to his GP a few years back with a whole host of symptoms: back pain, aching limbs, headaches, fatigue. Dr Arthurs had referred him for some tests and a scan, but everything came back clear. Joe was puzzled. He hadn't mentioned the insomnia, but Dr Arthurs had asked him on his second visit how much sleep he was getting, and Joe had had to admit, not very much. Dr Arthurs had looked at him seriously and said after a few moments, 'Have you considered getting some proper help?' For a foolish moment Joe thought he meant hiring a cleaner. As if Rose would allow that.

Then Dr Arthurs said, 'It might benefit you to talk to someone. There are people specially trained for this kind of thing. Bereavement counsellors. Psychotherapists.'

And Joe had said, 'No, no.' He felt awkward, embarrassed. 'It's nothing to do with that. I've got back pain.'

Dr Arthurs said gently, 'It's not uncommon for mental distress to manifest itself physically.'

'It's not that,' Joe said. Lucky I didn't mention the nightmares, he was thinking.

'Any nightmares?' Dr Arthurs asked.

'No.'

'Anxiety?'

'No. This is ridiculous.' Joe paused, trying to get himself under control. 'Please, can I have some painkillers? That's all I need.'

In the end, Dr Arthurs had sighed and prescribed him some painkillers, told him not to take them too often and to monitor the situation. Joe hadn't gone back since.

His back still troubled him, and the headaches hadn't got much better either, but he was more used to them now. He accepted them as a part of his life; a cross he had to bear. (This irritated him afresh. He hated the way religious language invaded everyday speech. Reminded him of Emma's religious craze, which, thankfully, seemed to have dampened down in recent months.)

He thought perhaps his body was starting to pack up. His mind didn't seem as sharp as it had once been. He got muddled these days, had trouble concentrating – the simplest tasks took longer than they should. He made stupid mistakes at work, forgot to get mortgage documents signed before sending off the money, forgot to do the land-registry searches before completion, mistakes which would have horrified him once, but now didn't seem to worry him the way they should. He'd wondered at first if he might lose his job if this carried on, but it did carry on and nobody said anything, so in the end it didn't really seem to matter whether he did the job well or not.

He remembered Chris coming into his office a few weeks after it happened, asking if he could have a quick word. Joe had thought it might be about ending his partnership, and had tried, unsuccessfully, to feel concerned. But Chris had asked him how he was getting on, and was there anything they could do? If he'd like more time off work, then Chris himself and David could help out with his caseload for as long as he needed. Joe had found himself suddenly close to tears at this unexpected kindness, and had had to shake his head almost rudely and say, no, no, everything was fine.

At night, he was haunted by the same dream. Always the same. He was at home, and Kit was somewhere in the house too, and in the dream he knew Kit was going to kill himself and he had to stop him. So off he went, searching for Kit from room to room, calling for him, growing more and more desperate. There seemed to be an infinite number of rooms in the house but all of them were empty. He started to think perhaps he'd missed a whole corridor out by mistake, but there were more rooms ahead of him to check. Should he go back or should he carry on going forwards? His search became more and more frantic as he started to realize that he was running out of time, that Kit must have done it already and if he didn't find him in the next few minutes it would be too late to save him.

He searched desperately on, night after night, waking in a panic after each dream. But he never found Kit.

He'd discovered things that helped, slightly. Distractions. Making things brought some relief. (He thought, involuntarily, of Jamie's castle.) He was killing time, just filling the hours. He had projects to focus on, calculations that required all his concentration. Lying awake at night, he tried to focus on small, technical matters like how he might prevent the expansion of the veneer on the dining room table. One problem that had kept him going for a while was the shelves he'd made for Emma's room; he wanted them to appear to be held up by magic. After much consideration, he'd designed an inconspicuous cantilever mechanism, which he thought worked reasonably well, although he wasn't sure Emma had fully appreciated the complications involved.

The mushrooms – now they were causing him a bit of a headache. He'd had a good many attempts already, but still hadn't got his technique perfect. He wanted them to look as realistic as possible, whilst staying true to their essential woodenness. A wooden mushroom, growing in the wild: that was his idea. One thing he was trying was leaving a little bit of bark around the edge of the cap so it had a frayed feel like mushrooms do. He wanted to use the grain pattern in the wood to imitate the circles and patterns on the underside of a mushroom cap, whilst having the top side appear smooth. Not straightforward, by any means.

Joe had planned to give Emma one of the finished mushrooms for her birthday, but he hadn't managed to get one right in time. He'd settled for one of his apples instead, using the wood he'd saved from the apple tree, and spent longer on it than usual; he wanted this one to be the best he'd ever made.

The outcome had pleased him – the grain pattern in the wood was particularly lovely. He was feeling so confident that he made her a pear as well, usually a trickier proposition.

He felt shy, handing them over. Was he making a fool of himself? He was ready to pretend the pieces of wooden fruit were just an afterthought, stupid little things he'd produced at the last minute. The jacket was her main present, although Rose had got her that, of course. But Emma's face as she opened them had enchanted him. She'd been so pleased, and it had moved him, made him feel that it had been worth soldiering through the past week to make her smile like that.

He wasn't making much progress on the mushrooms today. It was starting to frustrate him, and he decided he might as well take a break, so he headed inside to make a cup of tea. Rose was in the kitchen as usual, and he murmured a greeting to her as he went to put the kettle on. Then he reminded himself to make an effort, asked her politely, 'Would you like some tea?'

She looked delighted. 'Do you know, I was just think-ing how nice a cup of tea would be right now. There's something very fortifying about it, isn't there?'

He breathed deeply and tried not to be irritated by her. 'What kind would you like?'

'I'll have what you're having. But why don't you let me make it? I'll do it in the teapot.'

'I'm happy just to make two.'

'But the teapot will be more special, won't it?'

'I don't want it to be special. I just want a cup of tea.'

She seemed to pick up on his tone. 'Whatever you want, darling.' She went to the cupboard and got out the mugs. 'Would you like some Victoria sponge with it? I made it yesterday, so it's still nice and fresh.'

Joe was about to refuse – why on earth did she have to make such a song and dance about everything? – but caught himself in time. It would be unkind to refuse the cake. It wouldn't cost him anything to eat it.

'Yes,' he said. 'That would be very nice.'

They sat and drank their tea at the kitchen table, and Joe had a large slice of cake which Rose watched him eat. He could sense her pride as he tucked in.

'I wonder why it's called *Victoria* sponge,' she said after a moment. 'Perhaps it was Queen Victoria's favourite cake.'

'I don't know,' Joe said. He carried on eating his cake in silence, hoping Rose would drop the subject, and after a little more speculation on Queen Victoria's taste in cakes, she did.

'Emma seemed to enjoy her birthday, didn't she?' Joe

said after a bit, adding generously, 'That jacket you got her was very nice. She seemed to love it.'

Rose smiled at this. 'Yes, I was relieved about that. I bought it ages ago, you see, because she'd seen it and liked it, and I was worried they'd stop selling it. But then I thought, what if she's gone off it by the time I get round to giving it to her? But it all turned out fine, didn't it? And it was really thoughtful of you, those pieces of fruit you made her.'

Joe was impressed with both of them. Here they were, drinking tea together and chatting about their daughter. All the same, he found himself wanting to be away from her. He gulped the last of his tea, thanked her, and stood up to go.

'What are you making at the moment?' Rose called after him as he left.

'Oh, you know,' he said. 'Just bits and pieces.'

Back in the safety of his shed, he congratulated himself. He was getting much better at keeping his temper. He managed to be kinder to Rose these days – it just took a bit of effort. And he was determined to keep making that effort. Rose didn't deserve any more grief from him. Uncomfortably, he thought back to the months after Kit's death, when his anger had filled the house. Sometimes it frightened him how little he could control it. He couldn't talk to Rose without snapping at her. And any thought of his younger son had been accompanied by a vicious, blackened rage. He'd thought he might kill Jamie if he ever saw him again. The idea alarmed him but he couldn't banish it completely. Imagine if he had taken Dr Arthurs up on his offer of therapy and that kind of thing came tumbling out.

They'd been suffocating, all three of them, before he learnt to take himself away to the shed. Thank God for the shed.

He hadn't managed to seal himself off, though. There was no escape from what had happened; no turning away, no forgetting. And that was true now more than ever, because over the past months Jamie had insinuated himself into every corner of Joe's life, the letters arriving at his office with insidious, inexorable regularity. Paper nail-bombs. Why send them to his office, he wondered. Presumably because Jamie wanted to make it clear they were intended for his father alone.

Joe had been enraged after the first few, and yet perversely determined to feed his anger by reading on. He thought Jamie was deliberately taunting him, trying to goad him into a reaction, so he'd resisted giving any kind of response at first. But several sleepless nights had worn him down, and after lying awake for hours one night he got up and scrawled a short note telling Jamie not to contact him again. He posted it on his way to work the next morning, felt better, then regretted it almost immediately. He should have pretended he wasn't reading the letters. More dignified. It might have discouraged Jamie.

But the letters kept coming, and still he read on.

It became a kind of obsession. Each morning he'd wait tensely for Helen, his secretary, to bring him his post and would rifle through it, furious if there was a letter, deflated if there wasn't. Gradually, his anger dulled. He grew resigned; drawn slowly, painfully into Jamie's world. He recognized what Jamie already knew: that they would never be free of each other. Perhaps these letters were their mutual punishment. The bits about Kit – agonizing to read, impossible not to.

He could hear Jamie's voice with brutal clarity on every page, though lately there was a new quality to it that Joe didn't recognize, and wasn't sure how to describe – a kind of blankness, perhaps. The more he read, the more unsure he felt about Jamie's motives for sending them, whatever Jamie said. What was he hoping to achieve? Joe thought he could detect in the sometimes dislocated, fevered style a kind of compulsion; as if Jamie didn't want to write the letters any more than Joe wanted to receive them. It occurred to him eventually that his son wasn't well.

Jamie had said in his last letter that he wouldn't write again, but Joe had a feeling that Jamie hadn't finished with him yet. He didn't know what to do about his son, so he did nothing, simply carried on as before. Head down, struggling through the days. Keeping going, getting through. He'd always known, without having to consider it, that there was no chance of recovery. Not for him, not for any of them. The passing years hadn't changed a thing. There was no getting over this.

3

'You can open the biscuits and put them straight into the good tin,' Eileen said, and Rose obliged, wondering why Eileen persisted in referring to her one-and-only biscuit tin as the 'good' one.

'The gravy was £2.99 a tub,' Rose said, as she put Eileen's two pints of milk in the fridge along with the eggs, yoghurts, lamb chops and supermarket cottage pie.

'Good God!' said Eileen.

'I thought you wouldn't want it, with the price having gone up so much.'

'I certainly wouldn't,' Eileen said. 'They must think there's one born every minute.'

'I got you Bisto in the end. Granules. I hope that's alright?'

Eileen was still tutting to herself as she 'dealt with' her new box of tissues, which involved fitting it painstakingly into her floral tissue-box cover, setting it on the window-sill next to the postcards from her nephew's children, and standing back to admire it.

'Now,' she said. 'Tea or coffee?'

'Tea, please.'

'China or Indian?'

'Indian, please,' Rose said, and waited patiently for the next subcategory. Eileen prided herself on her tea selection.

'Darjeeling or Assam?'

'Assam, please.'

Eileen popped the teabags into her flowery teapot and poured hot water shakily from the kettle. Rose winced at the amount of milk Eileen slopped into the two cups.

'Could you lay out the biscuits, dear?' Eileen said. 'Three should do it.'

Rose laid the biscuits on a little plate, and put it on the tray with the cups and teapot.

'You'll have two,' Eileen said generously, indicating the biscuits.

They took their tea through to the sitting room, and Rose perched on the sofa whilst Eileen settled herself in her usual chair and began to talk about her nephew, who'd got himself a new job recently, something with computers.

Rose found these occasions rather trying, but it would seem unkind to insist on leaving immediately after dropping off Eileen's shopping. Besides, she reflected, she could spare the time.

'I took back your library books,' she said. 'I nearly forgot. I got you another one by Rosamunde Pilcher, and one by Mary Stewart.' She took them out of her bag and handed them over. Eileen seemed to interpret this as a prompt towards paying her back for the shopping, and fussed over getting out her purse and sending Rose off to the kitchen to fetch the receipt. Then she spent a long time rummaging through her purse for the exact change to add to her twenty-pound note, even though Rose assured her that twenty pounds was fine. They went through this performance every week, and Rose always found it embarrassing.

To change the subject, she said, 'I took a couple of books out for myself, as well. I thought I'd re-read *Cranford*. And I got another Barbara Pym.'

'*Cranford* is *wonderful*,' Eileen said, transported by the memory. 'I felt that the television adaptation was rather good, but didn't really do it justice.'

'Judi Dench was excellent though, wasn't she?' Rose said, sensing a fruitful conversational topic. 'The cast was superb. But it must be hard, adapting a book that's so well loved. Because it's never quite going to live up to people's expectations, is it? Even if the television version's wonderful, it'll still be different to how people have imagined it, not necessarily worse, but different – and that's enough to make people not like it.' Rose stopped at this point, feeling that she'd spoken for a little too long and probably lost Eileen's attention. She took a sip of tea.

'I think I shall re-read some of Mrs Gaskell's books next,' Eileen remarked. 'Perhaps you could get me one or two of those next time? *North and South* first would be best.'

'Of course.'

'Although I shall enjoy the Rosamunde Pilcher and Mary Stewart this week. Thank you, dear.'

Eileen talked on about her nephew for a bit longer, and the excellent job he'd done mending her shed roof, which had been leaking after all the rain they'd been having lately. 'A stormy spring we've had,' she said. 'Terribly unpredictable weather.'

Rose agreed, and said something vague about it being good for the garden.

'And how is Emma?' Eileen asked.

'She's fine,' Rose said. 'Just had her fifteenth birthday, and she seems so grown up, all of a sudden. The next thing I know, she'll be going off to university.'

'She must be a great comfort,' Eileen said, as she often did when Emma was mentioned. Rose nodded and let it go. It was no use explaining to Eileen, who'd never had children, that there was no comfort. She remembered the words of the priest at Kit's funeral, how moved she'd been by his graciousness, even in the face of what he must surely regard as Kit's sin. He'd referred to the moment in Luke's Gospel when Simeon takes the baby Jesus in his arms and celebrates his birth. But even in the midst of his blessing, Simeon tells Mary, *Yea, a sword shall pierce through thy own soul also.* Because Mary's son would die and she would have to live on without him. Joy and pain, pain and joy.

Rose decided it was time to go. She couldn't sit around here all morning drinking tea. It was Monday, so the fridge needed clearing out and cleaning, and she had to arrange the flowers she'd bought. She couldn't even remember the last time she'd cleaned behind the washing machine. Panicked, she stood up abruptly, startling Eileen.

'I must be off,' Rose said, trying to keep her voice calm. 'I've rather a lot to be getting on with this afternoon.'

'Alright, dear,' Eileen said. 'But don't work yourself too

hard. Be kind to yourself.' This was another thing she often said to Rose.

'See you next week,' Rose said. 'Ring me if you need anything before then.'

'I'm sure I'll be *quite* alright,' Eileen said, and Rose wondered if she'd offended her. Eileen often did ring midweek to ask for something she'd forgotten on the Monday, so she could hardly be affronted at Rose's suggestion.

At home, Rose allowed herself a light lunch of salad with beetroot and feta cheese before she got to work. She'd put the bunches of supermarket flowers she'd bought in water when she got home, but saved arranging them until most of the cleaning was done. This was her favourite task. She'd chosen some gorgeous pink roses and white stocks, along with some foliage she picked from the garden. She spent a while arranging them in her favourite white vase into a lovely, fresh, late spring bouquet. It looked delightful, sitting on the kitchen table. There was nothing like flowers for cheering up a room. She wondered if Joe or Emma would notice.

It was past four by now, and Emma would be home from school soon. Rose decided she'd have a nice cup of tea and a bit of time to herself until then. She settled down at the table to read her magazine. There was an extended feature on the '100 best summer dresses' which she lingered over, vaguely wondering if it might be time to buy herself something new as a treat. She was particularly taken with a purple wrap dress with a lovely floral pattern, so she got a biro from the drawer and drew a circle round it. And there was rather a nice shift dress in a light grey, which she circled as well, and then a V-neck linen dress in a daring crimson. There were a couple of lovely party dresses too, but Rose wasn't sure when she'd ever wear them, so she reluctantly left them uncircled.

She read a real-life story about a woman who'd left her abusive husband and started her own business, and then an article on the empowering nature of female friendship. Rose didn't recognize the kind of closeness the women in the article talked about. She supposed she didn't have many close friends, unless Eileen Draper counted, and Rose was fairly sure she didn't. But then, there wasn't much time when you had a family to look after. And of course it had been difficult in the years after Kit died – people felt awkward.

Rose was starting to feel low, so she put the magazine away and got out *Cranford* instead. That was the kind of soothing escapism she needed. But though she fixed her eyes on the first page, she wasn't really seeing the words; she was seeing Jamie again, answering the door to them in Sheffield, and none of them knowing what to say. She pictured him coming home from work each evening, with no one to ask him how his day was, or to make sure he was eating a proper supper.

Perhaps if he'd tried to come back, she thought. Perhaps if he'd tried to talk to us after everything had calmed down. It shouldn't have come to this – losing both of them.

She gave up on *Cranford* and stared out of the window, thinking of her younger son. She still blamed him, she thought. Of course she still blamed him. But mostly she just missed him, missed them both, every second she was awake.

The sound of the door roused her – Emma. Rose hurried out to meet her daughter in the hall.

'How was school, darling?'

'Fine,' Emma said.

'That's great!'

'No,' Emma said. 'Not great. Fine.'

'Would you like to come and have a snack?' Rose tried. 'I bought some bagels today. You could toast one, and tell me all about your day.'

'I'm not hungry,' Emma said. 'I think I might go straight up to my room. Homework. You know.'

'What would you like for supper?' Rose called after her, as Emma set off up the stairs. 'There's a choice of toad in the hole or quiche Lorraine with salad.'

'Don't mind,' Emma said, disappearing along the landing.

Rose went back to the kitchen. She must be firm. No more brooding and feeling sorry for herself. She didn't want a return to the bad days, those terrible months just after Kit died when she hadn't known what to do with herself. Some people had been ever so kind, just after it happened – neighbours bringing round meals and so on, and offering to look after Emma. But there came a point, of course, when everyone expected you to pull yourself together and move on. Rose had tried to do this, but it seemed an impossible task, especially as the visits and phone calls became less frequent and there were no longer any distractions. And the more stuck in the past you seemed, the less people knew what to say to you.

She wasn't sure what would have happened if Eileen, one of the few people who still rang up after the first few months, hadn't said one day in her tactless way, 'I suppose you should talk about it, dear. But goodness knows *I* wouldn't know what to say to you. Why don't you ring the Good Samaritans?'

'Do you mean the Samaritans?' Rose had said.

'Exactly,' Eileen said. 'I took the liberty of picking up a leaflet for you.'

And so in the end Rose had called them, and although she couldn't think of much to say to the nice man who answered the phone the first time, it had been a strange relief just to be able to say one sentence to him, the only sentence that mattered. It had been almost impossible to get the words out, but she had managed it in the end, saying jerkily into the patient silence at the other end of the phone: 'My son took his own life.'

On days like today she thought she'd like to call the Samaritans again, but she always resisted – she felt it would be somehow unseemly to continue to bother them now, years on.

She gathered herself. In half an hour or so she'd take a snack up to Emma and probably by then Emma would fancy a little chat. Until then, Rose would concentrate on really getting stuck into her book. Then, before she knew it, Joe would be home and it would be time to start supper. Quiche Lorraine was a lighter dish, more suitable for the time of year, but Joe might prefer something heartier after his long day at work. But really, Rose thought, it was no use getting in a tizz about which dish to make, because whichever she didn't make tonight, she'd just make tomorrow. The thing to do would be to ask Joe which he wanted when he got home. Perhaps she'd even meet him at the door with a gin and tonic. She hadn't done that for years. Yes, Rose thought, with a surge of relief, that was what she would do.

4

Joe had a splitting headache, even before the letter came; couldn't think, couldn't work. He forgot about the tea Helen had brought him until it had gone tepid, then tried to make up for it by gulping it down in one go; but the lukewarm milky liquid sat uncomfortably in his stomach.

Helen took one look at him when she came in with the post and went out again, returning a moment later with some paracetamol and a glass of water. She set them down unobtrusively on the edge of his desk. Joe was grateful, as always, but found himself unable to thank her.

The letter was thicker in its envelope than the others had been. He'd heard nothing for weeks, but when he sorted through the post and came across the familiar handwriting, he felt no surprise. He'd thought this might be coming.

A choice now: read it or destroy it. Perhaps he could pretend the letter had never come; he could tell himself he'd never heard from Jamie again. But no – even as the idea occurred to him he knew it was impossible. It was always, always too late to go back.

He waited until his lunch break, then walked out with

the letter in his pocket and found an empty bench in the park. He unfolded the letter and began to read.

*

I wanted to stop. I'd planned to stop. But the momentum's too great and it carries me on. You know that if I could stop without having written this letter, I would.

Kit outsmarted us again. He'd been waiting and planning for weeks, without any of us realizing it. By then, he'd been home from the hospital for a few months, and as far as we could see, everything was normal – or as normal as it could be, anyway. None of us knew what was going on in his head. None of us ever knew, of course.

You and Mum were taking Emma to London to see *Joseph and the Amazing Technicolor Dreamcoat* as a treat, and you were going to stay the night afterwards in a hotel. I was charged with keeping an eye on Kit for the weekend. Strange, in a way, that you could think of leaving me alone with him, given what had happened the last time. But he'd seemed so much better recently. And besides, Emma was becoming withdrawn and tantrum-prone, and you thought she needed some proper attention; some time out of the house, away from the whole situation with Kit. You couldn't put all your children first at the same time.

Of course you weren't happy about leaving Kit. It would never again feel safe to you. But you and Mum reasoned that it would be alright. It was just one night, and Kit was definitely on the road to recovery. He was starting to talk about going back to finish his degree next year. He was looking ahead.

And certainly when you left, Kit seemed OK. He chatted to you and Mum as you packed up, and helped you carry the bags out to the car. It felt a bit like old times. He picked Emma up, and even hugged you and Mum goodbye, an unusual gesture for him. I could see you were touched.

I didn't notice anything odd about Kit's behaviour that afternoon. In fact, he seemed pretty relaxed. We watched a film together and had some pasta for supper, then Kit said he was going to bed. It was only 8.30, but he'd been really tired since coming back from the hospital, so this didn't alarm me. I think the last thing I said to him was 'Sleep well'. He went upstairs and I stayed where I was, watching TV and chatting to Alice on the phone. I probably went up to bed around twelve. I stuck my head round Kit's door to check on him on the way to my room. He was fast asleep.

When I came downstairs the next morning, there was no sign of Kit. But this wasn't unusual. He often didn't emerge until around lunchtime. I made myself a coffee and went up to Kit's room to rouse him.

There was no answer to my knock, so after a moment I pushed the door open. The room was in darkness, but I could see the outline of Kit lying in bed. I said quietly, 'Hey, Kit – it's morning.' He didn't stir. 'Come on, Kit,' I said, and went over to draw the curtains, flooding the room with light. I stood looking out of the window, waiting for Kit's drowsy protests, but he still didn't move. I turned to look at him, and that's when I saw what I hadn't noticed the night before – the empty pill packets and the vodka bottle, pushed almost out of sight under his bed.

I stood where I was for a few moments, frozen in the bright pool of sunlight by the window. Then I darted over to Kit and grabbed his shoulder as if I could shake him awake, but I knew as soon as I touched him that it was too late. His skin was cold. I felt for a pulse, but couldn't find one. I carried on searching for it long after I realized he was gone.

The doctors said afterwards that Kit had suffered a fatal cardiac arrhythmia in the night. He would have been unconscious already – he wouldn't have known what was happening. He'd most likely already passed out when I checked on him around midnight, thinking him peacefully asleep. He may even already have been dead.

Will that do? I've told you about Kit's death, so it's all finished now.

Except, Dad, we both know this isn't enough. I knew I couldn't trick you, but I thought perhaps I could trick myself. My mind's so unreliable these days.

I've told you what I should have told you at the time, not what actually happened. If I'd lied then, instead of now, everything would have been different.

I lied now because I didn't then, because for a moment I wanted to try out a different version of events, and see how the weight of them felt on my shoulders.

But you know what happened already.

Forgive me for lying, and forgive me for telling the truth.

Kit's plan was foolproof. He wasn't one for half measures and he'd put a lot of thought into it. I got the feeling he'd been turning it all over in his head for a long time. He'd considered every possible method, and lighted on a drug overdose as the best – for everyone. He didn't want to hang himself, and he certainly didn't want to be found hanging.

He wasn't an amateur these days. He was well aware, from personal experience, of the unreliability of pills, the high chance you had of vomiting too soon or being found too early and revived. An overdose is one of the least-effective methods of suicide. But that's only because people don't do it right, Kit said.

He'd messed up before, but this time he did his research. A jumbled cocktail of over-the-counter painkillers and prescription sleeping pills wouldn't do it, even alongside an antiemetic. A tricyclic antidepressant would be a much better bet. Since Kit was now on one of these, he was in luck. He just had to take all his pills at once, washed down with a bottle of vodka bought specially for the purpose. That should do it.

All this Kit explained to me with clinical precision that weekend as we sat together in the living room after you three had left. If it sounds brutal to you now, Dad, imagine how it felt to me at the time.

'Jesus, Kit,' I said.

'I know. Sorry.'

Sorry? I thought. We sat in silence for a few moments whilst I tried to take it in.

'I had to tell you,' Kit said.

'Why?'

'Because of the roof.'

'That was the worst moment of my life,' I said.

'It wasn't brilliant for me, either.'

'Kit, it's not just your own life you're planning to ruin.'

'I know.' Kit's calm seemed to waver. 'But I have to do it. It's impossible for me to carry on.' When I didn't reply, he said again, 'It's impossible, Jamie.'

I put out my hand to him. 'We'll get you more help. Try another drug. Another doctor.'

Kit shook his head. 'You don't understand what it feels like,' he said. 'You think it's about not feeling happy, but it isn't. It's got nothing to do with that. It's this constant, terrible pain. It fills you up. I never would've believed it was possible to feel this bad.' He paused, looking away from me. 'Even if it eases for a bit, it always comes back. There's no hope of escape – it's always out there, waiting for me. I don't want that as my life.'

I shook my head slowly.

'It's not fair of people to ask me to endure it,' Kit said. 'This way's better for everyone. I'm ruining things for all of you, and I can't help myself, and no one can help me.'

'Kit.'

'Don't you understand, Jamie? There's no choice.'

'No. You've fought this off before, you can do it again.'

'I don't want to!' Kit's voice rose in frustration. 'I've been trying to explain it to you. You're not listening. I have tried, Jamie. I've tried for years. I didn't want it to turn out like this. And I really thought it might be OK this time. But I can feel it coming back, and I won't go through it again.'

'OK.' I reached out and laid my hand on his arm, trying to calm him. We sat in silence for a while.

After a bit, I said, 'Do you want to watch some TV? Try to take your mind off it? I'll sit with you.' This had occasionally worked in the past. Kit could sink into a sort of stupor whilst watching something he liked on television, and the distraction could ease his suffering, if only for a short while.

Now, though, Kit looked at me in exasperation. 'Jamie, I'm going to do it. I really am. And you can either make it easier or you can make it harder.'

I knew he was telling the truth. He was going to kill himself, however much anyone begged him not to. If he didn't do it now, then he'd do it another time. Better, then, to keep you and Mum out of it as much as possible.

Are you starting to see why I didn't tell you?

I know it drove you and Mum almost mad afterwards, replaying that last scene in your heads, outside by the car, saying goodbye to Kit. You must have tormented yourselves, asking how you didn't realize, how you could have left him. I know you blame yourselves, as well as me. I wish you wouldn't. There was no saving him.

I think afterwards you convinced yourself that I'd known in advance what Kit was planning. That it was some kind of terrible conspiracy. But I promise you I didn't know. Kit didn't tell me anything until you'd driven away and he and I were alone in the living room. Does that change anything?

There was another reason why he shared his plans with me this time. A little later, after we'd been sitting in silence for some time, he said, 'Jamie – will you sit with me? After I've done it. Will you stay with me?'

Comprehension dawned. I felt cold. 'Kit, I can't—'

'Please, Jamie. I know it's a lot to ask. Please, though. I don't want to be alone.'

Through all his talk of drugs and toxic doses and wanting to escape, I hadn't realized how frightened he was until then.

'How can I – watch you?'

'It'll be OK. It'll be easy,' Kit said. 'Just like going to sleep. I've checked it all out – it won't be messy or painful or anything. I just want someone there before I pass out. I want you there.'

I could have asked him then if he'd thought about what he was putting me through – asking me to watch him die. But he was exhausted and ill. He wanted desperately for it all to be over, but he was afraid of the final act. I understand that, and I don't blame him. I've thought about it a lot – about whether Kit was being selfish. But I don't think considerations like that are relevant. Kit had suffered so much already; more than the rest of us can imagine. He'd passed beyond any judgements of selfishness. I won't let anybody blame him.

Kit said, 'I don't think I'll mind it, if you're there. I think it'll be OK.'

I couldn't have said no, Dad. I couldn't have abandoned him. I knew then, and I know now, that in the same circumstances he would never have left me.

For a long time that Saturday, we stayed where we were in the living room. It was early afternoon by then.

Kit said eventually, 'It'll be easier for Mum and Dad, to know you were with me. They won't have to worry about me being scared or anything. You can tell them I wasn't.'

I still didn't say anything. I didn't want to think about what I was going to say to you and Mum. All my energy and attention were now focused on the part immediately ahead of us. If I allowed my mind to wander, I didn't think I'd be able to go through with it.

He was looking at me now. 'I'm ready. Is that OK with you?'

I nodded, unable to speak, and followed him up to his bedroom. Kit sat on his bed and produced a bottle of vodka and a stack of pill packets from his bedside drawer. I hovered by the door for a few moments, looking round the familiar room, full of remnants from our shared childhood: the Spurs scarf, the miniature Spartan helmet Kit had bought on our holiday to Greece, the array of Lego models, crooked from my attempts at rebuilding them, now piled into a large box in the corner.

I said, 'You probably should've got rid of your Lego a while back. Bit weird to still have it when you're twenty-three.'

Kit shrugged. 'Doesn't matter now.'

I thought then how unfair it was that Kit had never been teased for a hobby as nerdy as building Lego models, which he'd carried on even into his teens. Despite this, he'd always been the cool one. And he took the piss out of me all the time, for the smallest things. I felt like I'd missed a trick.

I wondered what would happen to his Lego models after he was dead.

Kit was watching me closely. 'Jamie, are you alright?'

'Yes.'

'Come and sit next to me.'

I did.

'I'm going to start now,' Kit said. Then he added, 'Thanks for being here.' His voice was steady. He seemed calm. My heart was beating uncomfortably fast, but if Kit was going to be matter-of-fact about this, then so was I.

Kit started popping pills methodically out of the packet, putting them in his mouth, taking swigs of vodka, shuddering slightly as it went down. He worked quickly and efficiently, whilst I sat beside him in silence.

At the end of the first packet, he said, 'I tried to write them a letter.'

I nodded, knowing he meant you and Mum.

'But it was no good,' Kit said. 'I couldn't seem to get across what I wanted to say, so I just – gave up.'

He carried on taking the pills. I could see he wasn't enjoying the vodka very much. He pulled a face every time he took a swig.

'What if you throw up?' I said.

'I won't. Besides, I probably won't have the whole bottle.'

He'd sunk about a third of it already.

I said, 'Is it definitely going to work this time, Kit?'

'Yes. Definitely.'

'I can only do this once,' I said.

'Once will be enough.'

He carried on. I said, without realizing I was going to, 'I'm going to miss you.' I felt like a child, and tried to fight back my sense of desolation.

Kit stopped for a moment. He said, 'I know you will, Jamie.' Slightly awkwardly, he put his hand on my shoulder, even though I was the one supposed to be comforting him. 'I'm sorry,' he said. 'I really hope you'll be OK after a bit. You've been . . .' He paused. This wasn't the kind of conversation we were used to having, and I wondered what he was going to say. 'You've been my best friend. More or less.'

'You've been mine, too,' I said.

'Your only friend, really.'

'Hilarious,' I said automatically.

We sat quietly for a few moments. Then Kit said, 'I think I knew it would turn out like this. In the end. I think I've known for a while now. I did try, though.'

'I know you did,' I said.

'I did my best.'

'I know.'

It didn't take him long to finish all the pills. He was halfway through his bottle of vodka now and was starting to look groggy.

He said, 'That's the hard bit done now. You don't have to stay if you don't want to.'

'I won't leave you.'

Kit lay down on the bed. Then he said, 'Actually, I might get under the covers.' I helped him climb in, and sat on the edge of the bed next to him.

'How are you feeling?'

'Bit drunk. Pretty alright.' He was silent for a few moments. 'Not sure what to do now. Might take a sleeping pill.' He got out a packet from his bedside drawer and swallowed a couple more pills. 'I suppose I'll drift off in a bit,' he said, looking uncertain.

I could see he was at a loss as to how to fill the time, so I said, 'Do you want to watch some TV? I could bring the TV in here and we could watch your Simpsons DVD.'

Kit said he'd like that, so I brought up the TV and DVD player and set them up on his desk. We settled down next to each other on Kit's bed, Kit lying under the covers and me sitting on top of them beside him, and watched *The Simpsons* together, like we used to when we were kids.

We didn't talk for most of the first episode, but Kit said towards the end of it, 'I'm starting to feel sleepy. It's such a relief.'

'Good,' I said. But my heart felt painful in my chest and my throat ached. I was suddenly aware that there would be things I'd remember afterwards that I should have said to him. I couldn't think of any of them now, but I found it almost unbearable, thinking of the regret I'd feel when he was gone and I couldn't talk to him any more.

I turned my attention back to *The Simpsons*, and tried

to keep myself under control. I'm glad I managed it. That was the moment I came closest to losing it, but I didn't – I stayed calm, and I think that helped Kit to stay calm. He wasn't frightened or upset before he died. It helps me sometimes to remember that.

We sat together quietly, watching the second episode of *The Simpsons*. I became absorbed in it, and even found myself laughing at one point. I turned to Kit to see if he was smiling, but he was asleep. I stayed where I was, and when that episode was over I put the next one on. Then I watched another after that.

Eventually I went to get my duvet and pillows from my room, and the old camping mattress. I settled down on the floor beside Kit's bed and lay there in the dark, feeling removed from everything. In the end I must have fallen asleep.

Kit had thought it would take him longer than one night to die – he'd made me promise not to call an ambulance until you and Mum and Emma were about to come home after lunch. By then it would surely be over. I hadn't thought so far ahead as to comprehend what Sunday would have been like, waiting alone in the house with my unconscious, dying brother. I doubt Kit had thought about it either.

But I was spared that, in the end. As we would later be told, the drugs had stopped Kit's heart at some point in the night. The best thing that could have happened, as far as Kit was concerned.

I slept deeply that night, as though I'd taken a sleeping pill as well, and woke at around 9.30 the next morning,

stiff and dull-headed on the floor. For a split second
I didn't remember how I'd got there, but then the
pieces of the previous day fitted themselves back
together in my mind.

I sat up slowly to look at Kit. He seemed to be sleeping
peacefully on his side, his face towards me. But after a
second, I registered that he looked too calm, too still. I
didn't need to feel for his pulse, but I did anyway. I think
I wanted to make myself touch his skin. It was startlingly
cool, and I drew my hand back quickly. He'd been dead for
several hours.

I sat on the edge of the bed and looked at him. Except
it wasn't Kit any more. It was just a body. This, I hadn't
anticipated – this total absence of Kit. I was suddenly
hyper-aware of my own body, which felt too heavy for me,
as though it was the wrong size. I thought I could feel the
warmth of my blood moving through me, the insistent
pulse of my heart. I've never felt so lonely; not even in the
years since.

While I was waiting for the ambulance and the police,
I moved my duvet and pillows out of Kit's room, and put
the camping mattress away. Then I put the TV and DVD
player back downstairs. When the paramedics came, I told
them I'd gone in to check on Kit as soon as I woke up and
had found him like this. They were very kind.

Then I had to ring you. You answered your mobile
straight away, and I found I didn't have any words at all,
so after a minute I recycled the phrase I'd used all those
months ago, when Kit jumped off the roof. I said, 'There's

been an accident.' I didn't add that Kit was dead, but I think you already knew.

There were so many lies I could have told to protect myself from your rage. But the stupid thing is, I didn't think I needed to lie at the time. I thought you'd understand. I even thought you might be grateful to me for staying with him. It hadn't occurred to me that you'd be angry.

When I told you the whole story much later that day, I hadn't planned what I should say. I've often thought I should have explained it better, so it wasn't such a shock to you. The facts are bleak, aren't they? I allowed Kit to die and did nothing to save him. And I kept you in the dark until it was too late, preventing you from saving him as well.

I do understand how it looked to you, Dad. Sometimes it looks that way to me, too.

You and Mum didn't give me away at the inquest, even though you'd had weeks to brood on it all by then; weeks to work up your hatred of me. You let me stick to my story about how I'd found Kit dead on Sunday morning, though perhaps I could have been arrested if you'd admitted the truth – I don't know how it works. Another thing Kit and I didn't think about at the time. But you let me lie to save myself. I've often wondered why you did that.

I could tell you I'm sorry, but why should you believe me? That's not the whole truth, anyway. Part of me wants you to be sorry, for being so angry with me, for hating me so much and refusing to realize that I loved Kit too. In any case, what good would forgiveness do us? What happened would still have happened, and Kit would still be dead.

I don't know why I started this. I don't remember what I felt when I first wrote to you. It seems so long ago, and it feels like so much has happened since, though in reality nothing has happened – not for years. The last thing I remember happening was Kit's death. And it keeps on happening, doesn't it? It doesn't ease off. It doesn't go away. I know it feels like that to you. Perhaps I just wanted to show you that it's the same for me.

I don't see him any more, but I feel him sometimes, usually when I've stopped looking. Occasionally I can fool myself into thinking he's in the bookshop, browsing amongst the history books, somewhere behind the shelves. And sometimes when I'm out walking, I realize he's there in the crowd, hidden amongst all the people in front – always just ahead of me; always just out of sight.

5

Rose bought the purple wrap dress in the end. And why not? She hadn't had anything new for ages.

When she was looking round the other shops, she'd seen a lovely necklace of purple beads which she thought would go well with her new dress, so she bought that too. And then she felt it would be nice to get a little present for Emma, so she'd chosen a silver bracelet with little charms attached.

She gave it to Emma as soon as she got home from school. Emma seemed really pleased with it, and followed her mother through to the kitchen to have a glass of Ribena.

'How was school?' Rose said when they were seated at the table, and waited for the usual irritable 'fine'.

But Emma said, 'It was good, actually. We're doing *Persuasion* in Literature Club and I've already read it. I said that I thought Anne Elliot was romantic underneath, even though lots of the other characters think she's just a spinster. But she goes on loving the same man for years, even though she thinks she'll never see him again. I said I thought Anne Elliot was more romantic than Marianne Dashwood in *Sense and Sensibility*, even though Marianne thinks she's really romantic and is always going on about it. But Marianne falls out of love with Willoughby and marries Colonel Brandon, whereas Anne Elliot goes on loving Captain Wentworth forever. Miss Griffiths said it was a very *perceptive comment*, and that I was a sophisticated reader,' Emma concluded, slightly breathlessly. 'So I think I may have turned out to be quite good at English. Actually.'

Rose felt tears welling up at the sight of her daughter looking so pleased with herself. She hadn't read *Persuasion* herself for many years, and struggled to recall much about this romantic Anne Elliot. She wondered if perhaps she should focus on re-reading Jane Austen instead of getting out another Mrs Gaskell, in case Emma wanted to discuss any more of her books.

'And do you know,' Emma was saying now, 'what one of Jane Austen's books is called? It's called *Emma*. And Miss Griffiths says it's her favourite. Olivia and I are going to read it next.'

'Who's Olivia?' Rose said, feeling rather at sea.

'My friend,' Emma said casually. 'She's very clever. She might come round this weekend. Is that OK?'

'Of course it is. I'll look forward to meeting her,' Rose said. It had been a long time since her daughter had had a friend round and Rose found herself rather excited all of a sudden.

'But you won't fuss too much, will you?' Emma said.

Rose wasn't quite sure what Emma meant by 'fuss', but she promised she wouldn't. 'Have you got much homework?' she asked.

'Just a bit of horrible Maths, and some English,' Emma

said, adding, 'I'm going to spend longer on the English.'
With another smile, she disappeared off to her room.

Rose stayed at the kitchen table for a while, finishing
her tea and thinking about Emma and her new friend. She
wondered if Olivia would come for lunch on Saturday. If
she did, Rose would be sure to make something special.
Homemade pizzas, perhaps, and the girls could add their
own toppings. Or if Olivia just came for the afternoon,
Rose would make sure she had a good selection of cakes
on offer.

Her thoughts turned to Joe, and how much he'd
enjoyed that Victoria sponge she'd made a couple of weeks
ago. She wondered if she should make another one for
him. A lemon cake, perhaps. There was nothing more
delicious than a lemon cake with thick, zesty butter icing
and lemon curd in the middle.

At that point Joe himself came into the kitchen. Rose
had been so lost in her thoughts that she hadn't heard the
door.

'Darling, you're home,' she said, and then was annoyed
with herself, because this was exactly the kind of silly
observation that usually elicited a sarcastic response from
him.

She waited, but Joe didn't reply, just leaned against the
kitchen counter and rubbed a hand over his eyes. Rose
thought he looked exhausted, but managed not to comment on it.

'Would you like a drink?' she ventured.

'Maybe a beer,' Joe said.

Rose fetched one for him, and poured it into a glass.

'There's an hour till supper,' she said. 'You'll have plenty of time in your shed.'

'I don't think I'll bother this evening,' Joe said. 'I'm a bit tired.'

'You look it,' Rose couldn't help saying. But Joe didn't react. He barely seemed to hear her. After a moment, he went and sat at the kitchen table, clasping his hands round his beer glass.

Tentatively, Rose sat down opposite him. He never usually spent any time in the kitchen, particularly if she was in it. She thought he probably viewed it as her sphere, like he had his shed, and didn't want to intrude. Rose wasn't quite sure what to do. After a minute, she said, 'How was your day?'

'Fine.'

'I bought a new dress.'

'That's good.' He was making an effort to be polite, and Rose was encouraged.

'And I got a bracelet for Emma,' she said. 'Just a little thing.' She paused, wondering if Joe would be hurt that she hadn't got him something as well. She said, 'I'm making sausage casserole for supper.'

'Lovely.'

They lapsed into silence for a while, then Rose said, 'Emma was in a good mood when she came home. I think things might be picking up at school.'

'Glad to hear that,' Joe said. He had nearly finished his beer already, and Rose was surprised – he wasn't usually much of a drinker. But perhaps it had been a particularly bad day. She wondered if she could ask him.

At length he said, 'Do you remember when we took the boys to that adventure park in the Gower? When they were quite little?'

Rose looked up at him quickly. It wasn't like Joe to reminisce. She said carefully, 'They had those carts on wheels that the boys went down the slides on, didn't they? I remember that.'

'Kit's face,' Joe said. 'That's what I remember. He was so excited.'

'And Jamie looked terrified,' Rose said, half-afraid of mentioning him, and feeling a stab of grief at the memory of her younger son's fear. 'He nearly threw up afterwards.'

'I suppose he only went on because Kit did,' Joe said. 'I wonder if we should have stopped him.'

'I don't think we could have done,' Rose said. 'You know boys.'

Joe smiled sadly down at his empty glass. 'We were camping that week, weren't we?'

'Yes. And there was that shop on the campsite selling that wonderful ice cream.'

'And we were right by the beach.'

They'd often been to the Gower when the boys were young. Rose saw it all again, the beach, the cliffs, the bright sky; Kit and Jamie running into the sea and her and Joe sitting on towels further up on the sand. She wondered what kind of couple they'd been back then. Did they joke together? She could hardly remember. How strange it was to be sitting here like this, talking about old times.

She said, 'Do you remember when we took the boys to

Blackpool Pleasure Beach? Jamie won tickets in the school raffle.'

'I remember,' Joe said, wincing slightly. 'Awful place. But Kit and Jamie had a good time.'

'And Jamie was too small to go on the big rides, and got upset about it.'

'Oh yes, and Kit sneaked him onto one of them,' Joe said, more animated now. 'I forget how he did it. I think he lifted him up or something.'

Rose was silent for a moment, wondering whether to say more. She decided she would. 'Do you know,' she said, deliberately casual, 'I had the most terrible fright on that ride. Jamie had slipped down in his seat so I couldn't see him any more, and I thought he'd fallen out. It wasn't until the ride stopped and he got out that I knew he was alright.'

Joe looked at her properly now. 'You didn't tell me that at the time.'

'I suppose I felt a bit silly.'

He was rolling his empty glass between his hands. 'They caused us a fair bit of trouble, didn't they?' he said after a moment. 'Do you remember the time they decided they'd stay the night in their dens, have a camp-out in the woods?'

Rose nodded. 'We thought they'd been kidnapped. Horrible.'

They sat quietly for a bit. Rose thought she'd offer Joe another drink – perhaps even have one herself. But just as she was about to speak, Joe stood up, rubbing his hand across his face again. 'I'd better go and get changed out of my suit,' he said, and the next moment he'd left the kitchen and Rose was alone.

Time to make a start on the casserole then, she thought. But as she was browning the sausages she was thinking what she often thought when she remembered Kit: how did this happen? From time to time, she wondered if Joe agonized over the same question, but she could never ask. He wouldn't thank her for bringing it up, and Rose had to admit that mostly she didn't want to talk about it, either. She was sorry for Joe, obviously. But always at the back of her mind was the knowledge that he wasn't a mother. He'd loved the boys, of course, but *he wasn't a mother.*

6

Alice had rung the bookshop a few days ago. She'd planned what she wanted to say in advance, so he didn't make her feel like an idiot again. When Jamie answered, she was going to say, 'I just wanted you to know that I forgive you. And I wish you the best.' That would be all.

But when she was put through to the History department, a woman answered, which for some reason Alice wasn't prepared for. She gabbled out, 'Can I speak to Jamie, please?' and the woman said, 'Sorry, he's not in today. Can I help?' Alice quickly hung up.

Often, since seeing Jamie again, she'd thought back to the weekend Kit died. She remembered her irritation on the Saturday, as she'd tried to get hold of Jamie, who wasn't answering his phone. Alice had been angry with him, and faintly nervous because he'd seemed distant lately. She wasn't used to being the one making the effort, and she thought Jamie needed a reminder of how desirable she was. Toby had been texting her for a couple of weeks, and after yet another unanswered call to Jamie, Alice told Toby she'd go for a drink with him.

When she'd got back from seeing Toby on Sunday night, she'd called Jamie again – and he'd finally answered. But when she'd asked why the *hell* he hadn't been picking up his phone all weekend, Jamie said, 'Kit's dead.'

And that was the end of everything. She had no idea how to act in the wake of this, no idea how to process the horror of the news that Kit had committed suicide and Jamie had found his body.

She'd gone round on Monday, had known she had to. No one had come to answer the door for ages, and she'd stood there on the doorstep feeling wretched and out of place. She'd almost decided to get on the train home again when she heard someone fumbling with the lock. But whoever it was didn't manage to get it open for some time, as if all the shock had caused them to forget how to use their own front door.

When it finally opened, Jamie's dad stood there, but he didn't say anything. Alice had to break the silence. She said, 'I'm so sorry.'

He stood looking at her as though he didn't understand her words. It seemed like an age before he turned and went stiffly back into the living room. Alice could see Jamie's mum through the doorway, half-sitting, half-lying on the sofa. Jamie's little sister was beside her, clinging to her arm.

There was something horribly wrong with the atmosphere of the house – it made Alice tremble just to be inside. The sadness she understood. But how to explain the violent hostility she felt as she stepped through the door? Alice had been sensitive to atmosphere her whole life, susceptible to the feelings of others and to the feeling of a room. Now it resonated almost physically.

She went quickly up the stairs to Jamie's bedroom and found him huddled on his bed, still in his pyjamas. There was an old film magazine open on the covers in front of him, but he wasn't reading it.

Alice hadn't expected to feel so nervous around him. But it was as if Kit's death had made them strangers.

'Jamie,' she said, hovering at the door. 'How are you?'

'OK,' he said. His eyes were red.

Alice didn't know what to say – there didn't seem to be anything she could offer him.

She made herself sit on the edge of his bed. 'Do you want to talk?'

He shook his head.

Alice was looking for the right words, looking for whatever a loving and dutiful girlfriend would say at a time like this. She tried again. 'I don't think you should be sitting up here all alone.'

'I can't go downstairs,' Jamie said. 'They don't want me.' For a moment, he looked like he might cry.

Alice took his hand. 'I'm sure they do,' she said.

'They hate me.'

'No they don't, hon,' she said, glad of an opportunity to provide reassurance. 'It wasn't your fault.'

She tried to put her arms around him, but he shook her off.

'You don't understand,' he said, and she was shocked by the coldness in his voice.

Alice didn't stay long after that. She didn't recognize this version of Jamie, didn't know how to help him. She caught the train home, with some relief, having been in the house for less than an hour.

That was almost the last time she saw him. She'd gone round once more, which had been little better than the first time; the same awful atmosphere, Jamie shut away in his room and refusing to go downstairs. Then the funeral. Jamie had sat at the end of the pew with his parents; but he didn't look at her, didn't look at anyone.

And that was it. Jamie simply left home, and stopped returning her calls. She found out later that he'd stayed with his friend Sam for a while, but then he left London and Sam said he didn't know where he'd gone.

It was grief, Alice had thought at the time. The cloud would lift eventually, and then he'd come back for her. She waited and waited, but he never did. Months went by with no word, and Alice started to realize she might never see him again. The pain of it had been terrible. Even now, years later, she was starting to wonder if she'd ever really get over it, or if the pain would be a part of her forever—

Her thoughts were interrupted by a question from Mark, and Alice found herself returned to the present, to her supper of fish pie and her husband.

'Sorry?'

'Are you OK?' Mark said again. 'You've gone very quiet.'

Alice looked down at her food, and then bravely met his eye. 'I was just thinking about the past. Everything that happened with Jamie.'

Mark was silent.

'I hate to think there's all this unfinished stuff between us,' Alice said. 'It makes it so hard to leave it behind.'

'I'm not sure Jamie would think it's unfinished,' Mark said, taking a slow sip of his wine.

'How can it not be?' Alice said. She thought for a moment. 'Maybe it would have been different if Kit hadn't been weird about our relationship. I think Jamie would've got back in touch with me eventually, if it hadn't been for that – but I suppose after Kit was dead, Jamie couldn't bear to go against him.'

'Why didn't Kit like you?' Mark said.

What made him ask that? Alice wondered. She hesitated. But she might as well tell him. 'It was a long time ago, but I once slept with someone else. Whilst I was going out with Jamie. It was just a stupid mistake, and Jamie saw that, but Kit never forgave me. Maybe that's why Jamie left me. Maybe he did it for Kit.'

Mark was looking at her thoughtfully. 'Is it possible that Jamie wasn't thinking about you at all when he left? That he was just distraught because his brother had died?'

'You have no idea *at all* what happened.'

Mark put down his glass. 'When is this going to stop, Alice?'

She was startled by his tone. 'When's what going to stop?'

'This *fixation* with Jamie. I know it was hard for you seeing him again, but you can't cling on to this forever.'

Alice sat back in her chair, so hurt and surprised that it was a few moments before she spoke. 'You weren't there – you can't imagine how terrible it was when Kit died. It ruined everything.'

'I think you need to let this go.'

'I can't,' she burst out. 'You don't get it. You don't understand how much his death affected me.'

'Of course it did,' he said sharply. 'It must have affected everyone. But *you*, Alice, are not part of his family. For *you*, it was sad, but not life-destroying. For Jamie it sounds like it was. That's terrible for him, but nothing to do with you any more. You can't go through your whole life hanging off the coat tails of someone else's tragedy.'

She was shaken by this, too shaken even to cry. Mark let her take it in silently for a few moments, then he moved his chair next to hers and put his arms around her. 'I'm sorry if this hurts you. You probably think I don't love you, but I do. That's why I said it.'

Alice was quiet for a long time, her face hidden in his shirt front. She half wanted to get up and storm out of the house. But she couldn't make herself pull away from his warmth, his steadiness.

'No more wallowing, OK?' Mark said eventually.

Alice thought she was going to tell him to leave her alone. She thought she was going to tell him again that he didn't get it.

But in the end, closing her eyes against his chest, she just said, 'OK. Alright.'

7

This is the end of the road, Dad.

I didn't see it coming, but how could I? I thought I was there already.

The door was open when I got home. Maybe I shouldn't have gone through it. Nothing was in my mind. They were still in there and I was so shocked I just stood where I was. Then one of them must have hit me, because I found myself on the floor, and they were gone.

They've taken the PlayStation and the TV and the stereo but that doesn't matter. Nothing matters now. I crawled over to the shattered castle where it lay in the corner. There didn't seem any reason for it to have been destroyed, but that's beside the point. It's the outcome not the cause that matters. But perhaps I've said that already.

I picked up some of the pieces and looked at them for a long time, but it still didn't seem real. Blood began to pool in my cupped hands, and I thought for a minute that the pieces themselves were bleeding. But then I saw the heavy drops splashing down on them from above and I realized it must be coming from me, which seemed to make more sense, and also less sense.

I thought of Kit breaking his Lego models, and how

I tried to rebuild them, and I thought: Nothing can ever be rebuilt. That's so obvious now that I can't believe I didn't realize it before. I suppose I deserved to be shown my mistake.

I put my head down on the floor next to the pieces of my castle and stayed there for a while. When I woke up I found I was holding one of the blue flags in my hand. I put it in my pocket. Then I knew I had to write to you one last time – and this is the last time, because there's nothing left now. But I had to tell you that I finally understand. About history and time, I mean. They're cyclical, not linear. There is a pattern. It was there all along, only I couldn't see it. Ebb and flow, like the waves of the sea. The wave came for Kit and then it drew back and now it's come for me. It was always coming back for me, ever since I saw him die. And I'm relieved, Dad. I don't think I really wanted to go on. Maybe that's why I've been standing still all these years. I was waiting in one place so the wave would be able to find me when it came back for me.

Slowly, Joe read the letter through again. The second reading offered no more comfort than the first – in fact, it became even harder for him to turn away from the fact that something was very wrong. The letter was hard to follow, even the second time round, but its tone was disturbing – especially as Jamie sounded firmly convinced of his own logic.

'Joe?' Helen stuck her head round the door, startling him. 'Mr Armstrong just dropped this off. It's his signed transfer.'

Joe tried to focus. 'Thanks,' he said. 'I'll check it in a minute.'

'Everything alright?' she said.

'Yes, yes,' he said abruptly, not looking up; then regretted his rudeness as Helen disappeared.

Joe went back to the letter. He hadn't expected another one, had been surprised to find an envelope addressed in Jamie's handwriting amongst his morning post. He'd wondered what there could be left to say.

It sounded as though Jamie's flat had been burgled, and that the thieves had hurt him, though it wasn't clear how badly. This was worrying in itself, but Joe was more concerned about Jamie's state of mind. Whichever way he looked at it, his son sounded unhinged. And try as he might to tell himself he was shocked, Joe knew deep down that he should have seen this coming; that in a way, he *had* seen this coming.

He'd briefly considered contacting Jamie after his previous letter, once the initial pain had subsided. He'd thought he might send a quick note, or even call him – just to check up on him. But he'd dismissed the idea in the end. He couldn't offer forgiveness; there was no forgiveness. And besides, Jamie wasn't interested in that.

He forced himself to picture again the scene that day, after they'd come back from the mortuary. Joe had gone into the living room and sat down on the sofa. On the mantelpiece was an old picture of Kit in his school uniform and he'd looked at it with unfocused eyes. Soon he would notice that Rose had come into the room and sat down beside him, but for now he remained where he was, oblivious. He had been struck by how unbelievable it was, that he could be here, sitting on his own sofa; and all the while his son was dead, his body in the mortuary.

A short while later, Jamie had come into the room and sat in the armchair opposite.

Rose said again through her tears, 'What was he thinking?'

Nobody replied. Rose suddenly cried out, making Joe start. It was almost like a scream.

'He must have been so scared,' she said.

'No,' Jamie said. 'He wasn't scared.'

Joe looked up at him, grateful for the attempt at reassurance, but not believing it for a second.

Then Jamie added, without looking at either of them, 'I was with him.'

There was a beat, before Joe understood what he meant. Then the realization, turning him cold, as Jamie began to explain.

'You let him die,' Joe said, as soon as he could speak.

Jamie replied, 'It was what he wanted.'

Joe felt the rage seeping in at the edges of his consciousness, making its way into his bloodstream. It had surprised him at the time, how little control he had over himself. But he didn't want to control himself. He wanted Jamie – who'd explained the situation to them so calmly – to *feel* for himself the damage he'd done.

Joe couldn't remember now what he'd said to Jamie that day. It could have been anything. In a way, the actual words didn't matter. They couldn't have been more vicious than the intent behind them.

Jamie had been visibly frightened – had turned to his mother for help. But Rose was incapable of helping anyone. She'd curled up on the sofa and put her arms over her head like a child. Over the next few days, she became unreachable, alternating between hysterical crying and sitting in listless silence. She ignored even Emma, who had transformed overnight from a cheerful nine-year-old into a needy toddler and developed a kind of nervous reflex which involved eating everything in sight.

Jamie took refuge in his room for the next few days, and he and Joe avoided each other. When Joe did see him, Jamie was blank and remote. Joe had been deeply unsettled at the time by this lack of emotion, interpreting it as a chilling absence of remorse.

Jamie had been with them at the funeral, but none of them spoke. He sat rigidly at the end of the pew, dry-eyed even as his parents wept. Then they'd had that terrible argument afterwards, at home, even though the day was supposed to be about laying Kit to rest. Joe still regretted that. He shouldn't have let it happen that day – not on the day they buried Kit. But there had been no holding back. He'd heard himself telling Jamie to get out, to go away and never come back. Jamie had taken him at his word.

They saw him once more, at the inquest a few weeks later. Perhaps if Jamie had displayed some grief then – had broken down and sobbed as he described how he'd found Kit's body – Joe might have begun to forgive him. But Jamie had delivered his evidence with a steady voice, as though he had no understanding of the magnitude of what he'd done, the suffering he'd caused. It occurred to Joe now that Jamie had probably been in shock.

Alone in his office, he found that he was trembling. He read the final section of the letter again, coming to a halt at the most disturbing sentence. *I don't think I really wanted to go on.* Joe stood up slowly from his desk but remained motionless for a few moments. He glanced over the letter again, and finally came to a decision.

8

The M1 looked bleak in the rain, a slicked grey runway. Joe queued impatiently in traffic up to Leicester, then hit a blank stretch and sped along in the fast lane. The wind buffeted his car, dragging the steering to the right, and the rain grew heavier the further north he got.

He'd told Helen he wasn't feeling well and needed to go home. It wasn't completely untrue – he certainly wasn't feeling himself – but it had felt strange lying to her. He trusted Helen. She'd been his secretary for eight years, and had proved herself invaluable through all kinds of crises. Deceiving her seemed somehow more of a betrayal than lying to his wife would be. But it couldn't be helped, he thought.

The journey seemed far longer now than when he and Rose had driven up in tense silence to collect Emma. And of course the weather wasn't helping. The Sheffield ring road appeared alien and confusing in the wind and rain, and Joe felt his throat constrict with panic – he wasn't used to being lost.

The rain had eased off to a mean-spirited drizzle by the time he drew up on Jamie's street. He turned off the engine, but stayed in the warm fug of the car for a while longer, trying to work out his next move. He was nervous, now he'd arrived. He wondered what he should say. Perhaps he could pretend he'd been to a conference somewhere in Sheffield, and thought he might as well look in on Jamie since he was passing. Yes, that would do.

Abruptly, he opened the car door and emerged into the chill, damp air.

But when he reached Jamie's front door, he saw it was held shut by a heavy bolt and padlock. The bolt was inexpertly screwed onto the door and doorframe at a slightly crooked angle – an amateur job. It was padlocked from the outside, so Jamie must be out. Of course, Joe thought, it was Monday. Jamie would surely be at work.

He was annoyed with himself: how stupid that this had never occurred to him. Jamie would be at the bookshop – that was all. He got back in the car and set off for the city centre.

By the time he found an NCP car park he was feeling rattled, having driven round in circles for what felt like hours, a prisoner of the crazed one-way systems. But he was relieved to find the bookshop easily enough, stumbling upon it almost straight away on the high street.

Squaring his shoulders, he marched inside and up to the History department on the second floor. He couldn't immediately see Jamie behind the desk or among the shelves, and realized with increasing discomfort that he'd have to find someone to ask.

'Excuse me,' he said, going up to the woman behind the desk. 'Do you know if Jamie Stewart's working today?'

'No, he isn't, I'm afraid,' the woman said, adding politely, 'Can I help you with anything?'

She must think I'm a customer, Joe thought. He made himself say, 'I'm his father.'

Now the woman was looking at him with interest. 'Jamie's father?'

'Do you know where I might find him?'

The woman shook her head. 'He was supposed to be in today and over the weekend, but he never turned up. We haven't been able to get hold of him.'

Joe's sense of unease was growing. 'When did you last see him?'

'Friday,' the woman said promptly. 'Working here. But he left much earlier than me. He was on early opening, you see. It's a new thing we're trying. We open at eight, to get more business. So whoever comes in to do the early shift gets to leave early, as well.'

If Jamie had gone home earlier than usual, Joe thought, perhaps that was why he'd run into the burglars. He said, 'Did he seem alright on Friday?'

The woman thought about it. 'Yes, I think so. Quiet, I suppose. But he's always quiet. Look, is he in some kind of trouble?'

'No, no,' Joe said. 'Nothing like that. I just want to talk to him.'

'I'm sorry not to be more helpful. I was thinking of getting his address from HR and going round there. Check he's OK.'

'I'm sure he's fine,' Joe said. But he was starting to feel the first flutterings of panic.

As he made to walk away, the woman said, 'When you find him, could you tell him to get in touch? He's probably just ill at home or something, but still. He should have rung.'

'Yes,' Joe said, but he was barely listening. He roused himself, and added, 'I'll tell him to ring you when I find him.'

He turned and headed back down the stairs. *When* I find him, he'd said. But standing shivering under the shop's awning, he was struck by a frightening suspicion that perhaps Jamie didn't want to be found.

9

He drove back to Jamie's flat, though he had no clear plan of what he was going to do when he got there.

The padlock was still in place, and Joe found himself standing on the doorstep again, at a loss. He couldn't go home now, not without checking Jamie was alright. But Jamie could be anywhere for all he knew, and he had no idea how to go about finding him.

He went round the side of the building to look through the windows for any signs of life, any clues as to how recently Jamie had been there. As he was peering in at the small kitchen window, he felt a hand on his arm and a voice said in a thick Sheffield accent, 'What do you think you're doing?'

Startled, Joe turned, and was confronted by a bulky man about his own age, an angry expression on his face.

'What are you doing?' the man said again. 'I saw you here earlier as well, snooping about.'

Alarmed by the man's aggressive manner, Joe took a step back. 'I'm looking for my son,' he said.

'Who's your son?'

'Jamie Stewart.'

The man seemed to relax at this, his manner becoming

friendlier. 'Ah, OK. Can't be too careful round here. We've had a bit of trouble recently. Break-ins.'

'I know.'

'Got to keep an eye out.'

It occurred to Joe that he didn't look a very likely burglar, a middle-aged man in a suit, but he didn't want to argue. He said, 'Do you live in this building too?'

'I own it.'

'You're Jamie's landlord?'

'Aye. I live upstairs.'

This, at last, seemed like progress. Joe said, 'Have you seen him recently?'

'What?'

'Do you know where he is?'

'Jamie?' the landlord said. 'He's gone. Thought you must have come to pick up his stuff. He left a fucking mess, if you don't mind me saying.'

Joe scarcely registered this last part. 'Gone where?' he said. 'Where's he gone?'

'How should I know?' the man said. 'I don't stick my nose into his personal life.' He seemed affronted.

'When did he leave?'

'Friday night. Left his deposit, I'll say that for him, but it's not exactly convenient, is it?'

'Did he say why he was going?'

'The break-in. He were in a right state. I tried talking to him, calm him down, you know, but he weren't staying.' The landlord looked at Joe sadly. 'You can see why. They did a few other buildings round here too. The police came, but there's not much chance of getting the stuff back. But it's a fact of life, right? It's not the first break-in in this area, and it won't be the last. That's why you get insurance, because there's people in this world that don't have respect for nowt.'

Joe nodded along. Eventually, he managed to get in, 'And you're sure he's not coming back?'

'He said he weren't. But I didn't know he'd left his stuff behind then. I couldn't get round to see the place till he'd gone.'

The panic was rising in Joe. He said, 'May I take a look at his flat?'

The landlord seemed to consider for a moment, then shrugged. 'Don't see why not. You could take some of his things, save me a visit to the tip. Hang on, I'll get the key.'

He set off on a laborious journey up the metal stairway to the flat above, and reappeared out of breath and brandishing a key. He led Joe up to Jamie's front door and unlocked the padlock.

'Had to put something temporary in place,' he explained, 'whilst we wait to get the locks repaired. They're closed on a Monday,' he added. 'Can you believe that? They're *closed* on a *Monday*!' Still shaking his head in disgust, he pushed open the door and Joe followed him into the narrow hallway.

'Haven't had a chance to clear up yet,' the landlord said, and Joe stood still for a moment, taking in the chaos of the living room. The naked spaces where the stereo, TV and games console had been were immediately obvious, and the sofa had been pushed over onto its back, which struck Joe as a gratuitous gesture. The floor was strewn with items that must have been emptied out of drawers but not deemed worth stealing: some takeaway menus; a spiral-bound notebook (empty, when Joe opened it); several CDs evidently not to the burglars' taste; a couple of books on castles. There was a scattering of Lego bricks amongst the other odds and ends.

'I brought some bin bags,' the landlord said, handing him a roll. 'To help you pack up the stuff. I'll leave you to it. Got things to do.' He headed towards the door, calling over his shoulder as he left, 'Lock up again when you're done, OK?'

Alone in the flat, Joe wandered through to the bedroom, where he saw an array of Alistair MacLean novels on the shelf and on the floor, along with more shattered remains of Jamie's Lego models. He couldn't find the base of the castle, just a few grey bricks strewn around. How odd, he thought absently, that Jamie should be reading Alistair MacLean. The whole place felt stale and airless, and he wanted to open a window, but already felt ashamed to have intruded this far.

He opened the wardrobe and had a look in the chest of drawers, which were both still full of clothes; Joe could see why the landlord had been irritated. He began to shove things into a black bin bag: pairs of jeans, T-shirts, jumpers and shoes, a stack of books.

He went numbly from room to room, packing up Jamie's possessions, clearing out the flat. This is what we should have done with Kit's stuff, he thought. Packed it up and given it away, rather than keeping his room exactly as it was. It wasn't healthy, having a mausoleum in the house. He'd thought that at the time, when the subject of Kit's room had come up in the weeks after his death. But Rose had panicked at the idea of clearing it out, and he couldn't argue with her. Though she never voiced it, he knew she believed her suffering outweighed his own. She'd been Kit's mother, after all. Joe was anxious and uncertain in the face of this. He started to feel almost ashamed of his own grief.

He'd often been overruled in the days after Kit's death. The funeral arrangements, for instance. They'd put a large photograph of Kit at the front of the church, one of him in his first year of university, smiling broadly at the camera. The photo in its frame was surrounded by white flowers Rose had chosen – roses and lilies and chrysanthemums. Joe had wanted to put Kit's Spurs scarf up there as well. Kit had had it since he was eight or nine years old, had worn it to all the games, so Joe had suggested draping it over the edge of the frame, but Rose had been upset by the idea. She didn't want anything interfering with the simplicity and purity of the flowers, and Joe had felt it would be insensitive to argue with her. He'd been so dazed at the time that he thought it probably wasn't important anyway. But it had been. All through the funeral he sat looking at the delicate white flowers, and thinking how they had nothing to do with Kit, that Kit would have preferred the Spurs scarf.

It occured to Joe as he consigned the remaining CDs to the bin bag that Jamie would have backed him up on the scarf if he'd asked him. But no one had considered at the time how Jamie felt.

He eventually found the base of the Lego castle under the chest of drawers in Jamie's bedroom, where it must have been kicked. Parts of the wall were still intact, and Joe retrieved as many bricks as he could find from amongst the broken pieces on the floor. Jamie's letter came back to him again – some things can't be rebuilt. Was this true of Kit? No way of knowing. Perhaps he would have recovered, at least for a while, if only he'd waited.

But that wasn't what Kit wanted to do, Joe thought suddenly. 'A while' wasn't good enough for Kit – and who was to say it should have been?

Slowly, he set the sofa back upright, revealing some final detritus which had been concealed beneath it: the Christmas card signed by Emma and Rose, and a crumpled business card for someone called Sam Locke, a Financial Advisor at one of the big London banks. Joe wondered when – and why – Jamie had needed financial advice. Then he realized that this must be Jamie's university friend, who'd come to their house once or twice years ago and whom Jamie talked about in his letters. He pocketed the card and collected the bin bags. Then, with a final glance around the flat, he went outside into the cool, white daylight, and padlocked the door behind him.

10

Sam replaced the receiver carefully and sat still for a few moments, staring at it. Jamie's father had sounded different on the phone to the way Sam remembered him – less sure of himself. Older. Sam had been caught off-guard by the phone call, and by the man's fear.

He got up from his desk and went to stand by the window. Usually the sight of the sleek, glass office buildings surrounding his own made him feel complacent, part of a powerful elite. Today they looked bleak and unwelcoming. Sam was struck for the first time by the little medieval church squeezed in amongst them. It looked sad, pushed out.

Call the police, he had said to Jamie's father. For God's sake, call the police.

That's what I should have done, he thought. I should have done it yesterday, not waited.

Miserably, he cast his mind back to Saturday, and Jamie's unexpected appearance. Going over it again, he looked for the point where he should have acted. Because now it was too late.

It had been a tedious Saturday: he'd cleaned the flat, taken himself off for a walk round Holland Park, cooked a chicken breast for his supper. The last thing he'd expected, when his buzzer went shortly after midnight, was to see Jamie, soaking wet and trembling on the doorstep. After a moment's silence, Sam had ushered him in out of the rain, and Jamie went through to the living room.

'You're lucky I'm still up,' Sam said. Then, 'You've got a bloody nerve – ignoring me for months, then turning up out of the blue in the middle of the night.'

'I didn't have anywhere else to go.'

'At midnight?'

'I slept in the train station last night.'

'What?' Sam saw now that the shaking wasn't from the cold, that Jamie's eyes were slipping anxiously around the room. Now they were in the light, he could see too that Jamie's face was badly bruised on one side, and there was dried blood on his collar.

'Sit down,' Sam said.

Jamie did as he was told.

'And you'd better take your jumper off – I'll get you a dry one.'

He chucked a hooded sweatshirt at Jamie and went through to the kitchen to make him a cup of tea. All kinds of frightening possibilities came into his mind. Had Jamie been attacked? Had he had some kind of breakdown?

He took a mug of tea back to the living room, and sat down opposite Jamie, who was huddled on the sofa with his knees drawn up to his chin.

'What's going on?' Sam said.

Jamie shook his head.

'What happened to your face?'

Jamie seemed surprised by the question, put his hand

slowly up to his face and touched the bruise. 'I don't remember.' His teeth were chattering and he slopped tea over himself when he took the mug. Sam retrieved it and set it down on the coffee table.

'You'd better tell me what happened.'

Jamie shrugged, then shook his head again. 'Kit died.'

'I know, Jamie.' Sam paused, anxious and at a loss. 'That was years ago. You know that, don't you?'

Jamie's next comment didn't register for a few moments, and Sam had to ask him to repeat it.

Jamie said again, 'I don't think I can do this any more.'

Sam felt suddenly overwhelmed with sadness. At length, he said, 'I know how much you miss him.'

Jamie looked at him properly. 'You're probably going to say at least he's not suffering.'

'Well, he isn't, is he?'

'But I am. *I'm* suffering.'

'I'm sorry. I'm so sorry. I know Kit wouldn't have wanted that.'

'You don't know anything.' Abruptly, Jamie was on his feet. Sam was afraid he was going to leave, disappear back into the night. But Jamie only paced towards the door, hovered indecisively for a few moments, then swung back towards him.

'I was in on it.'

'In on what?'

'Weird way of putting it, isn't it? But that's how it feels now. Like a plot. And I was in on it.'

'I don't understand.'

Jamie was leaning with his back to the door. A moment

before he'd been bursting with violent energy, but now he seemed to go limp. He slid into a sitting position, his back still to the door. 'I was with Kit when he died,' he said.

Sam's shock was so great he couldn't speak for a moment. Jamie put his head in his hands.

Gathering himself, Sam said, 'You knew?'

'He told me. I promised to keep it a secret.'

'Why?' The question was out before Sam had had a chance to consider it.

Slowly, Jamie raised his head. 'Because he wanted to die. Because he was ill and didn't believe he'd ever get better. Because it was *his choice*. Not mine. Not my parents'. We'd have chosen to keep him with us. Of course we would. But it wasn't up to us.'

'Your parents—' Sam began.

'They know what I did.'

Sam tried to say something else, and found he couldn't.

Jamie said again, 'I don't think I can do this any more. Kit should never have asked me. Sometimes I hate him for it. That's the real secret. Not that I helped him die. But that some days I want to kill him myself.'

Then he was shaking again, and the appearance of calm had gone. He tried to get to his feet, but was doubled up and retching the next minute. Sam tried to go to him, but Jamie pushed him away.

'Going to be sick.' He made a run for the loo, and after a moment Sam heard him vomiting. He went to get him a glass of water and found Jamie crouched on the bathroom floor, tears streaming down his face.

'I can't do this,' he said. 'I have to get away – find somewhere safe to go.'

Sam crouched next to him and put an arm round his shoulders. 'You're safe here, OK? Jamie? You can stay as long as you want.'

'I'm not safe anywhere.'

'You'll feel better when you've had some sleep. You're not thinking straight.'

'I *can't* think straight. It's all happening at once. I need to get away—'

'You can stay here.' Sam gripped Jamie's shoulder to still the trembling.

Jamie looked at him in appeal. 'I just want to – disappear.'

He finally fell asleep on Sam's sofa sometime in the early hours of the morning. Sam, who'd been keeping an eye on him up to that point, went through to the kitchen and drank a pint of water in one go, then remained standing at the sink for a while. He felt light-headed with exhaustion, and frightened. You didn't have to be an expert to realize Jamie was seriously ill. With anyone else, the first thing you'd do would be to call their parents. But in Jamie's case, there was no one to call. If Jamie needed help, it would have to come from Sam himself. Jamie trusted him – as much as he trusted anyone, at least.

It was to Sam that Jamie had come in those awful days after Kit's funeral, when he couldn't bear to be at home – or wasn't welcome there, Sam realized now. For several weeks, Jamie had stayed in the little flat in Shoreditch Sam had rented during his first year at the bank; he'd been silent, self-contained, impossibly shocked – crying only occasionally, and never mentioning Kit.

Then, after the inquest, he'd suddenly decided to move on, had gone away up north without even telling Sam where he was headed. It had taken Sam several weeks to track him down again, many anxious calls and texts – but eventually Jamie had replied saying that he was in Sheffield, and had a job in a bookshop. Sam had gone up to check on him, and tentatively began to relax. Jamie was doing OK. He was keeping his head above water. He wasn't the same, of course. Sam's sharp, lively friend from university had been replaced by someone else entirely.

Still, you had to deal with what was in front of you, not with what you wished for or remembered. What was clear now was that Jamie was no longer OK, no longer keeping his head above water.

Exhausted, Sam finally went to bed, and didn't wake up until late the next morning, feeling more hopeful. Jamie would probably be more coherent after a good night's sleep. But when Sam went through to the living room to check on him, he found the sofa unoccupied, and a quick search of the rest of the flat revealed what he already knew – Jamie was gone.

That's when I should have done something, Sam thought, not just sat around waiting and trying his mobile over and over. It had been awful, relaying the night's events to Jamie's dad, who'd already sounded panicky enough. Imagine Jamie's father being involved, after all this time. It was this more than anything that had brought the gravity of the situation home to Sam. He was going to drive home,

Jamie's dad had said, and tell his wife. And then he was going to call the police.

Sam went back to his desk and tried to focus on his computer screen, but couldn't concentrate. He sat still for a moment, then got to his feet again and headed out of the door.

11

Rose saw Joe's face as he came into the kitchen and knew immediately that something was wrong. Her mind went quickly to Emma, but she was able to reassure herself – Emma was safely upstairs in her room.

'Can I talk to you?' he said.

Rose sat down at the kitchen table and waited as Joe seated himself opposite her and clasped his hands in front of him. But after that he couldn't seem to get any words out.

'Tea?' she offered after a moment.

'Yes,' he said. 'Yes, please.'

Whilst she made the tea, Rose was steeling herself for bad news, though she couldn't think what it might be. Something to do with his job? The mortgage? She found she couldn't summon up much alarm. In reality, there was nothing left to fear, nothing on earth. The worst had already happened.

She set the tea down on the table, and Joe took a swig from his mug, wincing as he burned his mouth. 'It's about Jamie,' he said.

When had she known, Rose asked herself afterwards. At what stage in her husband's faltering narration of events

– of the letters he'd been receiving for months now, of the abortive journey he'd made to Sheffield, of his troubling conversation with Sam – at what point had she known that Jamie was dead?

A mother always knows. That was something her own mother used to say, although now Rose couldn't remember the context. Not this, certainly – the dizzying sense that your child was lost. Her own mother, for all her stern self-conviction, had no idea what that was like.

Rose had felt it the night Kit died. She'd woken up beside Joe in the hotel room in London, winded and panic-stricken. Joe had put his arm out to her, had told her to settle down, that everything was OK. And so she'd made herself lie back down, had tried to breathe deeply. Eventually she'd fallen back to sleep. And all the while, at home, her son was dying.

But in truth there had been many nights like that after Kit's first suicide attempt. Countless nights of panic and terror. Perhaps it was wrong to single out one in particular, just because that night had turned out to be the one on which it finally happened.

All the same, she still believed she'd known. Yea, a sword shall pierce through thy own soul also.

She remained where she was in the kitchen while Joe made the call to the local police station. She heard him from the next room, explaining that their son was missing, that they were concerned for his safety. Rose felt suddenly faint, and put her head in her hands. The worst had not yet come after all. The worst was building around them at this very moment, ready to engulf them.

Joe came back through and said, 'They took some details. They're sending someone round in the morning to talk to us.'

He sat back down at the table, and Rose could see his awkwardness.

He said, 'I should have told you about the letters.'

'Yes.'

'I'm sorry.'

This, Rose found, was not enough. She said, very slowly, 'You drove him away.'

'Yes.' Joe had his hands clasped on the table in front of him, and now she saw their grip tighten, his knuckles turn white.

'You blamed him – for it all.'

'I know.' He sounded infinitely weary. 'Didn't you?'

And this time Rose had nothing to say in response, because she knew it was the truth, that she had blamed Jamie too, and if Joe was responsible for driving him away, she was just as guilty for not protecting him.

They were still staring at each other when the doorbell rang. Rose stood up to answer it.

'Just leave it, will you?' Joe said, but Rose ignored him.

On the doorstep was a fair-haired young man in a slightly rumpled suit. Rose thought for a moment he might be a door-to-door salesman, or even a Jehovah's Witness. But then she realized that he looked familiar, and everything slotted into place. He didn't seem to know what to say, so Rose spoke for him.

'You're Sam,' she said. 'I remember you. Jamie's friend.'

'I came to see if I could help at all,' he said. He seemed shy. 'I hope you don't mind.'

'It's good of you,' Rose said. She might have assumed that the presence of one of Jamie's friends would be a blessing, helping her to feel closer to her missing son. But now she felt bleaker still, as though Sam's presence signalled the end of all hope, as though he'd arrived for the wake.

'Come through, dear,' she said.

Joe jumped up to welcome the young man, and relayed his conversation with the police operator to him whilst Rose made some more tea.

'They said a lot of missing people come back of their own accord,' Joe said. 'Or just turn up somewhere after a few days. They're going to circulate a description, in case anyone sees him.'

'He'll be OK,' Sam said, not sounding convinced. He wrapped his hands round the mug of tea Rose placed in front of him as if for warmth.

Rose said, 'Did you see much of Jamie over the past few years?'

'A fair bit,' Sam said. 'Every couple of months, maybe. He isn't the easiest person to be friends with – not very sociable at times.'

Rose was grateful for his use of the present tense. On impulse, she reached across the table and put her hand on his. 'Thank you for sticking by him,' she said.

Sam seemed embarrassed, tensing up and staring down at the table top. 'I haven't been a very good friend to him recently,' he said at last. 'I hadn't spoken to him for some time before this. And now, of course, I keep thinking of all the things I could have done differently. *Should* have done differently. Because even though he could be a total dick – sorry – he was still my friend. I should have kept more of an eye on him.'

His speech had become rapid towards the end, but now he lapsed into silence again, seeming uncomfortable at having said so much. Rose was searching for the words to reassure him, but could find none. In the end, it was Joe who spoke.

'But he was my son. *I* should have kept an eye on him.'

There was another silence. Sam took a hurried swig of tea. Rose contemplated getting up to make more, but couldn't summon the energy.

'Is there anyone else you can think of?' she asked Sam. 'Any friend he might have gone to?'

'I already tried everyone from Warwick,' Sam said, 'though he hasn't been in touch with most of them for years. I even tried Alice, his ex-girlfriend, but she hadn't seen him. She'll call me if he contacts her, but I don't think he will.'

Silence again.

'He'll come back,' Sam said, almost to himself. 'I know he'll come back.'

The kitchen door opened and Emma came in, startling them all. In her terror over Jamie, Rose had temporarily forgotten that her daughter was still upstairs, working her way through *Jane Eyre*.

'What's for supper?' Emma said.

Rose started to reply, 'Lasagne,' but fell silent at the look Joe gave her.

Emma didn't seem to notice. She was too busy staring at Sam. Rose realized that it must be unusual for her to see a visitor in the house.

'Hello,' Sam said, when no one else spoke. 'You must be Emma. I'm Sam. I was at university with Jamie. I've actually met you once before, when you were much younger.'

'Have you?' Emma said, lighting up. 'I think I remember.'

Joe cut off any further conversation. 'Sit down, love. We need to talk to you.'

What kind of effect would this have on Emma, Rose wondered, hearing of Jamie's disappearance? It occurred to her that perhaps this was the end of Emma's childhood – a life-altering trauma. But no, Rose dismissed the idea almost immediately. She was starting to see things more clearly this evening. Clearly enough, at any rate, to see that if there was the potential for damage then it had already been done. Probably years ago.

Emma didn't cry. She was wide-eyed, stricken, but fuelled with passionate energy. 'We'll find him,' she told her parents. 'We'll look everywhere until we find him.'

Joe and Rose had exchanged a look. Sam had stared down at his hands.

'We'll see what the police say tomorrow,' Joe said eventually.

Then Sam left to drive back to London, saying he would call the next day, and Joe suggested that they all go to bed.

In their bedroom, Joe stood mutely by the door as Rose busied herself with getting her nightie out from under the pillow. He turned away, almost squeamish, as she started to undress. How bizarre, he thought, that they still shared a room, still shared a *bed*; when they never touched each other, whether in bed or out of it, not even a casual hug or stroke of the arm.

Rose climbed into bed and sat silently, waiting for him to get in. Feeling suddenly self-conscious and exposed, Joe took his pyjamas through to the bathroom to change.

When he came back, Rose still didn't speak. Joe began to feel frightened of her anger. He thought about apologizing again for not telling her about the letters, but there didn't seem to be much point. What's done is done. And if Jamie was lost to them forever, no amount of apologies would be able to mitigate his wife's fury, or his own guilt.

How short-sighted to have blamed Jamie for tearing the family apart, Joe thought. It was he himself who'd done that. And what was perhaps even worse was that somewhere, deep down, he'd blamed Kit as well. He shouldn't have. He shouldn't even have allowed that thought to cross his mind. It had been so easy at the time to see Kit's death as the end of everything. But of course it wasn't, Joe thought. It was up to us to make sure it wasn't. Kit tried his hardest to live, and we couldn't have asked for more.

'I'm sorry,' he said to Rose, uselessly. 'I'm so sorry.' He was going to say more, but she cut him off.

'Would you like some Ovaltine? I could pop down and make you some.'

'I've already brushed my teeth,' Joe said. So this was how it was going to be. No outright accusations, just offers of warm milky drinks.

'Thank you anyway,' he said.

It was no less than he deserved to be reproached like this – nothing direct, just continual reminders of what a good wife Rose had always been. No one could deflect like Rose. It had been making him angry for years, all this pretending. He'd never been able to counter it. Even his own rage was incapable of making a dent in the facade she'd put up, the gilded impression that their family life was perfect, that they were coping admirably, that *life went on*. It had always seemed to Joe a kind of betrayal. Now he realized that it must have taken courage, too.

'Shall I turn out the light?' he said.

'Yes.'

Lying in the darkness, he was minutely aware of Rose's rigid form beside him. He said, 'The police will find him.'

But the comment sounded sinister rather than comforting. Because if the police ever did find missing people, they didn't often find them alive.

Sometime after midnight, Rose fell into a light, fitful sleep. Joe remained stranded in wakefulness beside her, the same harrowing carousel of possibilities going round in his mind. Maybe Jamie was alive somewhere, and really had just needed to get away. But if this was the case, he would almost certainly never get in touch with them. Whether he was alive or dead, they would never see him again. That kind of fear – that terrible certainty. Joe hadn't expected ever to feel it again after Kit. How foolish to believe it could only happen once.

He thought of that other, awful time many years ago when he and Rose had been on the verge of calling the police: when Kit and Jamie had decided to stay the night in one of their woodland dens, and hadn't thought to tell their parents. Joe and Rose had sat at the kitchen table minute after minute, hour after hour, as the boys' supper grew cold on their plates. Rose had rung round all their school friends, and every family member or acquaintance they could think of, but nobody knew where Kit and Jamie might be. And then it got to nine o'clock and Joe had said, 'Right. I'm calling the police,' making himself sound far calmer than he really felt, because Rose was becoming hysterical. But as he was in the act of picking up the phone, the boys trailed in through the door, cold and deflated, but completely oblivious to the nightmare they'd caused. He'd been *furious* with them, blistering with anger because he'd been so frightened. Kit had been defiant (the whole thing had most likely been his idea), but Jamie had wept for hours.

This time, though, there was no getting them back. He saw himself taking the phone call, the one from Kit's housemate that first time saying Kit had cut his wrists and overdosed. He recalled how he'd put down the phone and lay back in bed for a few moments, dazedly trying to assimilate this new knowledge into his former view of the world. Then he'd had to turn and wake Rose.

He tried to go back in his mind, to retrieve memories that didn't hurt him. He saw Kit and Jamie pedalling off on their brand-new matching bikes, Kit's blue, Jamie's green, and slightly too big for him. He saw them kicking a football around in the garden, saw them sitting side by side in the living room playing computer games, their dark heads almost identical from the back. Thinking of those years, Joe found, could still make him happy. Whatever had happened afterwards, their childhood was safe.

This stirred something in his mind, made a connection that he couldn't immediately identify. Something to do with what Sam had said on the phone, a phrase of Jamie's he'd repeated.

He lay frozen, letting the idea spread out and fill his brain. For a few moments he was breathless, heart-stopped, with the possibility. It was so unlikely. And yet –

He left Rose sleeping, and went to wake Emma. She was drowsy and confused at first, but agreed to show him the way. She didn't ask him why he wanted to go, which was how Joe knew she was worried about him.

He left a note for Rose on the kitchen table saying they'd gone for a walk. Then he set off with his daughter in the cold dawn light.

12

The darkness was starting to peter out; he noticed the daylight gathering around him with sinister, martial patience. For hours, he'd lain content on the ground, cocooned in the night and guarded on each side by the stiff silhouettes of the trees. But now, as the morning light began to seep into his bones, he felt cold for the first time. As his limbs were returned to him out of the darkness, he thought they looked strange, odds and ends that didn't belong to him.

Jamie retreated back into the shelter, pulling the tarpaulin doorway closed, a defence against the daylight. He put his second coat on and wrapped it tightly round himself.

The nights tended to be better. He felt calmer, more together. But with the light it all came back again. The panic was stirring, that strange, shivery feeling in his gut. The invisible walls were closing in.

He'd known that if he kept still it would catch up with him. The silence in his head was gone, replaced by a roar. He'd tried to do what he'd always done, let nothingness fill him up, take him over. But it was all gone, all used up. Now there was only terror. He'd tried to visualize the dens, to picture himself in the woods. But it wasn't enough. The panic came for him, again and again. That's when he knew he had to make it to the woods – away from the noise and the fear. There, everything could stop.

In the shadow of the trees, he tried to calm himself. However frightened he was, nothing could touch him here. He made himself look in his bag, ate his last apple, had a few swigs of water.

He was starting to warm up now. He dared to peek out through the doorway and registered the straight backs of the trees around him, their unassailable presence. He listened, but there was no sound in the woods beyond the faint rustle of small animals moving through the leaves and twigs on the ground, and the quiet calls of birds.

He lay back, nestled inside his two coats. Eventually, he fell into a doze.

Then he was awake. He was jerked, hurled headlong into consciousness. He was rigid, alert – his ears straining to catch again whatever noise it was he'd heard. He had no idea what the sound was – but somehow he knew it was a noise that had woken him.

He lay completely still, straining to listen, searching for the sound amongst the trees. The woods remained quiet. Somewhere high above him, he heard the shrill, flute-like call of a blackbird – was it frightened too? But no, he knew the alarm call of the blackbird, a piping rattle. This was just a song. He tried to relax. He'd probably just heard a larger animal moving close by, perhaps a fox. He closed his eyes.

There it was again. No mistaking it this time. A rustling, the sound of twigs being broken, dry leaves stirred and trodden down. Too loud for a fox. The movement was too heavy – it could only be human. Somewhere in the woods, someone was walking. Someone was coming towards him.

Jamie felt the hairs on the back of his neck rise. He retreated into the furthest corner of his shelter and crouched there, tensed, listening as the noise grew louder, as the person came closer and closer. His heart was pounding as though about to burst out of his chest and his breath came fast and shallow. He felt the dampness of sweat pooling down his back. Then he heard his own name called.

Kit, he thought. Kit was coming.

He was almost sobbing now. He knew the end was close, and found that he wasn't ready after all. There was no relief – only terror. Someone pulled back the tarpaulin doorway and Jamie gasped as the lethal light flooded his little room. He tried to ward off the silhouette in the doorway with his hands. 'Please,' he said, shrinking back into the corner. Kit's face was in shadow. He came closer, and said Jamie's name. Jamie put his hands in front of his face, rubbed the dirt into his cheeks. The darkness came to meet him, folded itself over and over him.

Now he was being pulled out of the shelter. He didn't resist. It was all over, and there was nothing he could do now. Someone was pulling him to his feet, holding him up, and he realized suddenly that something was wrong. This wasn't Kit. He tried to look closer but his eyes wouldn't focus and everything seemed to be moving very slowly.

He said, 'Dad?'

And the person said, 'It's alright.'

'Is Kit here?'

'No, Jamie. You're half-asleep. You'll be alright.'

Jamie felt the tears streaking the dirt on his face. Kit wasn't coming; he was never coming. 'I'm sorry,' he said.

'It's alright,' his father said. 'It's alright.'

13

Emma had to be strict with herself afterwards: Jamie's reappearance was not a miracle.

It had been kind of amazing, though. Her heart swelled as she remembered the sight of her father lifting Jamie up out of his woodland shelter, putting his arms around him to keep him on his feet. And Emma herself had played a part in it, because she'd remembered the way to the dens, even so many years later.

But the days of miracles are behind us, she thought. She had to be firm about it, because she often longed to read the Bible again. Phrases and passages from it came back to her as she tried to go about her life, and sometimes the old words made her ache with missing them. But she knew she could never return to the CU. That was all done with now, even though the cool group hardly ever went any more. Last week, Kayleigh had come to Emma specially and asked her if she wanted to help plan a series of meetings based around Jesus' miracles, and for a few seconds Emma had been tempted. But the feeling passed. She told Kayleigh she couldn't because the CU meetings clashed with Literature Club.

Nevertheless, she occasionally got the sense that Jesus was still there, slinking along behind her and then dodging out of sight, as though He was playing a game of Grandmother's footsteps.

It wasn't surprising then that Emma had thought for a moment she could feel His presence in the woods. It was remembered faith. *Thy brother was dead, and is alive again; and was lost, and is found.*

But it wasn't enough. People let themselves be deceived too easily, because they wanted to be deceived; they saw miracles in the burn-pattern on a slice of toast. Bringing Jamie home had been wonderful, but Emma didn't think God had been involved. Now, if they could go back a few years – if they could undo everything that had happened, and start afresh – then that would be a miracle. Picking up the pieces afterwards wasn't.

It was something, though.

All the same, it was best to see things for what they were. In the Bible, Jesus gave people back. *Our friend Lazarus sleepeth; but I go, that I may awake him out of sleep.* But He didn't give everyone back, Emma thought.

She'd been sitting in her bedroom for some time reading *Wuthering Heights* when the doorbell rang. Reluctantly, she put the book aside and padded downstairs to answer it.

Jamie's friend Sam stood on the doorstep looking unusually scruffy in jeans and an old sweatshirt. He was holding two small bunches of flowers. Emma smiled shyly at him. 'Hello.'

'Hello, Em.' He handed her two bunches of flowers. 'One's for your mum. The other's for you.' He paused. 'It seemed like a nice gesture about half an hour ago, but now it's coming across as a little weird.'

'*I* don't think it's weird.'

'Well, that's a relief, then.'

He stepped across the threshold and wandered through to the living room, where he stood absent-mindedly peering at the family photos on the piano.

Emma said, 'You're not wearing a suit.'

'I didn't realize there was a dress code.'

Emma grinned, and managed to counter him. 'We'll let it pass, just this once.'

'That's generous of you.'

They smiled at each other. Emma was still holding the flowers. She got a vase out from the cupboard and pushed the two bunches into it – they just about fitted – and then placed it next to the photos on top of the piano.

'I think you might need to add water, too,' Sam said tactfully.

'Oh, yeah – I forgot.' She headed off to the kitchen, filled the vase with water and left it on the kitchen table for her mum to see when she came back.

Returning to the living room, she said, 'Mum's out, by the way. She has a new job in town.'

'Doing what?'

'Working at the tea shop. She makes the cakes. And sometimes serves the customers.'

'That's great.'

'It means we get fewer cakes at home,' Emma said. 'Because she has less time now. But that's probably for the best.' She paused, wondering whether to tell Sam about the new healthy-eating chart she'd made. She decided against it, and went on, 'Jamie's in the shed with Dad at the moment. They're making a chair.'

'Just one?'

'Shall I go and get him?'

'No hurry.' Sam paused. 'How is he now?'

Emma thought about it. 'I'm not sure,' she said eventually. 'He doesn't say very much.'

Sam acknowledged this with a nod. 'Well, I'm dragging him out for a pub lunch. I'll report back.'

A moment later, Emma's dad and Jamie came in from the shed. Both of them seemed pleased to see Sam, although Jamie hung back by the door at first.

'How's the chair?' Sam said earnestly.

Emma's dad said, 'It's coming along nicely. Isn't it, Jamie?'

Jamie nodded.

Their dad said, 'We're making good progress. Especially as Jamie's getting more used to the tools now. I don't think he's exactly a natural, but he's doing very well.'

Emma saw Jamie roll his eyes slightly, and thought it was an encouraging sign.

'What will you do when you've finished it?' Sam asked.

'I suppose we'll – sit on it,' Emma's dad said.

Jamie gave a small smile. 'On very special occasions.'

'Actually, we're planning to make a full set,' their dad said, sensing that his chair was being made fun of.

'Well I hope you'll invite me along when they're finished. For the great unveiling,' Sam said. He paused, thoughtful. 'For the great *chair*-emony . . .'

Jamie shook his head, visibly pained. 'Please don't.'

Sam was grinning now. 'It'll be so exciting I . . . might need to sit down.'

'Stop.'

'Should I book in advance to be assured of a *seat*?'

Jamie turned to his dad. 'I'm sorry about him.'

After Jamie and Sam had left, Emma and her dad sat in the kitchen, her dad having a cup of coffee and Emma some hot Ribena. Emma told him a bit about the Brontë sisters and he seemed quite interested. Eventually they heard the sound of the door and Emma's mum came into the kitchen. She smiled at Emma and sank into a chair.

'Busy today,' she said. 'We were rushed off our feet. What beautiful tulips!'

'They're from Sam,' Emma said quickly, worried that her mum would think they were from her dad. 'One bunch was for you, and one was for me.'

'How sweet of him! Is he with Jamie now?'

'They've gone to the pub,' Emma said. 'Haven't they?' she added, to include her dad. He'd got stiffly to his feet as soon as Emma's mum entered the room, and was standing by the counter.

Emma thought he was about to go back to the shed, but he said after a moment, 'Would you like a cup of tea, Rose?'

Emma saw her mum look at him, and hesitate. Then she said, 'Yes, please. That's kind.'

There was silence whilst Joe made the tea. Emma sipped the rest of her Ribena and wondered if she should try to make conversation. She'd already used up her material on the Brontë sisters.

Her dad's back was turned as he stirred the tea, but after a bit he spoke again. 'He seemed alright today.'

'That's good,' her mum said.

'He was a bit quiet this morning, but we got some useful work done. He seemed interested. He asked some questions about woodworking.'

'It'll do him good to be out with Sam.'

Emma's dad came back to the table and placed a mug of tea in front of Emma's mum. He sat down at the table. Emma saw that he'd made one for himself, too.

Her mum said, 'Do you think I should ask Sam to stay for supper this evening?'

Emma's dad wrapped his hands round his mug. 'That sounds like a nice idea.'

'I thought we'd have toad in the hole. I hope Jamie still likes that.'

'I'm sure he does.'

Emma decided to slip away and leave them to it.

14

The following Monday, something strange happened. Emma was summoned, out of the blue, to see the school chaplain. She was perplexed and slightly anxious. Was she in trouble for not being a Christian any more? Was he going to denounce her as a heretic?

She went up the stairs by the vestry and knocked nervously on the door of his office, but the chaplain greeted her with a smile.

'Emma,' he said, 'thanks for coming. Have a seat.' He gestured towards the threadbare sofa, and Emma perched on the edge. At first she couldn't even remember his name. She always thought of him as 'the chaplain'. She groped around, and after a moment came up with Reverend Scott.

The chaplain, meanwhile, had seated himself in the armchair opposite her. He pushed his glasses up the bridge of his nose, and folded his hands in his lap. Emma recognized his mannerisms; they signalled earnestness. She waited.

'There's something I want to ask you,' the chaplain said. 'But first, if you don't mind my mentioning it, I've noticed you stopped going to the Christian Union meetings a while ago.'

Emma felt awkward – she hoped he wasn't taking it personally, but she supposed that a slight against Jesus might feel like a slight against the chaplain as well. She didn't know what to say.

Noticing her hesitation, the chaplain said gently, 'It's none of my business, Emma. But I'd hate to see the interference of others, with –' he paused thoughtfully, '– shall we say, mixed motives, damaging your own faith, or making you feel pushed out.' He looked seriously at her and Emma knew he was talking about the cool group. Mixed motives. So he thought they were Pharisees too.

'I don't care about them,' she said, and he nodded, satisfied.

'Well, that brings me to what I wanted to ask you,' he said. 'I imagine you're aware that every year I appoint a pupil sacristan to help with chapel duties, setting up before services and so forth. It's an important position. The sacristan attends prefect meetings, and has a good deal of responsibility within the school. And I was wondering if you'd like to take over that role next term.'

'Me?'

'I know, traditionally, it's tended to be a Sixth Former. But I think we can waive tradition in this case. If you want the role, it's yours. If you don't, well that's fine too, and we'll say no more about it.'

Emma considered the matter in silence.

'Do you want a bit of time to think it over?' the chaplain said.

'Yes, please,' Emma said. Then she added, 'If I was a

sacristan, would I have to start going to the CU meetings again? Would it look bad if I didn't?'

The chaplain shook his head with a small smile. 'Your faith is no one's business but your own.'

Emma went to the chapel to think it over. She hadn't spent a lunchtime there for months. Usually now she hung out with Olivia. But it felt peaceful to be back, and she settled into her usual pew and wrapped herself in the heavy silence. She knew that once she would have regarded the chaplain's offer as divine intervention, God working through His servant to draw her back to the fold; now she thought it was just Reverend Scott being nice. All the same, she found she was already turning over in her head the various psalms she could pick for different moods and occasions. And it would be kind of cool to go to prefect meetings.

She stared up at the stained-glass cross in the window above the altar. The sunlight was bursting through it, setting it on fire in the way she loved. Probably not a sign from the Lord – but it was beautiful to look at.

She and Olivia went to find the chaplain at the end of the day, and Emma accepted his offer. He seemed pleased, and Emma was touched. On the bus home, she planned how she might tell Jamie, how to communicate the magnitude of her new role. They hadn't had sacristans at Jamie's and Kit's school, but Emma thought if she explained that she was now allowed to help choose the psalms, Jamie might appreciate the importance of her position.

She decided to dig her Bible out when she got home, and start selecting psalms. She thought of Psalm 55, her favourite. Although perhaps that wouldn't be appropriate? She could pick some which were more cheerful, she supposed, but they didn't seem to stick in her head as much as the sorrowful ones. They knew a thing or two about suffering, the psalmists. So did everyone in the Bible, actually. Emma saw Jesus on the cross, crying out with his last breath: *My God, my God, why have you forsaken me?*

She found her dad in the kitchen when she got back, and was pleased to be able to tell him about being sacristan straight away. He didn't seem to get what a big deal it was, but he said well done all the same.

'Where's Jamie?' Emma said.

'In the shed finishing off the chair,' her dad said, but as he spoke, Emma saw Jamie through the window.

'No, he isn't. He's standing at the end of the garden.'

Her dad turned and looked. 'Oh – he must be having a break. I'm taking us out some tea in a moment.'

'I've already decided on what psalm I want for my first service,' Emma said.

'Good!'

It was nice, she thought, that he was pretending to be interested in the Bible.

'It's a sad one,' she said. 'It's Psalm 55.' Then she added, without realizing she was going to, 'It's my favourite, even though it's so sad, because it makes me think of Kit.'

Her dad went very still for a few moments, and Emma was afraid she'd annoyed him. But then he said, his voice low, 'How does it go, love?'

And so Emma began to recite it for him, finding that she was word-perfect. Her father listened.

To Emma's surprise, her voice shook slightly as she spoke the words, 'My heart is sore pained within me: and the terrors of death are fallen upon me.' And when she looked at her father, she saw that he had tears in his eyes. She thought perhaps she should stop, but she didn't. Instead she recited, clear as a bell, her favourite part:

'And I said, Oh that I had wings like a dove! for then would I fly away, and be at rest.'

Jamie, standing alone in the garden, was staring out across the fields towards the woods. After a moment, he closed his eyes and let the images come. He saw them mostly without pain. There was his father helping him to his feet in the woods; there was his mother running out of the house to meet them, her face ablaze; and Emma, anxiously taking his hand.

And he saw himself and Kit, always a pair in his memory: Kit unfazed in the sinking rowing boat, Kit next to him on the roller coaster, Kit passing the ball to him in the garden. He pictured himself and Kit on the beach in Wales, trying for the thousandth time to dig all the way down to Australia. They'd never made it. But they'd given it a good go. Jamie smiled at the memory.

Then he opened his eyes to the present, and felt the

misery afresh. There was no end to it. There would never be an end to it. *Kit*, he thought. There were a thousand things jumbled up in his head that he wanted to say to him. But finally he put them all away and looking out at the distant woods, thought only one thing.

God, I miss you.

So he closed his eyes once more.

And there they were again.

Acknowledgements

I'd like to say a huge thanks to my agent, Caroline Hardman, my editors, Francesca Main and Sophie Jonathan, and everyone at Picador. Nothing would have been possible without them. I'm also grateful to the following for encouragement and suggestions: Will Haig, Jack Skinner, Philip Knox and Archie Davies. Thanks particularly to Clare Garbett for showing me the dens when we were children, Mike Scott for telling the strangest anecdotes, my brother Tim for his Lego habits, and Helen Wyatt for pretty much nothing beyond making me feel normal by comparison. Finally, thank you to my parents for enduring with me the dark time that led to this novel, and Dave Young, for his generosity and unexpected common sense.